BEVERLY LEWIS

The Postcard

BETHANY HOUSE PUBLISHERS
MINNEAPOLIS, MINNESOTA 55438

The Postcard
Copyright © 1999
Beverly Lewis

Cover by Dan Thornberg

Bird-in-Hand, Pennsylvania, is a village located in central Lancaster County; however, with the exception of Bishop Jacob J. Hershberger, the characters in this novel are fictional, and any resemblance to actual persons, living or dead, is purely coincidental.

Scripture quotations identified NIV are from the HOLY BIBLE, NEW INTERNATIONAL VERSION®. Copyright © 1973, 1978, 1984 by International Bible Society. Used by permission of Zondervan Publishing House. All rights reserved. The "NIV" and "New International Version" trademarks are registered in the United States Patent and Trademark Office by International Bible Society. Use of either trademark requires the permission of International Bible Society.

Scripture quotations identified KJV are from the King James Version of the Bible.

Published by Bethany House Publishers
A Ministry of Bethany Fellowship International
11400 Hampshire Avenue South
Minneapolis, Minnesota 55438
www.bethanyhouse.com

Printed in the United States of America by
Bethany Press International, Minneapolis, Minnesota 55438

Library of Congress Cataloging-in-Publication Data

Lewis, Beverly, 1949–
    The postcard / by Beverly Lewis.
      p. cm.
    ISBN 0–7642–2211–2 (Trade paper)
    ISBN 0–7642–2224–4 (Hardcover)
    ISBN 0–7642–2225-2 (Large print)
    ISBN 0–7642–2223-6 (Audiobook)
    1. Amish—Pennsylvania—Lancaster County Fiction. I. Title.
PS3562.E9383 P67 1999
813'.54—dc21
                                                              99–6378
                                                               CIP

The Postcard

By Beverly Lewis

THE HERITAGE OF LANCASTER COUNTY

The Shunning

The Confession

The Reckoning

❖ ❖ ❖

The Postcard

The Crossroad

❖ ❖ ❖

The Sunroom

To Dave,

my beloved helpmate and husband.

To the memory of my dear aunt,

Gladys Buchwalter,

who, along with her co-worker in the Lord,

Dorothy Brosey,

led many souls—young and old—

to Calvary's Cross.

About the Author

$\mathscr{B}$everly Lewis was born in the heart of Pennsylvania Dutch country. She fondly recalls her growing-up years, and due to a keen interest in her mother's Plain family heritage, many of Beverly's books are set in Lancaster County.

A former schoolteacher, Bev is a member of The National League of American Pen Women—the Pikes Peak branch—and the Society of Children's Book Writers and Illustrators. Her bestselling books are among the C. S. Lewis Noteworthy List Books. Bev and her husband have three children and make their home in Colorado.

A cloud, unforeseen, skidded across the ivory moon and darkened his room, if only for a moment. He lit the kerosene lantern and set about rummaging through his bureau drawers, searching for something—anything—on which to write, so eager was he to pen a prompt reply to his beloved's astonishing letter.

Amish words poured from his joyous heart as he wrote on the back of a plain white postcard. . . .

Prologue: Rachel

□ ❖ ❖ ❖ □

It's all I have to bring today,
This, and my heart beside,
This, and my heart, and all the fields,
And all the meadows wide.

Emily Dickinson (circa 1858)

I used to dream of possessing a full measure of confidence. Used to wonder what it would be like to have at least "a speckle of pluck," as Mamma often said when I was a girl.

Growing up Plain, I come from a long line of hearty women. Women like my grandmothers and great-grandmothers, who believed in themselves and in working hard, living out the old proverb "The Lord helps those who help themselves."

Yet, in spite of all that hereditary determination and spunk, I was just the opposite—overly timid and shy. Nearly afraid of my own voice at times. A far cry from the stories told me of my ancestors.

Elizabeth, my next oldest sister, seemed awful worried about me when, upon my sixteenth birthday, I was too bashful to attend my first Singing. Turning sixteen was an important milestone in the Amish community. The wonderful coming of age offered long-awaited privileges, such as socializing with boys, being courted.

Lizzy was so concerned, she confided in one of Bishop Fisher's granddaughters, explaining in a whisper so I wouldn't hear. "Rachel was born shy" came her tender excuse.

I *had* overheard, though the reason my sister gave for my perpetual red face didn't make me feel any much better. 'Least back then it didn't.

And it didn't help that all my life one relative or another felt obliged to point out to me that my name means *lamb*. "Rachel puts herself out, she does. Never mind that it costs her plenty," Lavina Troyer had declared at a quilting years ago. So my course was set early on. I began to live up to my father's distant cousin's declaration—working hard to keep the house spotless from top to bottom, tending charity gardens as well as my own, eating fresh in the summer months, putting up more than sufficient canned goods for the winter months, and attending work frolics.

Now that I've been married for over six years—a mother of two with another baby on the way—I've come out of my shell just a bit, thanks to my husband, Jacob, and his constant encouragement. Still, I wonder what it would take to be truly brave, to develop the kind of admirable traits I see so clearly in my eleven siblings, most of them older.

As for church, Jacob and I left the strict Old Order behind when we married, joining the ranks of the Amish Mennonites, which broke Mamma's heart—and she never forgot it! I 'spect she's still hoping we'll come to our senses and return someday.

Beachy Amish, that's what the non-Amish community ("English" folk) call us now—after Moses Beachy, who founded the original group in 1927. Our church does *not* shun church members who leave and join other Plain groups, and we hold public worship in a common meeting-house. Often our bishop, Isaac Glick, allows the preachers to read from the newly translated Pennsylvania Dutch version of the New Testament instead of High German, which the young people don't understand anyhow. We embrace the assurance of salvation, and we use electricity and other modern conveniences like telephones, but a few church members rely on horse-drawn carriages for transportation.

Still, we dress Plain and hold fast to our Anabaptist life-style. Besides my husband, I am most grateful that the Lord has seen fit to give me a confidante in my cousin Esther Glick. Confiding my deepest thoughts to my Pennsylvania-turned-Ohio cousin is always a joy. It seems easier to pour out my heart in a letter than face-to-face with any of my sisters. Esther and I had often shared our deepest secrets as youngsters—we go back as far as I can remember. Maybe further. I've heard it told that Esther's mother—Aunt Leah—and my mother experienced the first twinges of labor at the exact hour. So my cousin and I are a faithful reflection of our mothers' sisterly love.

Every Friday, without fail, I stop whatever I'm doing and write her a letter.

Friday, June 17

Dearest Esther,

It has been ever so busy here, what with the summer season in full swing. Jacob says we will soon have enough money saved to move to Holmes County.

Oh, I miss you so! Just think—if we do live neighbors to you, we'll quilt and can and raise our children together once more!

Tomorrow's a busy day at Farmers Market. Jacob has handcrafted lots of fine oak and pine furniture for our market stand. He's worked especially hard at restocking the little wooden rocking chairs and toy trucks. Lancaster tourists snatch them right up—hardly think twice about opening their pocketbooks. We cater too much to outsiders, I fear. But then, tourism is our main industry these days. Not like it used to be when Lancaster farmland was plenty and not so dear. Things are changing rapidly here.

Remember the times I hid under the market tables at Roots and the Green Dragon? Remember how Mamma would scold? Every now and then, I look in the mirror and still see a young girl. Running alongside Mill Creek at breakneck speed, through glimmering shadows of willows and maple, I used to pretend I was the wind. Imagine that! I did enjoy my childhood so, growing up here in the country, away from the noise and bedlam of Lancaster.

Speaking of childhood, I see signs of friskiness in young Aaron. So much like Mamma he is, and only five! Annie, on the other hand, is more like Jacob—agreeable and companionable. My husband laughs when I tell him so, though deep down I 'spect he's awful pleased.

As for our next little Yoder, I do believe he or she will be a mighty active one. The way this baby wrestles inside me is a new experience altogether. I daresay the baby is a boy, probably another mischief in the making! Not a single one of my children shows any signs of shyness, like their mamma, and I 'spose I'm glad 'bout that.

Ach, forgive me for going on so.

Stopping, I adjusted the waistline of my choring dress, letting my eyes roam over the letter. *Jah,* I was downright uncomfortable these days. Oughta finish hemming the maternity dress I started yesterday. But first things first . . .

Jacob's itching to get his fingers back in the soil. Won't be long and he'll have his twenty-sixth birthday. I'm close behind at twenty-four, still young enough to hold on to certain dreams, you know, trusting the Lord to help make them come true. Even though we married young, we've worked mighty hard for a chance to buy some land, like you and Levi. We're both eager for that day—farming's im blud— in the blood.

Jacob's a good provider and a kind and loving husband. We're good friends, too, which isn't too often the case among some husbands and wives. (I have you to thank for setting us up. If it hadn't been for you, I might never have gone to my first Singing back when!) 'Course, I'd never want to return to my single days—ach! My face was always that befuddled pink. Remember?

When I look into Aaron's bright eyes, I can't help but see the hope of the future. Such a spirited disposition he has, and I am indeed grateful. When Annie points out the colors of a dewy rose garden at early morning or the changing sky at sunset (she really does have a keen eye for nature at just four)—it makes me stop and count my blessings. So very many!

Sometimes I think the dear Lord has showered too many wonderful-gut things down on me. But you know my reticent heart, Esther, that I do have much to be thankful for.

Mam and Dat are finally settled one hundred percent in their new place. Just didn't seem right, them moving out of the old farmhouse. But they're happy about the new business—Zooks' Orchard Guest House B&B—not far off Beechdale Road, on Olde Mill Road. I'm amazed, at their age (Mam's already sixty-three!), yet they want to do something completely different now that Dat thinks he's too old to farm. At least the homestead didn't change hands to strangers. It stayed in the family the way Dat always wanted. My two older brothers and their wives are keeping *the place going. The dairy farm, too. I think my parents really do have a ministry to the weary traveler. Offering a retreat in the midst of Amish country is something more of us ought to consider.*

Well, this is getting long, and news is scarce. Please write soon.

I remain your loving cousin,
Rachel Yoder

Ohio and Esther were both on my mind as I folded the letter, then placed the envelope on the buffet at the far end of the kitchen.

"Time for evening prayers," Jacob said, looking up from the *Budget.* He'd spread the weekly Amish newspaper out all over the kitchen table, open to the ads for carpentry tools.

"I'll go call the children." I watched from the back door as Aaron and Annie came running, their hands and faces smudged from digging in the dirt. "Pop's gonna read the Bible," I said, hurrying them to the sink to be washed up.

Jacob took the Bible down from its usual place in the corner cupboard and sat in his grandfather's old hickory rocker—his favorite chair. "Listen carefully, children," he said, his face tanned and smiling.

Aaron and Annie sat cross-legged at their father's knee. "What Bible story will it be tonight?" asked Aaron. Then, not content to wait for an answer, "Can we hear about David and Goliath again?"

Jacob grinned and ruffled the boy's head. "Something *friedlich*—peaceable—will do."

I pulled up a chair next to Jacob, grateful for our special time together. But the house was so warm, nearly too hot and humid to expect our little ones to sit still. Both the back and front doors stood wide open, the screen doors allowing circulation through the house, yet keeping out flies and other pesky insects. There had been an abundance of mosquitoes, my least favorite of the summer pests.

We listened as Jacob read from Psalm 128—a hymn of celebration, possibly sung by King David himself. Yet I found my thoughts drifting off to the move to Ohio. Probably wouldn't happen till the dead of winter. Still, the realization of our dream was fast approaching.

Jacob's soothing voice brought me out of my reverie. " 'The Lord shall bless thee out of Zion: and thou shalt see the good of Jerusalem all the days of thy life.' " He paused, his eyes bright with affection as he looked over the heads of the children . . . at me. I felt a little giddy as our eyes met and locked.

Dearest Jacob, I thought, smiling back at him.

He began to read again. " 'Thou shalt see thy children's children, and peace upon Israel.' "

I was delighted with the Scripture Jacob had chosen for this summer night. This balmy evening, brimful of peace and contentment, before the chaos and stress of market day. . . .

Once Aaron and Annie were safely tucked into bed, I scurried down the hall to Jacob's waiting arms. I recalled the words of the psalm, still clear in my memory. *Thou shalt see thy children's children*. . . .

Sighing, I smiled into the darkness. Ohio was just around the corner. At long last, we would see the desire of our hearts. The Lord willing, we would.

We talked into the wee hours, yet it seemed the night was young. "We have much to look forward to," Jacob whispered.

I felt a twinge of confidence. "A new beginning, ain't so?"

He gave a chuckle, and we sealed our love with a tender kiss before settling down to sleep.

There was no way I could've known then, but that night—that precious, sweet night—was to be our very last. Nor could I have foreseen that my sensitive, shy nature—a persistent hound throughout my life—would change my course and, in due time, plunge me into darkness and despair.

Part One

The best mirror is an old friend.

German proverb

One

❖ ❖ ❖

Something as insignificant as sleeping past the alarm—getting a late start—always set things spinning out of kilter.

The hurrier I go, the behinder I get, Rachel thought, feeling awful frustrated about having to rush around. Quickly, she washed her face, glancing in the oval mirror above the sink. That done, she brushed her longer-than-waist-length hair, parting it down the middle and working it into the plain, low bun at the back of her neck, the way she arranged it each and every morning.

She had lived all her life in rural Bird-in-Hand, in the heart of Pennsylvania Dutch country. Her parents and siblings had found great fulfillment in working the land, all of them. But, as was their custom, only the youngest married brothers had been given acreage, divvying up sections of the original family farm. There was only so much soil to go around, what with commercialism creeping in, choking out precious land—the very reason Levi and Esther Glick had packed up and bid farewell to their close-knit families. All for the sake of owning a parcel of their own.

Still, the historic village and outlying area had offered everything she and her now-grown brothers and sisters ever wanted, and more. There was the grace of swaying willows, the tranquillity of clear, chirping brooks, the honesty of wide-open skies, and the blessing and abundant love of the People.

"Our Father God, thy name we praise," she whispered, starting the day—late as it was—with a prayer of thanksgiving.

Reverently, she placed the white prayer veiling on her head and turned to see her husband standing near the window, his tall, stocky frame blocking the path of the sun.

"We best hurry," she said, moving to his side. "Can't be late for market."

"We'll take the shortcut, then we won't hafta rush so," he said, drawing her close.

"The shortcut?" Rachel was cautious about the roads that led to the Crossroad—a dangerous intersection—where a number of fatal accidents had occurred in the past.

Jacob reassured her. "It'll be all right. Just this once." When she relaxed in his arms, he whispered, "What if we moved to Ohio a bit sooner?"

"How soon?" Her heart beat hard with excitement.

"Say late December . . . after Christmas maybe."

Delighted, she reminded him of her cousin's many letters. "Esther says there's still ample farmland where they are." She thought ahead, counting the months. "And the new baby'll be two months old by then, if I carry full term."

Jacob nodded thoughtfully. "A right gut time then, prob'ly."

Rachel couldn't deny that Esther's persistent letters had caused a stirring in her, and now to hear Jacob talk so!

"There's plenty time left to discuss the details." He looked down at her, his eyes serious. "The woodworking shop brings in nearly more business than I can handle, so we'll have enough money to make the move by December."

"The Lord willing," she whispered. God's will was always uppermost in their minds, yet she longed for the cutting sweet smell of newly mown hay and the earthy scent of cows herded into the barn, ready for milking.

Rachel's parents and both sets of grandparents, clear back to the sturdiest aging branches of the family tree, had been dairy farmers. Some of them had raised chickens and pigs, too, spending grueling hours in the field while they spread manure to insure bountiful crops.

According to snippets of stories she'd overheard growing up, there was only one of her ancestors who'd forsaken his upbringing. Considering the two hundred or so conservative folk connected to her through blood ties or marriage, losing a single member was ever so slight compared to some families. Age-old gossip had it that Great-uncle Gabriel, her mother's uncle, had turned his back on the Plain community sometime during his twenty-seventh year, long past the time a young man should've joined church, making his commitment before God and the People.

There were various spins on the story. Some said Gabe Esh was a self-appointed evangelist. Others had it that he'd been given a so-called "divine revelation"—only to die weeks later.

As far as Rachel was concerned, no one seemed to know exactly what happened, though she wasn't the sort of person to solicit questions. Truth was, most everyone closely acquainted with Gabe had long since passed through the gates of Glory. Except, of course, Old Order Bishop Seth Fisher and his wife, and Jacob's and Rachel's parents, though none of them seemed inclined to waste time discussing a "rabble-rouser," which was just what one of the preachers had said of Gabe in a sermon some years back. And there was Martha

Stoltzfus—Gabe's only living sister. But the brusque and bitter woman refused to speak of him, upholding *die Meinding*—the shunning that must've been placed on him, for what reason Rachel did not know. Lavina Troyer was rumored to have been a schoolmate of Gabe Esh, though none of that was talked about anymore.

So there was a broken bough on Rachel's family tree, and not a single Esh, Yoder, or Zook cared to recall the reason for the fracture.

She headed downstairs to cook the usual breakfast for her dear ones. Abandoning thoughts of the past, she turned her attention to the future as she scrambled up nine large eggs, made cornmeal mush and fried potatoes, and set out plenty of toast, butter, grape jelly, and apple butter. Just knowing that she and Jacob and the children could move so far from home, that a Bible-based conservative group was expecting their arrival—or so Esther had said—filled her heart with gladness. The future was ever so bright.

Rachel and Jacob sat down with the children to eat, but the minute Jacob was finished, he dashed outside to load the market wagon. Rachel gently encouraged the children not to dawdle as she washed and dried the dishes.

Soon, Jacob was calling to them from the yard. "Time to load up the family. *Kumme*—come now!"

Rachel dried her hands and gathered up her basket of needlework. It was always a good thing to keep busy at market, especially if there was a lull, though that would hardly be the case on a summer Saturday. Tourists generally flocked to the well-known Farmers Market this time of year.

Spying the letter to Cousin Esther on the buffet, she snatched it up just as Jacob came indoors. "I think we're all ready," she said, shooing the children in the direction of the back door.

The Yoders settled in for a twenty-minute ride, by way of the shortcut. An occasional breeze took the edge off the sun's warm rays as Jacob hurried the horse. Still, they were forced to reflect on the day, allowing the primitive mode of transportation to slow them down, calm them, too. Truth be told, Rachel was glad they still drove horse and buggy instead of a car, like a few of her young Beachy relatives. The thought of buzzing highways and wide thoroughfares made her shiver with fright. She hoped and prayed Holmes County might be far less bustling.

"Plenty of time left," Jacob had said about scheduling their moving day. More than anything, she wanted to bring up the topic as they rode along. But she thought better of it and kept her peace.

It was Aaron who did most of the talking. Jabbering was more like it. After several minutes of the boy's idle babbling, Jacob reprimanded him. "That'll be enough, son."

Instantly, Aaron fell silent, but Rachel heard Annie giggle softly, the two of them still jostling each other as youngsters will.

Children are a gift from God, she thought, glancing back at the darling twosome. How very happy they all were in this life they'd chosen. And her husband's quiver was surely on its way to being full of offspring.

She allowed her thoughts to wander back to each of her children's home births. Seemed like just yesterday that Mattie Beiler, Hickory Hollow's most prominent midwife, had come at dawn to help deliver Aaron. Rachel kindly rejected her mother's suggestion to have a hex doctor come to assist—even after twenty hours of excruciating labor. Her first-born would make his appearance when he was good and ready, she'd decided, in spite of Susanna's pleadings. For once, Rachel had spoken up and was glad of it.

One year and two months later, Annie, all sweet-like, had arrived with the mildest, shortest labor on record in the area—around midnight. No sympathy healer was hinted at for Annie's birth. And no midwife.

Rachel cherished the memories, yet tried to lay aside her ongoing concern over the powwow doctors. Especially one *die blo Yonie*—Blue Johnny. *Dokder* was the name the children called him, though she knew he was not a real doctor at all. Not Amish either.

The tall man with bushy brown hair came a-knocking on one door or another nearly every Tuesday afternoon. Last month, he'd come to the Yoder house quite unexpectedly. He'd reeked of the musty scent of pipe tobacco as he rubbed his little black box up and down her son's spine and over his shoulders, never waiting for Rachel's consent whatsoever. Yet in no time, he knew about a tiny wart, hardly visible, growing on Aaron's left hand.

"To get rid of it, just roast the feet of a chicken and rub the wart with them, then bury the chicken feet under the eaves of your house, and the wart will disappear," the man had said, eyeing her curiously.

Because of her wariness, Rachel never roasted any such chicken feet. She honestly wished she hadn't opened the door to Blue Johnny that day, what with Jacob working clear across the barnyard in his woodshop. Even so, she was too timid to speak up. Such folk, calling themselves faith healers—with charms for this and herbal potions for that—had frequently called on Plain folk for as long as she could remember. Some of them were Amish themselves, though the powwow doctors among her own family had died out years ago. She herself had been looked upon as a possible choice because of certain giftings manifest in her as a young child. But due to her extreme shyness, she had been passed over.

As for Blue Johnny, she felt uneasy around him and others who claimed "healing gifts," even though he'd graciously cured Lizzy of rheumatism years ago. He'd come to the Zook farmhouse and taken the disease away by tying a blue woolen yarn around her sister's painful limbs, repeating a charm three times. In the process, the man had taken the disease on himself. And she knew that he had, because he limped out of the house and down the back steps, while Lizzy was free of pain in the space of five minutes!

Most of the Plain folk in the area never gave powwow practices a second thought. Sympathy healers and folk medicine came with the territory, brought to Central Pennsylvania by early Dutch settlers. Such healers were believed to have been imparted gifts by the Holy Spirit and the holy angels, but there were others—a small minority—who believed the healing gifts were anything but divinely spiritual, that they were occultic in nature.

Rachel knew precisely where her own uncertainties concerning powwow doctors had come from—an old column in the *Budget*, the popular Ohio-based newspaper for Amish readers. There had been an article written by one Jacob J. Hershberger, a Beachy Amish bishop living in Norfolk, Virginia, back in 1961. Esther had stumbled onto it when she cleaned out the attic before their Ohio move.

For some reason, her cousin had thought the article important enough to save, so she'd passed it along to Rachel and Jacob. The writer had spoken out strongly against enchantment and powwowing, describing such as the work of evil spirits. Jacob Hershberger had also admonished Amish communities everywhere to abandon their superstitious beliefs "handed down by godless heathen." He instructed them to "lay on hands, anoint with oil, call the elders of the church, and pray" for the sick as God's Word teaches, instead of turning to witchcraft—powwow doctoring.

After reading the column, Rachel initially wondered if there might be some truth to the notion that powwow doctors received their abilities from the devil rather than God. Could that be the reason she'd always had such a peculiar feeling around them? Yet if that was so, why didn't others in the community feel uneasy—the way she did?

Since Rachel didn't have the courage to speak up and share her apprehension with either her bishop or the preachers, she was glad she could confide in at least one other person besides Jacob. Esther was always kind enough to say, "Jah, I understand," or gently beg to differ with her. Esther was either black or white on any issue, and Rachel had come to trust that forthright approach. It was that kind of thoughtful and compassionate friendship they'd enjoyed throughout the years.

❖ ❖ ❖

Rachel gazed lovingly at her husband's strong hands as he held the reins, urging the horse onward. She looked ahead to the narrow two-lane road, taking in the barley and wheat fields on either side. Bishop Glick's place, with its myriad rose arbors bedecking the side yards, would soon be coming up on the left-hand side. Then another two miles or so and they'd pass the stone mill and the homestead where she'd grown up amidst a houseful of people.

She marveled at the beauty around her—the sun playing off trees abundant with broad green leaves and the wild morning glory vines entwined along the roadside. Ambrosial fragrances of honeysuckle and roses stirred in the summer air.

"Will we miss Lancaster, do you think?" she asked Jacob softly.

He reached over and patted her hand. "We always miss what we don't have. 'Tis human nature, I'm sad to say." His was a knowing smile, yet his words were not of ridicule.

"Living neighbors to Esther and Levi will be wonderful-gut," she replied, thinking out loud. "We'll be farmers again . . . after all these years."

Her husband nodded slowly, his well-trimmed beard bumping his chest. "Jah, the soil tends to pull us back to it, I'd say. But I'm a-wonderin' if you and Esther don't have somethin' cooked up." Jacob looked almost too serious. "Maybe Levi and I oughta keep you and your cousin apart, for good measure."

Rachel didn't know whether to laugh or cry. "Surely you don't mean it."

He looked at her and winked. "You know me better'n that."

She had to laugh, the mere pressure of the moment bursting past her timid lips. "Jah, I know," she said, leaning her head on his strong shoulder. "I know you, Jacob Yoder."

They rode that way for a spell while the children twittered playfully behind them. She closed her eyes, absorbing the sounds of baby birds, newly hatched, and the rhythmic *clip-clop* of the horse. The familiar sound of a windmill told her they must be approaching her parents' homestead. She felt close to the earth; the back roads made her feel this way—riding in the long, enclosed market wagon, pulled by a strong and reliable horse down provincial byways that wove the farm community together.

It was the intersection at Ronks Road and Route 340— the Crossroad—that put the fear of God in her. But the junction was a good twelve minutes away and the unfortunate accidents long since forgotten. Thankfully, a traffic light had been installed after the last tourist car accident, making the crossing safer.

She would simply enjoy the ride, let her husband humor her, and put up with Aaron's increasing silliness in the back of the wagon. Then, once they settled in at market, she'd have the children run over to the post office and mail her letter to Esther.

Two

*W*ith great expectancy, Susanna Zook watched through her front room window as an open spring wagon, drawn by a veteran horse, rumbled up the private lane to the Orchard Guest House.

Unable to restrain herself, she sailed out the screen door, letting it *slap-slap* behind her. She leaned on the porch post, catching her breath as her husband and his English friend climbed down from the wagon and tied the horse to the fence post, then proceeded to unload a large cherrywood desk.

Home at last! she thought, reliving the recent weeks of haggling with the Mennonite dealer over the handcrafted piece. The minute she'd caught sight of the fine tambour desk on display at Emma's Antique Shop she had coveted it, secretly claiming it for one of their newly refurbished guest quarters. She *had* thought of asking her son-in-law Jacob Yoder to make one, perhaps even suggest that he inspect the desk—see what he could do to replicate it. Something as old and quite nearly perfect didn't often show up in shop windows. Such handsome items usually ended up at private estate sales and family auctions.

Rumor had it that the rolltop desk had been in old Bishop Seth's family, unearthed and in disrepair in his wife's English nephew's shed up near Reading. Someone at the store let it slip that the 1890s desk had been restored in recent years, though when Susanna pushed for more background information, she was met with vague responses. She soon discovered that it was next to impossible following up on former antique owners.

Watching from the porch, Susanna held her breath as the men tilted, then lifted the enormous desk off the wagon. She could picture the space she'd set aside for its permanent new home. Upstairs in the southeast bedroom—newly painted and papered—ready for an overnight guest. All four of the other bedrooms had been completed in just a few short weeks after she and Benjamin had taken possession of the historic structure.

The architectural mix of colonial red brick, typical white porch, and country green shutters was both quaint and attractive, made even more fetching by the gentle backdrop of nature: the apple orchard and mill stream beyond the house to the north, a pine grove to the south, as well as expansive side and front lawns. Relatives and friends had come to help fix up the place, and in a few weeks, the rambling two-story house was ready for tourists.

Sighing with sheer delight, she watched as Benjamin and his friend hauled the desk up the red-and-pink-petunia-lined walkway. "It's awful heavy, jah?" she called.

Ben grunted his reply. It was obvious just how burdensome the ancient thing was, weighing down her robust man—her husband of nearly forty-five years.

She hadn't brought up the subject, but she figured Ben had encouraged her to purchase the desk as a sort of anniversary gift. "It's not every day a find like this shows up at Emma's—walks up the lane and into your house," he'd said, with a twinkle in his eyes.

She knew then he honestly wanted her to have it, and she was tickled pink. But then, Benjamin was like that, at least about special occasions. He, like many farmers, didn't mind parting with a billfold of money, so long as it made his wife happy. And Susanna had never been one to desire much more than she already had, which, for an Amish farmer's wife, was usually plenty, especially when it came to food, clothing, and a roof over their heads. Just not the worldly extras like fast cars, fancy clothes, and jewelry, like the modern English folk.

She held the door open as the men hoisted their load past her and into the main entryway. Deciding not to observe the painstaking ascent to the upstairs bedroom, she made herself scarce, going into the kitchen to check on her dinner of roast chicken, pearl onions, carrots, and potatoes.

When she was satisfied that the meal was well under way, she went and stood at the back door. Their new puppy, a golden-haired cocker spaniel, was waiting rather impatiently outside—as close as he could get to the screen door without touching it with his wet nose.

"You're just itchin' to come in, ain'tcha?" she said, laughing as she pushed the screen door open just wide enough to let him scamper past. She shooed away the flies, thinking that she'd have to go around with her flyswatter now, hunting down the pesky, germ-ridden insects. How she hated them!

Still amazed that Benjamin hadn't nixed her idea of having a house pet, she freshened the puppy's water dish, chattering with pleasure as he lapped up the cool refreshment. She'd grown up believing that animals—wild animals and farm animals alike, as well as dogs and cats—were meant to live outside in a barn or some other such place. Never in

31

the house. So when she'd spotted the beautiful pup at the pet store, she didn't quite know why she changed her mind, wanting to raise an animal indoors. Maybe it was the dejected, yet adorable way the puppy had cocked his head to one side, as if to say, "Won'tcha please take me home?"

In the end, Benjamin was more than generous about purchasing the sad-eyed thing, giving Susanna full sway with the decision. Maybe he was softening in his old age, though he was just in his mid-sixties. Still, she assumed the purchase of a pet was somehow a joint retirement present to each other, possibly for optional companionship should one of them die in the next few years. How very strange such a house pet might seem to any of the People, especially when a host of cats and dogs were multiplying themselves monthly back on the farm they'd left to Noah and Joseph, their youngest sons, and their wives.

"Copper, baby, come here to Mamma," she cooed down at the shining eyes and wagging tail. "You want a treat now, don'tcha?"

The dog seemed to agree that a midday snack was quite appropriate and followed her across the commodious kitchen, complete with all the modern conveniences, and stood near the refrigerator, wagging his bushy tail, eager for his treat.

She was secretly glad they'd bought a house with electricity already installed. And the modern kitchen—what would her sisters and cousins give to live like this! Thank goodness Bishop Seth had given special permission to conduct their B&B business this way. Only one requirement: She and Benjamin were not allowed the use of electricity in their private quarters, and, of course, there was to be no television or radio anywhere in the house, which was quite all right with Susanna. Such worldly gadgets made too much racket for overnight guests anyway.

She heard her husband and his friend chatting on the upstairs landing. *Gut*, she thought. They must be finished with the weighty chore.

"Here we are, pooch." She handed Copper a pale green treat in the shape of a miniature bone. Leaving the kitchen and rounding the corner, she hurried through the breakfast room, situated in the center of a plant-filled conservatory, then through the formal dining room. There, she met up with the men.

"Your writing desk looks mighty nice," Ben said, jerking his head toward the stairs. "I daresay, if I hadn't seen it squeeze past the doorjambs, I wouldn't have believed it myself."

"*Denki*, Ben." She included her husband's friend in her thanks, offering him hot coffee and a sticky bun and inviting him to stay and sit a spell. But the man declined, shaking both his head and his hands, backing away toward the front door.

Ben stood there with a silly grin on his face. "Well, go on now, Susie. You know you're just achin' to have a look-see."

She *was* eager. "Jah, I'll get up for a peek at it." And with that, she hastened up the stairs to the well-appointed guest room. Her eyes found the desk immediately, and she stood a moment, admiring the central placement on the long, papered wall. "It's *lieblich*—lovely," she whispered, heading for the linen closet in the hall where she kept cleaning supplies.

Before she set about dusting the desk, she pulled up a chair. After sitting down, she proceeded to roll back the rounded wooden covering, peering into every nook and cranny. Each little drawer and opening was just as she'd remembered, and she thrilled at the opportunity to own such a magnificent piece. "I will not be proud," she said aloud. "I will be thankful instead."

She dusted the organizer, complete with pigeonholes, and all the intricate woodwork where dust might've found lodging. Taking her time, she polished all the compartments except for one wide, thin drawer off to the left. She jiggled and pulled, but there was no budging the tiny niche, and she made a mental note to have Jacob take a look.

It was after she had finished polishing the desk, as she made her way down the hall to the stairs, that she heard the wail of a siren. The dismal sound came closer and closer, then swept past the turnoff to Beechdale Road, just south of them on Highway 340. Momentarily she cringed as she often did when she heard an ambulance or a fire truck in the area. But she dismissed the worrisome thought and went about the task at hand—preparing the noon meal for her husband.

Three

❖ ❖ ❖

*J*acob brought the horse and wagon to a complete stop, waiting first in line for the light to change at the Crossroad. "There's much traffic today," he mentioned, his eyes fixed on the highway.

"Public schools are out already," Rachel said, seeing the cars whiz past them on Route 340. "Tourists are here from all over."

"'Tis gut for business." Jacob looked at her quickly, then back at the road just ahead.

"Jah, and for us movin' to Ohio sooner," she replied with a nervous titter, eyeing the busy intersection.

Aaron, behind them, pretended to be attracting tourists, laughing as he talked. "Come on, now, folks, have a look at these handmade toy trains and helicopters! You won't find toys like this anywhere else in the whole wide world."

Glancing around, Rachel saw her son holding up the wooden playthings, one in each hand. "Dat's crafts won't last long today," she replied.

"If we ever get through this light, they won't," Jacob muttered.

Just then, an unexpected gust of wind snatched Esther's letter out of Rachel's hand, and it floated out the window and somersaulted—end over end—landing on the roadside to the right of the wagon.

"Aw, your letter," Jacob said.

"I'll run 'n get it right quick," Rachel said and got out before Jacob could stop her. But the wind played chase, sending the envelope into the field, and she stumbled after it, glancing over her shoulder to see if the light was still red. *Gut*, she thought, seeing that it was, and hurried to catch the stray envelope.

Just as she rescued the letter, pushing it down into her apron pocket—just at that moment—she turned and saw the horse rear up, spooked by traffic.

"*Himmel*, no . . . no," she whispered, running back toward the road, her heart in her throat.

Jacob was involved in a contest of wills, holding the reins firmly, pulling back hard. But the mare was up . . . up on her hind legs again, neighing loudly and shaking her long black mane.

"Hold steady, girl," Rachel begged, clenching her fists at her sides, helpless to do a thing.

She could see that Jacob was trying his best to control the horse, but after moments of struggle, the frightened animal lunged forward, still snorting and stomping.

Rachel screamed, but her cries did not keep the mare from pulling the market wagon forward into the busy intersection. In a split second, a surge of terrifying sounds filled the air—brakes squealing, car horn blaring. The noises accompanied a speeding car as it crashed broadside—Jacob's side—into the wagon.

Rachel stood gasping, frozen in place, as she witnessed the impact, seeing with her own eyes the market wagon splinter apart like so many toothpicks. Oh, dear Lord, her family . . . how could they possibly survive the crushing blow?

Moments passed. Everything around her fell silent.

Suddenly, strength returned to her legs. She began to stumble across the field to the accident scene, sobbing as she searched for her precious little children and dear, dear Jacob.

Rachel combed through the wreckage, calling frantically, "Aaron! Annie! Mamma's here. Aaron . . . Annie! Can you hear me?"

Unable to find her children, she wrung her hands, running here and there, nearly insane with dread.

Continuing her search, she winced at the sight of her husband lying in the highway, surrounded by dozens of damaged toys and mangled wood and metal from the shattered market wagon. She knelt on the road, its blacktop blistering her knees as she lifted her husband's battered face to hers. Lovingly, she cradled him as if he were a small child. "Oh, Jacob . . ."

He moaned pitifully as she held him, though she dared not rock or move him the slightest, so badly hurt he was. "Lord, please let my husband live," she prayed with trembling lips, all the while looking about her for signs of her little ones.

Jacob was breathing; she could feel the slow and labored movement of his chest. Still, she was frightened, alarmed by the gashes in his head, the torn shirt and suspenders. She hesitated for a moment, then touched the wound in his left shoulder, allowing her hand to linger there as if her touch might bring comfort. That shoulder had supported her weary head on countless nights as they lay talking into the wee hours, whispering in the darkness of their Ohio dream as they planned their lives together with God's help. Jacob's shoulder had soothed her when, at nineteen, she'd experienced the first unfamiliar pangs of childbirth.

Now . . . she heard voices as if there were people near, though she couldn't tell for sure, so murky and muddled things seemed, like a dream that she was actually living, unable to sort out the real from the illusory. She thought she might be dying, too, so dizzy and sick she was.

A distant siren sang out, moving toward her with a peculiar throbbing motion. The rhythm of its lament seemed to pulse up through the highway, into her body as she held Jacob close.

Compassionate hands were touching her husband, lifting his eyelids, putting pressure on his wrist. Then he was being carried away from her on a long stretcher. She felt faint just then and lay down in the road. "Where are my children?" she managed to say. "I must find my little ones."

"Several paramedics are with them." This, the voice of a man she did not know. "What are your children's names?"

"Aaron and Annie Yoder," she said softly, the life withering within her.

"And your husband?"

She attempted to speak his name, but pain—deep and wrenching—tore at her, taking her breath away. Then everything went black.

When she came to, she felt a cool hand on her pulse, followed by a sharp, brief prick in her arm. Though she had no sense of time, she knew she was being lifted onto something smooth and flat, the sun blinding her momentarily. The movement caused her great pain, and when she heard pitiful moaning, she realized that it was she herself.

"You're suffering from shock" came a voice in her ear. "We're going to take good care of you . . . and your unborn child."

The overwhelming emotion was that of helplessness as she was transported through the air, though she had no idea where she was being taken or who was taking her.

"Mamma!" a child cried out.

In her disoriented state she could not identify the source of the utterance, though something inside her wrestled to know. "Aaron?" she mumbled, beginning to shake uncontrollably. "Oh, Lord Jesus . . . help us, please."

A warm covering embraced her body, and for a fleeting moment, she thought her husband's strong arms were consoling her. Then came stark flashes of bewildering images. Two roads meeting, a horse lurching, children screaming . . .

"No . . . no," she said, fighting off the visions. Yet they persisted against her ability to stop them.

The sound of rushing feet startled her back to the here and now. Where *was* she? Struggling to raise her head even the slightest, Rachel tried to take in her surroundings, feeling horribly and completely alone. The noises about her ceased and outward awareness faded with the deep, prevailing pain in her womb.

The wail of a siren jolted her nerves, and gradually she gave in to the attentive urgings of those around her. *Relax . . . rest . . . please rest. . . .*

She sensed that she was weakening, letting go—surrendering to the tremendous pain. And fear so black and ferocious, such as she had never known.

❖ ❖ ❖

In the hours following the accident, Rachel was unable to divide reality from haunting impressions. She knew only one thing: Her parents were near, along with several of her brothers and sisters and their spouses. Her semiprivate room at Community Hospital was lovingly cushioned with Plain folk, close relatives with concern stamped on each face.

Suffering the ill effects of her miscarriage, Rachel was finally able to speak the burning question in her mind. "Where are Jacob . . . and Aaron and Annie?"

Her parents stood on either side of the bed, their faces grim. "Annie's doin' fine," her father said. "Her right arm is broken and there are bruises, but she will be all right."

"What about Jacob and Aaron?" came her frightened reply.

Such a look passed between Mam and Dat that panic seized her, and she thought she might faint. "I must know about my family!"

When neither parent responded immediately, she felt something rise up in her. Something strong and defensive. "Please tell me what happened. I must know *everything*," she pleaded.

Their pallid faces told the dreadful truth. "I'm sorry, my precious daughter," Dat said at last.

"You don't mean . . ." She paused, trying to breathe enough to speak. "Jacob isn't . . ." She simply could not voice the impossible word. "Is Aaron. . . ?"

Mamma nodded slowly, eyes glistening. "Jacob and Aaron died in the accident."

"It's a miracle of God that Annie is alive," added Dat, his voice sounding strangely stiff.

Mam took Rachel's hand in her own. "We'll stay right here with you, till you're released to go home."

Home . . .

Rachel moaned; her whole body shook. Home could

never be the same for her. Not without Jacob and Aaron. Overcome with grief, she closed her eyes, blocking out her mother's somber face. Mam's words were compassionate and true, yet Rachel could not comprehend a single one.

Jacob . . . Aaron dead? How can this be?

Her head throbbed with the truth, like a cumbersome weight against the long, flat hospital pillow. How it pained her to lean back. No matter what she did, her head ached, and her heart anguished for her dear ones. She wished she might've held her sweet little Aaron as he lay suffering on the road. It plagued her that he had died alone at the accident scene, that he might've called out for her—"Mamma, oh, Mamma, I'm hurt awful bad!"—or worse, that he could not utter her name at all.

She placed her hands on her womb, her flat, lifeless womb, longing for her unborn child as well.

More than anything, she wished to join her husband, her son, and their tiniest little one in heaven. Life without Jacob would be ever so lonely. Unbearable. Life on this earth without her darling boy would be intolerable. How could she face the years ahead? How could she bear the pain, missing them so?

Someone wearing white floated into the room, and although Rachel assumed it was the nurse coming with a sedative, a blanket of numbness fell over her before she ever felt the needle penetrate her skin.

❖ ❖ ❖

Esther and her husband arrived the next afternoon. They had hired a Mennonite van driver to rush them from

Holmes County to Lancaster. In the space of half a day, they'd come.

The reunion was a tearful one, and Rachel repeatedly searched Esther's dewy brown eyes, taking in the familiar rosy cheeks and the oval shape of her cousin's face. Esther had worn her best blue cape dress for the occasion, though her black apron was a bit wrinkled from the trip. "You'll need someone to look after you and little Annie for a while," she insisted, kissing Rachel's forehead and holding her hand. "Levi and I will be more than happy to stay till you're back on your feet."

"I'm so glad you're here."

"I came to help, to bear your sorrow," Esther pledged. "Levi and I can stay as long as need be." She explained that their children were with close Amish friends in Holmes County.

"I don't know what I'd do without you," Rachel said, her voice breaking. "Didja know that I must've written you a letter the night before the accident? But I don't remember writing it now. Mamma found it in my apron pocket." She motioned to the small closet. "It's in there somewhere," she said before giving way to a fresh spasm of grief.

Esther hugged her cousin. "Shh. I'm here now. We'll get through this, jah?"

When Rachel was able to compose herself, Esther sat on the edge of the hospital bed, their hands clasped. They talked quietly of Annie and how glad they were that the child had been spared, along with Rachel. "The Lord surely kept the two of you alive for a special reason," Esther said, her eyes still wet with tears.

Rachel didn't quite know what to think of that—being kept alive for a *special* purpose. God's sovereign will was not to be questioned, of course. Yet it was difficult to hear Esther go on so, especially when Rachel sincerely wished the Lord had taken her home to Glory, too.

Why *had* God let her live?

Mamma and Esther moved quietly to the window, encouraging Rachel to rest a bit. She heard the lull of their discreet whispering—Jacob's or Aaron's name slipping into the air every so often—but, honestly, she did not care to know what was being discussed. Funeral plans, most likely.

With the thought of such a thing—a funeral for her dear ones—horrifying mental pictures flashed before her eyes: the car roaring into the wagon, Jacob's body broken beyond recognition. She shook her head as if to shake off the visions, shutting her eyes tightly against the persistent images. "No!" she cried out.

Mam and Esther turned their heads. "What's that, dear?" Mam called to her. And Esther rushed to Rachel's bedside again.

She breathed heavily as the painful memories slowly receded. Then suddenly a new insidious notion sprang at Rachel—that the accident had been her fault. *Hers.* Taking a deep breath, she blurted, "I never heard the alarm! We slept through. If we hadn't overslept—if I'd heard the alarm clock like always—we'd never, *never* have taken the shortcut. We wouldn't have been at the Crossroad, and Jacob and Aaron would be alive today."

"Mustn't trouble yourself," Esther was saying, stroking Rachel's arm. "Mustn't go blamin' yourself."

But Rachel felt she had to express herself while this one memory was still alive in her. "We were rushing to market . . . requiring the horse to gallop. Oh, Esther . . ."

"The accident wasn't your fault," her cousin repeated. "Believe me, it wasn't."

Mam was on the other side of the bed now, leaning over to reach for Rachel's free hand. "The horse became frightened and leaped into traffic, is all."

"I . . . I don't remember any of that," she confessed as she wept. "How do you know this?"

"There were witnesses," replied Mam. "People saw what happened and told the police."

This was the first she'd heard any talk of police and witnesses. Why, the whole thing sounded like some made-up story.

Esther continued to hover near. "You mustn't dwell on what *was*, Rachel. Think on the Lord . . . how He watched over you and Annie," she said, her eyes filled with concern and love. "We will trust the Lord for His continued watch over you. And all of us will pitch in and help, too."

"Jah," she said, feeling calmer, knowing that what Esther said was precisely true. Still, she felt she was going through the motions, agreeing with Mam and Esther, yet not feeling much conviction, if any. She was now intended by God to be a widow, to raise Annie, her only child.

By herself.

Esther remained close as Mam looked on. "Rest now," she urged, squeezing Rachel's hand. "Please, just rest."

She wouldn't rest much, not the deep, life-giving rest that comes from a long day of toil. She would nap, but it would not—could not—possibly be restful.

That night, Rachel was alone for the first time. Mam and Esther had left Rachel to sleep, but her slumber was fitful and intermittent. Terrifying visions continued to haunt her as she fought to repress the nagging remnants of memories involving the accident, repeatedly refusing to see the sights her mind thrust upon her.

Giving up, she turned on the bedside lamp to read her New Testament, only to find that the room remained engulfed in hazy darkness. She blinked her eyes, trying to brush away whatever it was, assuming that her eyes were overly tired, strained perhaps. Slowly the darkness subsided.

She had been reading her New Testament only a short time when the words began to rill together like a gray smudge on the page. Thankfully, the distortion lasted only a few seconds, then cleared up. She said not a word to the night nurse but fell into a troubled sleep, the Testament still open in her hands.

Hours later, she awoke to a night sky, a starlit view from her hospital room. Getting up, she wandered to the window, looking up at a shimmering half-moon. "Oh, Jacob, I wish you hadn't had to die," she whispered. "You were such a peaceable man. Why did you and Aaron have to go that way?"

Her dreams just now had been filled with more nightmarish images. A horse—a sleek bay mare—lay sprawled out on a highway. Dead. And what might've been an Amish market wagon was twisted and on its side, all burst to pieces. She shuddered anew and rejected the repulsive visions. She would not, *could* not allow herself to see the memories that had torn her world apart. Yet with the shunning of images came shooting head pains, like long needles piercing her skull.

She closed her mind to the recollection of distant screams as well. The ear-piercing cries of a child.

Aaron? Annie?

Turning from the window, she limped back to her hospital bed, though it afforded little comfort. Once again she fell into a troubled sleep, dreaming that she was searching about her on the road, the sharp pain in her womb and the spasms in her head keeping her from moving much at all. She saw Jacob lying helplessly, wounded and bleeding. She began to cry out in her sleep, awaking herself with a jolt, only to find that the dimly lit hospital room had turned hazy beyond recognition.

❖ ❖ ❖

The next morning, Rachel was sitting in a chair near the hospital bed, wearing her own bathrobe that Esther had so graciously brought to her from home, when the nurse carried a large breakfast tray into the room.

"Good morning, Rachel," the nurse greeted her, though Rachel could make out little more than a filmy white shape.

"Gut mornin' to you," she replied, not able to determine where the coffee or juice or eggs or toast were located on the tray. She didn't feel much like eating anyway, so she sat silently till Mam and Esther began coaxing her to "just taste something."

"Honestly, I'm not very hungry."

"Ach, now, what a nice selection of things," Mam prodded discreetly.

"Looks mighty tasty to me, too," Esther said, getting up and picking up something on the tray—maybe a glass of juice or milk; Rachel couldn't be sure. "Here, why don'tcha just have a sip?"

Though she felt they were treating her like a reluctant toddler, Rachel went along with the suggestion, reaching out toward the shadowy figure. But she fumbled and missed making contact, and the glass crashed to the floor. "Oh, uh, I'm awful sorry."

"Rachel? What'sa matter?" Mam asked as Esther wiped up the mess.

"I guess it's my eyes . . . I've been havin' a bit of trouble, that's all."

"What sort of trouble?" asked Esther.

"Just some blurriness every so often . . . it comes and goes."

"Well, have you told the doctor about this?" Mam wanted to know.

Rachel sighed, feeling awful about the broken juice glass. And terribly uneasy having to answer so many questions. What she really wanted was to be left alone to grieve her husband and son. "I hate to bother anyone about it, really. Prob'ly nothing much at all."

But when the nurse came in to pick up the tray, Esther inquired anyway. "What could be causing Rachel's eyes to blur up?"

"Can you describe your symptoms, Rachel?" asked the nurse.

"I don't see so clearly anymore. Everything's all murky."

"Do you see light and shapes?"

"Jah, but it's a lot like lookin' through a cloud."

Esther spoke up just then. "Doesn't seem normal, her having foggy vision—not after a miscarriage, does it?"

"Well, I'll certainly mention this to the doctor," the

nurse said. "He'll probably want to do a preliminary check on Rachel's eyes, then, if necessary, refer her to an eye specialist."

"Thank you ever so much," Esther replied.

When the nurse left the room, Rachel reached out for her cousin's hand and squeezed hard. "Thank *you*," she whispered.

The doctor wasted no time in coming. He marched into the hospital room carrying Rachel's chart, a stethoscope dangling around his neck. "I hear you're experiencing some eye discomfort."

"No pain, really. Things are just all blurry."

"Well, we can't have you going home like that, can we?" he said casually, lifting her left eyelid and flashing a pen light into it. "Just exactly how much can you see now?"

Rachel struggled to describe her vision loss as the doctor led her through a series of probing questions.

"I don't need to tell you that you've been through a lot, Rachel. You're still reeling from having witnessed something no one should ever have to see. You'll need time to recover."

Recover?

She couldn't see how she would ever recover from such a loss as this. And she didn't want to be reminded of the grim accident scene. No, she desperately wanted to forget.

"But what would cause her eyes to blur?" asked Dat, sitting on the other side of the room, pressing for more explanation.

"I couldn't say for sure, Mr. Zook, but from what Rachel has just told me, the disruption in her vision may be related to what we call post-traumatic stress."

"How long will it go on?" Dat asked, his voice sounded thinner now.

"My guess is no longer than a week" came the cautious reply. "Only in rare cases does it persist. But if it does continue, I'd recommend you see an eye specialist and . . . perhaps a psychiatrist who specializes in grief counseling."

Rachel's vision was blurry, but she could see well enough to notice the nervous glances exchanged between Mam and Dat. Esther listened quietly, her gaze intent on the doctor.

He continued. "I'm confident that with love and support of those close to her, Rachel should recover very soon if this is, indeed, the reason."

Rachel mentally replayed the doctor's strange description of her condition. It sounded as if he thought she needed a head doctor. *I'm not crazy*, she thought.

Dat and Mam quizzed the doctor for several more minutes before he left to make his rounds, and Rachel took some comfort in his comment that her eyes would likely return to normal soon.

No longer than a week. . . .

In all truth, she was so discouraged by grief and the suppression of dreadful memories, her eye problem seemed almost trivial by comparison.

Four

The joint funeral for Jacob and young Aaron was delayed a full twenty-four hours, making it possible for Rachel, though sickly and sorrowful, to attend. Her parents and siblings—and Jacob's family—lovingly surrounded her. And there was Esther, attentive as ever.

Rachel needed help walking to and from the buggy and into the Yoders' farmhouse. There had been times after her hospital release when her vision actually seemed to be improving. Today, however, things were rather dim again.

A blistering sun beat down on the People, nearly two hundred strong, as they traveled for miles—most of them by horse and carriage—to gather at the farmhouse of Jacob's father, Caleb Yoder. The Yoders, both Caleb and his wife Mary, had wanted the funeral at home, due to the tragic nature of the deaths and the fact that it was a combined funeral for father and son.

"Has nothin' to do with us bein' Old Order," Caleb had assured her. "A home setting always makes for better." He said this with eyes hollow, his wrinkled face gray as death itself.

Rachel knew enough not to question, for Caleb Yoder was not a man to tolerate interference. And she wouldn't have thought of doing so anyway. Being submissive was a result of having been the last daughter in a string of siblings

51

prob'ly. And one of the twelve character gifts her father liked to talk about. Benjamin Zook believed certain traits were handed down through all families, through the ages. "Old" gifts, he chose to call them. Values such as generosity, responsibility, serenity, and simplicity. And, yes, submission.

Three expansive rooms had been prepared by removing the wall partitions so the People could see the preachers from any corner. The air was thick with heat and humidity as folks gathered, sitting on closely spaced wooden benches the length of each room. Women sat on one side of the house, men on the other. A large number of Jacob's English woodworking clients and friends also showed up to pay their respects. The house was filled to capacity, chairs being added here and there at the end of a bench row, squeezing in an additional person wherever possible.

Rachel sat stone-still, facing the coffins—one large, the other heartbreakingly small—seated with her relatives, Jacob's and Aaron's closest kin. Her back to the minister, Rachel recalled the painful, nagging memory of how they'd scurried about that last morning. She held her daughter close, letting Annie lean back against her, careful not to bump the broken arm. Rachel was glad her little one was still small enough to hold on her lap this way. There was something comforting about embracing a child, and she thought perhaps it was because she had lost the tiny baby growing inside her.

While they waited for the service to begin, she struggled with her circumstance, wishing she could go back and unravel the hours, relive their last morning together. A thousand times a day she wished it.

What was it Jacob had said—that they had plenty of time? She dismissed her keen thoughts for now, till her dear ones were safely buried in the ground, though the tragedy was as real to her as the precious child in her arms.

The People waited silently, reverently, for the designated hour. Then the various clocks in the house began to strike nine times, and the first minister in a lineup of several preachers removed his straw hat. The others removed their hats in unison.

The first preacher chose a spot, standing between the living room and kitchen. Rachel didn't have to turn and try to focus her eyes on him; she knew the scene by heart, from having attended a number of traditional Amish funerals. It was her place to face forward, to keep her eyes, though cloudy and dim, on the handmade pine coffins.

"The gathering here today is an important one," the preacher began. "God is speaking to us—all of us—through the death of our brother and his young son."

Rachel listened intently, adjusting Annie's position on her lap. Her little daughter might never even remember this solemn day, but Rachel wouldn't have considered not bringing her.

The preacher continued. "We do not wish either our brother Jacob Yoder back into this life or his son, Aaron, but rather we shall prepare ourselves to follow after these departed ones. Their voices are no longer heard amongst us. Their presence no longer felt. Their chairs are empty; their beds are empty."

He expounded on the grimness of dying in one's sins, though Jacob Yoder had chosen that good and right path— the only way a just and upright Amishman could stand before God on the Judgment Day, assured of where he stood for all eternity.

Their presence no longer felt . . .

Rachel stared over Annie's shoulder, down at her own black dress and apron. It was a blessing in disguise that the Lord had allowed her to be this calm and sedate at Jacob's and Aaron's funeral. By not looking so much at the small coffin, slightly wider at the shoulders and narrowing at both ends, she was able to keep her emotions in check. Her first-born lay silent and still inside that box, dressed in crisp white trousers and shirt. She had combed his hair gently, though she hadn't had the courage to push his little feet into the "for good" shoes before the funeral. Rather, she had kept the black shoes, putting them away in her own bedroom closet. There was something dear about the feet of a child. So Aaron would be buried stockingfooted, in clean black socks. Not something the Lord would mind, she was sure. To the contrary, she was almost positive her Aaron would be running barefoot in heaven—his father, too. It was what they were most accustomed to. Jesus would see to it that their feet were washed and cooled at the end of each day in Paradise.

As for the untimely deaths, she did not question God, for she had been taught to believe that His supreme will was above and over all. Yet the utter sadness had already begun to carve out a hole in her heart.

Their chairs are empty. . . .

The second minister stood to give the main address. "We come together this afternoon, united in spirit under the blessing of God, our heavenly Father, to bury our brother, Jacob Yoder, and his young son, Aaron Yoder." His words reverberated through the long front room of the farmhouse.

Rachel missed the spirit of her church. It was sadly absent here today, though she'd refused to insist on her opinion. Caleb and Mary Yoder had had their say as to the type of funeral service. Still, she would have been more inclined to have at least Aaron's service at the familiar meeting-house, where she and Jacob and the children attended Sunday school and church, packed out each week with Amish Mennonite friends and relatives. By the looks of things, the folk had turned out strong for the somber occasion, despite the traditional service. She would not have been so bold as to request a separate funeral anyhow.

What's done is done, she determined, paying close attention to the Scripture reading from John, chapter five.

" 'Verily, verily, I say unto you, the hour is coming, and now is, when the dead shall hear the voice of the Son of God: and they that hear shall live.' " The preacher read through the verses until he came to the thirty-fourth. Then he began to expound on the reading, saying that the text spoke of passing from death unto life.

When the People turned and knelt at their benches, Annie folded her hands in spite of the arm splint and leaned in close to Rachel. As the preacher prayed, Rachel realized for the first time since the accident that her knees were awful sore. She kept her eyes closed for the lengthy rote prayer, yet she reached down and pulled her dress away from her legs, touching curiously the blistered areas on her knees. She wondered how on earth the welts had gotten there, what had happened to cause them, having no recollection of ever scraping her knees . . . or burning them.

The People stood for the benediction. There had been no music, which seemed awful empty and even more sorrowful to Rachel. She loved the rich harmonies of a cappella singing. Another sigh slipped from her lips, and she hoped Jacob would forgive her for not having the sort of funeral service he would've preferred. When it came time for her to pass on to Glory, she would try to explain the sticky situation to him. Jacob would understand, she knew.

It was then, thinking of heaven again and the hope of seeing her husband someday, that her tears began to flow, unchecked. Try as she might, there was no stopping them, even as the preacher recited the ages of both Jacob and his son—the only formal obituary statement given at the end of the funeral.

"Jacob Yoder's memory is a keepsake, as is his son's. With that we cannot part. Their souls are in God's keeping. We will have them in our hearts," the preacher said finally.

We always miss what we don't have. . . .

Rachel wept silently, accompanied later by uncontrollable sobs at the graveside service. Quickly, little Annie was surrounded by Rachel's mother and sister Elizabeth as the pallbearers began to shovel gravel and soil, filling the graves.

The thumping sounds of the dirt hitting the coffins made Rachel quiver, and she was grateful for her mother-in-law and cousin Esther, who held on to her, standing with their arms linked through hers as the traditional hymn was read and the men removed their hats one last time.

That night Rachel slipped Aaron's black shoes under the covers, on Jacob's side. Then, when she got into bed, she reached over and held the shoes near her heart, thinking of the little barefoot boy with the bright, happy eyes . . . and his fun-loving father. She knew she would not speak of this deed to anyone. Not to Esther or to Mam.

It was her secret. Hers and God's.

Five

$\mathcal{I}$n the days that followed, Rachel was beholden to Esther for her care and supervision. Overwhelmed with despair, she slept around the clock some days, only to become too dizzy to stand when awake. So Esther cooked and cleaned and sewed, doing the things Rachel would normally have done if she'd felt strong enough.

By the end of the week, Rachel got out of bed due to sheer willpower, helping with a few chores indoors. She was grateful, especially, for Esther's loving attention to Annie and for her cousin's fervent prayers for Rachel as well.

"Can Esther stay with us, Mamma?" Annie asked as Rachel tucked her in for the night.

"'Twould be nice." She sat on the edge of the bed, touching her little one's brow. "But Esther and Levi must return to Ohio soon to care for their own family."

Annie was silent for a moment, her blue eyes the color of the summer sky. "Is God taking care of Dat and Aaron?"

"Jah, my *liew*—dear one, the Lord is taking gut care of them." She kissed Annie's cheek and held her in her arms long past the child's bedtime.

"I miss Dat and Aaron," Annie said, sniffling.

Sighing, Rachel fought the urge to weep. "I miss them, too, but we'll see them again in heaven."

After tucking Annie into bed, Rachel stood in the doorway, lingering there. Often, since the funeral, she'd questioned the wisdom of leaving her child to fall sleep alone. As hard as it was for *her* to sleep peacefully, she hoped Annie wasn't struggling that way, too.

"Don't think twice about bringing Annie into your room to sleep once in a while," Esther said when Rachel mentioned it to her privately. "The dear girlie's feeling awful alone in the world—and she's still just a baby, really. She needs to know that her mamma doesn't mind sharing that great big bed."

"She's blessed with many relatives who love her," Rachel added quickly, knowing full well that Annie would never want for fellowship. She would grow up completely loved and looked after by the whole of their church community, Beachy Amish and Old Order alike.

"Annie is not to be pitied," Esther commented. "And neither are you. Pity parties can only last so long, then one must put a hand to the plow, so to speak. Life goes on."

For you it does, Rachel thought, suppressing the idea as having been spiteful, then immediately asking the Lord to forgive her. She knew her cousin meant well. There was no doubt in her mind about Esther's motives.

❖ ❖ ❖

Once Esther and Levi had departed for Ohio, Rachel allowed herself to confront the extent of her loss, agonizing over the guilt that hung weighty in her mind. She sat up in bed each and every morning, greeting the dawn just as the sun was about to break over the horizon, though not without tears. Her outward mourning was her soul's response to the pain in her heart—especially at night—though she purposely put on a smile for Annie during the daylight hours.

Mam seemed wise to what was happening, though, and one morning while helping Rachel with her gardening, Susanna broached the subject. "Your eyes are forever swollen and red. Are you crying for Jacob and Aaron or for yourself?"

Rachel felt her heart constrict, wondering how to explain the pain inside. The guilt was present with her always, along with such feelings of worthlessness. "I should've been the one to die," Rachel replied, tears choking her voice.

Mam's expression was filled with tender concern. "It is not for us to question God's ways."

"Jah" was the only answer she could give, though she thought of telling her mother the truth, that she wished she might die even now.

"We must trust the Lord to work His will among us," continued her mother. "Each of us must come to accept it in due time."

In due time . . .

Rachel's eyes filled with tears. "It is not so hard to submit to the will of God." She paused, having to breathe deeply before she could go on. "It's knowing that things might've been—*should've* been—different, oh, so much different." She could not attempt to describe the ongoing gnawing in her heart, that she felt responsible for the accident. Accepting the deaths of her beloved ones would have been far easier had it not been for that singular fact.

"Time to move on, Daughter, past your agony," Mam said, though such a pat answer was nothing new. "For Annie's sake, you must."

In essence, her mother was saying the same things Esther had spoken to her before leaving—time's up on the pity party! Say what they may, she wondered how either of them might be coping with the unexpected and violent deaths of their own husbands. Cautious not to brood, Rachel pushed the thought out of her mind and prayed for grace to bear the loss, as well as the correction of her elders.

She trudged up the back steps and into the kitchen, carrying a large plastic bowl filled with mounds of leaf lettuce and a fistful of new carrots from the garden. Her vision shifted and the room seemed to float about. Things cleared up again just as quickly, and she wouldn't have thought much about it, except the English doctor had said all this would go away. *Less than a week*, he'd said. Well, now here it was two full weeks since the accident, and her eyes were still playing tricks on her.

She and Mam began to chop green peppers and cucumbers for a salad. But when the fuzziness returned, Rachel was hesitant to say anything, holding her knife silently. The blurring lasted much longer than usual, and she pushed the knife down hard into the butcher block, waiting. The longer the fog prevailed, the harder her heart pounded. Still, she attempted to stare down at a grayish-looking green pepper.

"What's wrong, Rachel?" Mam said. "You all right?"

She blinked repeatedly, trying to shake off whatever was causing the frustrating distortion. Steadily, she directed her gaze downward at the knife she knew was in her hand and the pepper on the cutting block, willing herself to see clearly, to focus on the shapes. Hard as she tried, she was engulfed in a misty world of grays and whites.

"Rachel?" She felt Mam's hand on her arm. "You're pale. Come sit for a spell."

She released the paring knife and followed Mam to the rocking chair—Jacob's favorite. She thought if she did as

Susanna suggested and sat there, relaxing and fanning herself for a bit, everything would be all right soon enough.

Sitting in the hickory rocker, she realized how very dismal things had been these past weeks, pining for Jacob's jovial nature. Oh, how she missed his hearty laugh! She missed other things about him, too. But it was the thought of his good-natured chortle that brought more tears.

"Ach, Rachel, must ya go on so?" Mam was saying. Yet she stood behind the rocking chair, stroking Rachel's back.

"I hafta tell you something, Mam," she said softly, wishing she knew where Annie was just now. She felt the swish of her mother's long dress against the chair and heard the patter of her bare feet against the linoleum floor.

Susanna seemed to understand, taking her hand and squeezing it. "If you're thinking of your miscarriage . . . well, believe me, I *do* know how you're feeling, Rachel." And she began to explain the empty sadness associated with the loss of a baby born years ago.

Rachel listened, though she continued to weep. "What I want to tell you isn't about the baby I lost," she whispered. Then, pausing, she asked, "Is Annie anywhere about?"

"Why, no, she's outside playing in the side yard—out diggin' in the dirt. You know, the way she and Aaron always . . ." Susanna stopped. "What do you *mean* asking if Annie is near? Are ya still having trouble with your eyes?"

"Well, right now, I can't see much of anything."

"I think we oughta have Blue Johnny come and take a look at you. He's been known to heal a wheal in the eye within twenty-four hours," Mam was quick to reply.

Rachel flinched at the mention of the pipe-smoking hex doctor. "I don't believe there's anything growin' in my eye,

Mam. It's just that my spirit's awful troubled . . . I can't shake it off."

"If I told your pop this, he'd say you're crying your eyes out. Plain and simple. That's just what he'd say."

Rachel blinked again and again, holding her hands out in front of her now, turning them over, trying to see them clearly. Still, she could not make out even the contour of her own thin fingers. "What's *really* causing this?" she pondered aloud. "Do you believe what the hospital doctor said?"

"You witnessed a *greislich*—terrible thing, Rachel. And if you ask me, I don't think it's something we oughta be foolin' with. Why don'tcha let me contact Blue Johnny?"

"I'm sorry, Mam, but no." She felt herself straighten a bit, determined not to let Susanna get the best of her, in spite of her distorted sight.

True, the powwow doctors were much cheaper—most of them worked for nothing—that was common knowledge, and most of the time they were quite effective. Still, she hadn't made a practice of calling on them and wasn't much keen on starting now.

Mam's voice rose in response. "I wouldn't be so quick to turn up my nose at the powwow doctors. 'Specially if you keep havin' trouble."

Rachel leaned her head against the rocking chair. "I think I'd rather go back to an English doctor, if I go to anyone. Besides, Jacob . . ." She paused. "Well, if my husband were here, he'd prob'ly tell me to stay far away from Blue Johnny."

"But Jacob's not here to see what you're goin' through, Daughter. He'd want what's best for you, jah?"

What's best for me . . .

She figured it was just as well she hadn't told Mam about

the sharp, penetrating pain that came sometimes at night, just after she lay down to sleep. It came most often with the sound of horses and carriages *clip-clop*ping up and down the road. And it came with the recurring noise of an automobile motor. She feared that one day the pain might come and stay put, with no relief ever again.

Sighing, she got up from the rocking chair, her vision having cleared up somewhat, enough to find her way to the back door and call Annie inside for lunch.

❖ ❖ ❖

Truly, she might not have gone to bed so early that evening—might've put off giving in to fitful sleep—had she known the needlelike affliction would grow nearly unbearable.

She sat up the next morning to watch the sun rise, the very dawn she had always greeted with joy. In an instant, the tormenting images returned, and she cried out in agony, renouncing them. "No! I *will not* see these things. I will *not* see!" She repeated it again and again, closing her eyes, shutting out the persistent mental pictures as she rocked back and forth.

How long she remained crumpled in her bed, she did not know. But when at last she opened her eyes and ceased her weeping, the earliest rays of morning had turned to a dark and dreary shade of charcoal.

She swung her legs over the side of the bed and stood up, groping her way across the room to the window. She and Jacob had stood and looked out together on this very spot, their last hours together. Yet no longer could she make out the rows of neatly tilled farmland beyond. So cloudy were the trees, the four-sided birdhouse, and even the neighbor's silo that they might not have existed at all.

The darkness persisted as she attempted to dress, then brush and part her long hair. No longer could she see the golden brown hues of her tresses. Neither outline nor color was visible in the mirror. Only murky, shadowy images shifted and waved, taunting her.

She had to call on past memory to place her prayer veiling in the correct location. Fear and panic seized her as she let her fingers guide the *Kapp*. Jacob and Aaron were never coming back, no matter the amount of hoping. Her life as Jacob Yoder's wife was a thing of the past. *This* was her life now. She'd had everything—*everything* right and gut and lovely—and all of it had been swept away in a blink of time. Why, she did not know, nor did she feel she could question the Almighty. Yet in the quiet moments—just before falling asleep—she had allowed herself to think grievous thoughts of anger and fear, sinful as they were.

Feeling her way along the wall, she stumbled back to the bed. This, the bed she and Jacob had shared as husband and wife. She dared not permit herself to recall the love exchanged here, nor the dreams spoken and unspoken. Denial was the only way she could endure the heartache of her life.

She made an attempt to smooth out the sheet and coverlet, to fluff the lone pillow. But the fiery pain in her head stabbed repeatedly, and in the depths of her troubled heart, she perceived that the light had truly gone from her eyes. Even as tears spilled down her cheeks, she resigned herself to the blindness, that self-imposed haven where no painful image could ever intrude.

"What's done is done," she whispered.

Part Two

❖ ❖ ❖

Midway this way of life we're bound upon,
I woke to find myself in a dark wood,
Where the right road was wholly
lost and gone. . . .

Dante

The Lord is slow to anger, abounding in love and
forgiving sin and rebellion. Yet he does not leave
the guilty unpunished; he punishes the children
for the sin of the fathers to the third and fourth
generation.

Numbers 14:18, NIV

Six

Two years later

*P*hilip Bradley checked into the first Amish B&B he could find off the main drag. Somewhat secluded and picturesque, Olde Mill Road was the kind of setting he'd wished for—made to order, actually.

The Lancaster tourist trade was like a neon sign, attracting modern-day folk who longed for a step back in time to the nostalgic, simple days—by way of shops offering handmade quilts and samplers, crafts and candles, as well as buggy rides and tours of Amish homesteads.

But it was the back roads *he* wanted, earthy places where honest-to-goodness Amish folk lived. Not the establishments that lured you with misnomers and myths of painted blue garden gates and appetizers consisting of "seven sweets and seven sours." Above all, what Philip wanted was to get this assignment researched, written, and turned in. Bone-tired from the pace of recent travels, he thought ahead to his writing schedule and deadlines for the next month.

At twenty-seven, Philip was already weary of life, though he wouldn't have admitted it. Even as a youngster he had been reticent to call attention to himself—the private side of Philip Titus Bradley, that is. His public image was a different story, and though he had risen to the top tier of feature writers for *Family Life Magazine*, he clung hard to his privacy, guarding it judiciously.

Sitting on the four-poster canopy bed, Philip stared out the window at a cluster of evergreens. The open space to the left of the pines captured his attention. In the distance, he spied a white two-story barn, complete with silo. A gray stone farmhouse, surrounded by tall trees, stood nearby. He wondered if the place might be owned by Amish. His contact, Stephen Flory of the Lancaster Mennonite Historical Society, had informed him that nearly all the farms in the Bird-in-Hand area were Amish-owned. The minute it was rumored that an English farm might be for sale, a young Amishman was sure to knock on the door, inquiring about the land and offering the highest bid.

Philip raked his hands through his thick dark hair, gazing at the streams of sunlight pouring through the opening in the tailored blue drapes, its gleaming patterns flickering against a floral wallpaper of blues and greens. The large desk had caught his eye upon entering the room, and now as he studied it, he fancied that if he were ever fortunate enough to own such a piece, it, too, would be made the focal point of its surroundings. Though such a colossal desk would be out of sync with the contemporary decor of his upper Manhattan apartment.

It was odd how the desk, centrally situated on the adjacent wall, seemed remarkably fashioned for the room. Lauren would *not* have agreed, however, and he chuckled at the fortuitous notion. Thank goodness they'd parted ways long before this present assignment. Were they still dating, she would be totally disinterested in his Lancaster research. On second thought, she might have made some crass remark about the back-woodsy folk he planned to interview.

Lauren Hale had been the biggest mistake of his adult life. She had completely fooled him, displaying her true colors at long last. To put it bluntly, she was an elitist, her intolerant eyes fixed on fame and fortune.

Nor had Philip measured up to Lauren's expectations. She had had a rude awakening; discovered, much to her amazement, that beneath his polished journalistic veneer, there was a heart—beating and warm. And no amount of wishful thinking or manipulation could alter that aspect of his character. So thankfully, he had won. He had let her have her way that final night, let her break up with him, though he'd planned to do it himself had he not been so completely exhausted from the recent European trip.

Philip observed the antique bow-top bed. King size. *Handmade canopy*, he thought, noting the delicate off-white pattern. Thanks to his vivacious niece, he knew about stitchery and such.

Young Kari had pleaded with him to let her accompany him on this trip. She'd giggled with delight when he called to say he was flying to Lancaster County. "That's Dutch country, isn't it?" she exclaimed. "And aren't there horses and buggies and people dressed up old-fashioned?"

"They're Amish," he'd told her.

"*Please*, take Mom and me with you, Uncle Phil. We'll stay out of your hair, I promise."

Regrettably, he had to refuse, though it pained him to do so. He made an attempt to explain his deadline. "You wouldn't have any fun, kiddo. I'll be busy the whole time."

"Won't you at least *think* about it and call us back?" She was eager for some fun and adventure, though she needed to stay close to home, follow through with her homeschooling—the sixth-grade correspondence course her parents had recently purchased. Public school just wasn't what it used to be when *he* was growing up in New York City. He had tried to get his sister and brother-in-law to see the light and allow him to assist them financially to get Kari into one of the posh private schools, but to no avail. They had joined a rather evangelical church and gotten religion, or the equivalent thereof, thus their desire to protect and groom Kari in the ways of God. Which wasn't so bad, he'd decided at the outset. After all, it hadn't been very long ago that he himself had knelt at the altar of repentance and given his boyish heart to the Lord, though too many dismal miles and even more skirmishes with life had since altered his spiritual course.

Before hanging up the phone, he'd promised his niece another trip instead. "Some other time, maybe when I go to London, I'll take you and your mother with me . . . when I'm not so tired."

"Tired of living and scared of dying?" She was a spunky one. "Okay, Uncle Phil, I'll take whatever I can get . . . if that's a promise. About London, I mean."

In no way did he wish to think ahead to the overseas assignments. Not then and not now.

He knew if he gave in to the abrasive feeling behind his eyes and the overall lassitude of the moment, he might not awaken in time to conduct any research or write a single sentence. Which now, as he considered the idea, seemed an exceptionally grand way to dispose of three days.

It was the notion, however, that he might miss out on the candlelight supper included in the night's lodging that caused him to rouse himself and forego the possibility of a snooze. Mrs. Zook, the hospitable owner's wife, had promised pork chops fried in real butter. Bad for the arteries but tasty on the tongue. The woman, who'd insisted that he call her Susanna, had welcomed him with such enthusiasm that he wondered at first if he were the only guest staying the night.

He discovered, soon enough, that the historic dwelling was solidly booked through October. "Most of the smaller rooms, that is," Susanna Zook had told him. Such was the Zooks' Orchard Guest House. A popular B&B indeed.

In dire need of a shower, he pushed himself off the comfortable bed, noting the handmade Amish quilt. He carried his laptop across the room to the handsome desk. The rolltop portion had already been pulled back, as though a welcome sign were attached. He was glad for the desk's spacious accommodations and would use every inch of space it could afford.

After setting up the computer, he turned his attention to unpacking. He would stay three days, depending on how solid his research connections were, though he'd called ahead to the Lancaster Mennonite Historical Society, setting up a specific appointment with Stephen Flory, a research aid, who, in turn, had promised a private interview with a "talkative Amish farmer." In addition to that, the owners of the B&B certainly seemed like a good possibility. They appeared to be retired farmers, though he couldn't be positive. There was something intriguing about their gracious manner, their kindly servant mentality. Only hardworking farmers emulated such character traits, or so his grandpap had told him years before. Grandfather Bradley had informed him about farm folk back when Philip was a boy, visiting his daddy's parents in southern Vermont. What a spread they had just outside Arlington, not far from Norman Rockwell's former home.

On first sight of Grandpap's place, his seven-year-old heart had actually skipped a beat or two. He immediately envied anyone who lived under a sky that blue and wide. And what enormous trees! Not a single towering building to block the sunlight, no blustery canyons created by skyscrapers that swayed in the wind. His heart felt free on Grandpap Bradley's land.

Philip's grandfather had built the hideaway in New England as a summer cottage, on the steep bluffs overlooking the Battenkill River. The five-room house possessed all the knotty-pine appeal a city boy might imagine, though prior to that first summer, Philip had had no knowledge of vacation spots of this sort. Especially summer places where lofty trees swept the expanse of sky instead of finger-thin structures—ninety or more stories high—and vegetable gardens were planted firmly in rich mahogany soil instead of imported box gardens on top of drafty penthouse roofs.

And there were llamas. Grandpa had a penchant for the long-necked, hairy creatures, and though they were gentle enough, Philip never quite got over the feeling, even as a teenager, that he ought to give the animals a wide berth. He'd read that llamas sometimes spit if they were aggravated or apprehensive. Young Philip could hardly begin to imagine the slime of a llama's spittle on his face. Such an experience, he'd decided early on, was to be avoided at all costs.

The oversized cottage was a replica of surrounding farmhouses, though less opulent and more quaint, in keeping with the unpretentious charm of the red Chisselville Bridge, the covered bridge not more than a mile away. Philip particularly enjoyed the miles of hiking trails and wilderness cross-country skiing near his grandparents' home. In summer, he pretended to be an explorer in those woods; in winter, just the opposite—he launched search-and-rescue missions for imaginary folk.

His grandmother's African violets were always on hand to cozy up the southern exposure of the large breakfast nook. From everything he'd read about Amish kitchens, the one set back in the hills of Vermont might have easily rivaled any Old Order kitchen, complete with buck stove and long wooden table and benches. He was yet to find out, of course, because the modern and convenient kitchen where Susanna Zook prepared supper, was, no doubt, a far cry from the turn-of-the-century-style kitchens he hoped to discover.

After he showered and dressed, he wandered downstairs for afternoon tea. Passing the parlor area, he caught sight of a young woman dressed in a long gray dress and black apron, dreary as any mourning clothes he'd ever seen. Yet it was the color and appearance of her hair that caught his attention—subtle flaxen rosettes mingled with light brown tones, parted down the middle and pulled back in a low bun, partially hidden by a white see-through head covering. She sat motionless, her hands folded gracefully in her lap. He thought at first that she might be asleep but saw that her head was erect, eyes open.

A small girl, wearing a long dress of pale green, her honey brown hair wrapped in braids around her head, came running past him and into the room. She was as cute as she was petite, and he was compelled to stand still just to see what she would do next.

Sweetly, the young woman turned and reached up to touch the child's pixielike face. "Ach, Annie, it's you."

"Jah, it's me, Mamma. Do you want somethin' to drink?"

"A glass of water will do," the woman answered, her hand still resting on the child's cheek. "Thank you, little one."

The encounter was like none Philip had ever seen. Yes, he'd felt the hand of his own mother on his brow, but to stand back and observe such a tender gesture from afar was pure poetry.

Moments of compassion were worth watching—savoring, too—even if one felt entirely removed from those involved. He had experienced a similar emotion the first time he'd seen a boy and girl holding hands as they ran down the steps of the Eighty-sixth Street subway station, laughing as they tried to squeeze through the turnstiles together. Moments like that, he'd decided, were priceless in the overall scheme of things.

Even if it were only his innate journalistic curiosity, he found himself drawn to the scene, especially to the woman, though her child intrigued him as well. Not one to gawk, however, he turned and made his way to the common area, featuring a bonnet-top highboy with slipper feet, as well as two sofas and several wingback chairs. A primitive butter churn stood sentinel in one corner, near a wood-burning fireplace.

Susanna Zook, the plump Amish hostess and owner's wife, had encouraged him upon his arrival to make himself at home. "Feel free to read, relax, and mingle with the other guests," she'd said. So he located the pleasant room, complete with floor-to-ceiling bookshelves built in across one wall and a marble-topped coffee table with ample reading material—all this within yards of a well-appointed dining room. He congratulated himself on having made an excellent choice for his stay, sight unseen.

A young couple was curled up on a settee near a fireplace marked by eighteenth century delft tiles, quietly exchanging intimate glances. He greeted them, then settled down in a chair to thumb through a Lancaster tourist guide.

"Oh, there you are again, Philip." He looked up to see the round and jubilant face of his congenial hostess. "Would you like something to drink?" she asked. "I can get you coffee, tea, a soft drink, or a glass of milk."

"Black coffee, thank you."

"Don't forget to save room for supper, served promptly at five o'clock, two nights a week—Mondays and Wednesdays," Susanna replied, including the couple in her remark. "You're always welcome to help yourself to snacks, before and after supper. Anytime, really." She turned to a corner table, arrayed with a variety of cheeses and fruit, chocolate chip cookies, and scones. "Homemade specialty breads are also handy, if you know where to look for them." She opened a cabinet door under the table, producing a wooden tray of additional delicacies. "Now, let me get you that cup of coffee. Black, you say?"

He nodded, sinking back into the chair just as the little girl he'd seen in the parlor came scurrying through the room, carrying a tall glass of water.

"Careful not to spill," Susanna called to her, then turning to Philip, said, "That's Annie, our six-year-old granddaughter. She's busy as a honeybee."

"I can see that." As they engaged in small talk, he listened carefully, paying close attention to the inflection of the woman's unique speech pattern. "Does Annie live with you?" he asked when there was a lull in the conversation.

"Both she and her mother do."

He waited, thinking that an explanation might be forthcoming. Was Annie's mother divorced, a young widow . . . what? But no clarification was given, and Philip decided it was none of his business anyway.

The Amishwoman turned toward the kitchen, and it was then he noticed the midcalf length of her blue cape dress and black apron, similar to the style of the younger woman's. She wore, also, the accompanying white netting head covering made familiar to moviegoers by Hollywood's portrayal of Lancaster County Amish. The see-through cap was referred to as a prayer covering by non-Amish folk; a Kapp or veiling by the Amish themselves. That much he knew.

He had a strong desire to get chummy with some Amish folk; maybe even volunteer to help pitch hay somewhere. Simple enough. It was what he was paid to do, his *gift*, or so his young niece had mischievously informed him last time he'd visited. Yet he knew he'd have to temper his questions, choose each one carefully, especially those he asked the Amish directly. He had been warned by his sister, who had been corresponding with an Amish pen pal near Harrisburg for several years now. Drained and wondering why he'd even agreed to this assignment, he now wished he had grilled Janice in more detail. Mainly, though, he had been caught up in his own affairs—too busy as always to delve into his only sibling's casual friendships.

"Most importantly," Janice had advised, "you must prove that you're a trustworthy sort of guy before *any* Amishman will give you the time of day. And I'm not kidding."

He had appeased her by listening with one ear, thinking that when he arrived in Lancaster, there would certainly be folks who'd be willing to talk. For money, if for no other reason. But now that he was here, had been offered a sampling of the conservative lifestyle, had met Susanna and observed Annie with her mother, he was having second thoughts about the silver-tongued approach. Maybe his sis knew what she was talking about. Lest he start out on the wrong foot, maybe he should mention to Susanna or her more reticent husband that Janice was close friends with one of *their* relatives. After all, weren't all Amish connected by blood or marriage? Yes, maybe some old-fashioned name-dropping would open a few doors for him.

He wracked his brain, trying to remember the name of the Harrisburg woman, Janice's pen pal. Was it Stoltzfus? Something fairly uncommon.

Scanning the room, he observed the brown tufted velvet chair and settee. Not exactly the most vigorous choice of color for such a grand room, considering the large tan hooked rug beneath his feet. Although coupled with the backdrop of yet another floral wallpaper pattern, the earthy tones actually worked.

He was beginning to wonder if Plain folk purposely chose to decorate their homes a whit better than they adorned themselves, though the bright blues and purples he'd seen several Amishwomen wearing as they scurried about Bird-in-Hand Farmers Market weren't entirely unattractive. At least, he hadn't seen anyone else sporting the dismal gray that Annie's mother wore as she sat alone in the parlor, completely still.

He took note of the pink- and cream-colored hurricane lamp. Antique, no doubt. Most everything in the house was of the Victorian era. That, or New England Country. Susanna surely had an affinity for old things, same as his sister.

He wondered how the two might get along if ever they were to meet.

Culture clash, he thought, suppressing the urge to laugh. Then again, they had the potential to get on famously, especially since it was Janice who'd told him in no uncertain terms to slow down and live. The Amish seemed to know how to enjoy a slow-paced life. "You're rushing through life, Philip, and it makes no sense . . . especially since you seem so absolutely miserable," Janice had said.

"But I *need* to keep busy," he'd responded, a bit put out. "I function best that way." He'd laughed, but he knew the truth. If he stopped working so hard, stopped filling up every second of his life with appointments and interviews and social events, he'd have to think. About the state of his life, for instance.

"I'd rather die than sit around twiddling my thumbs," he'd tossed off, hoping to end the uncomfortable Q and A.

"So you're addicted to work, is that it?" Janice never quit. She always pushed until he clammed up. "You know what I think? I think you're running from yourself, and if you slow down, you're afraid you'll have to take a long, hard look at who Philip Bradley really is."

Nailed again.

Truth was, of course, he *did* long for a simpler, slower life. But it was easier, by far, to keep running on this insane but safe treadmill called life, going faster and faster, never allowing himself to stop.

Susanna startled him slightly as she came with a generous mug of steaming coffee on a saucer. "Here we are. Feel free to take it to your room if you like." She glanced about her. "Or you may stay here . . . for as long as you wish. We also have a number of footpaths, leading to the orchard and beyond, to Mill Creek. It's a wonderful-gut afternoon for a walk."

"Thank you, I'll keep that in mind . . . and I'll look forward to supper as well." He offered a smile to the friendly hostess, and to the cozy couple who paid him no mind.

"I think you'll be mighty pleased with the pork chops." Susanna's smile was warm.

"Yes, I'm sure I will," he agreed, heading toward the stairs and to his room high above the parlor—that room where he had witnessed the sort of thing most writers would give their eyeteeth to see. A heartfelt, unposed portrayal of love between two human beings. Little Annie and her mother, no doubt.

He thought of his photographer friend on staff at the magazine. Henning would travel any number of miles if assured of such a tender photo opportunity. The vision of the child and mother was implanted in Philip's memory, and as part of his research, he decided to write the description, along with his emotional response to it. In fact, as he rehearsed the maternal scene, he realized with sudden enthusiasm that he was eager to begin.

Mighty happy, indeed, he thought, letting the quaint expression sink in. The Pennsylvania Dutch twaddle might take some getting used to, but he would be mindful of his sister's admonition and be a trustworthy kind of guy. The instant this assignment was finished, he would think about taking a much-deserved vacation. Janice would be happy to hear of it. So would Kari, who might even be allowed to sneak off with him to Vermont and hide out at Grandpap's old summer cottage. A pleasant thought, though he doubted he could ever bring himself to pull off such a fantasy.

First, though, the assignment—Plain folk and their family traditions. Tonight at supper, he would get his research rolling by saying all the right things. And hopefully he could get Susanna Zook talking. Maybe Benjamin, too.

Then he remembered Susanna's adorable granddaughter. *"Busy as a honeybee,"* the woman had said of the child.

Annie's perfect, he thought.

Seven

❖ ❖ ❖

Susanna poked a sharp meat fork into the pork chops, testing them for tenderness. "We'll have us a right fine supper tonight," she said, nearly singing the words. "Wouldja care to join us, Rachel?"

Rachel, who was counting out the utensils with Annie's help, shook her head. "Nothing's changed, Mam. I don't eat with our guests at breakfast, so I wouldn't feel comfortable joining in at supper. You know how I feel about eating with strangers."

"Strangers—*so en lappich Wese*—such a silly matter! Our guests are no longer strangers once they hang their hats in the vestibule." She sighed, a trifle exasperated.

Rachel wore a pained expression. "I'm all right, just keepin' to myself."

Susanna feared she'd hurt her daughter's feelings. "Well, then I'll leave it up to you." Which was pretty much the way things turned out most of the time—leaving Rachel to wallow in her grief. Had it not been for Annie, full of vim and life, Rachel might never wander any farther than their property, in either direction. She wondered, too, if her daughter would ever think to be wearing dresses of blue or purple again, instead of the humdrum gray of mourning. 'Course if she couldn't see, then what did it matter?

"Annie and I will have supper in the parlor, with the

81

door closed," Rachel said softly. "It's all right with you, ain't so, Mam?"

"No, Daughter, it's *not* all right." She was surprised at herself, revealing her true feelings at long last. She probably should've said something a year or more ago, after the appropriate time for mourning had ceased. But Rachel's grieving seemed endless, and she worried that her daughter was downright content with it.

The peculiar symptoms of lingering blindness bothered her almost as much as her daughter's indifference to life. She viewed Rachel's condition as something other than a true affliction. A Philadelphia doctor—an eye specialist—had conducted a battery of tests, even attached sensors to Rachel's head. Measured her brain-wave activity no less, and had found nothing physically wrong. Not mincing words, he'd said there was no medical basis for Rachel's inability to see. According to the tests, her brain was actually registering sight!

He'd termed Rachel's problem a conversion disorder—a hysteria of some sort—like hysterical blindness, which the specialist said sometimes comes on a person who has witnessed something so appalling that the mind chooses to block out visual awareness. He had also mentioned studies of refugees from Cambodia, mainly women, who, after being forced to watch the slaughter of their families, experienced one form of this hysteria or another, including temporary blindness, deafness, or paralysis. "I've heard of cases lasting as long as ten years or more," the English doctor had told them, "but that's very rare."

Susanna sighed, thinking back to that trip to Philadelphia and the specialist's peculiar comments. Honestly, she *had* suspected something mental, and to compound her suspicion, Rachel continued to shy away from talk of powwow doctors, which wasn't the only thing her poor, dear daughter was disturbed about these days. She also avoided talk of the accident that had taken her husband's and son's life, even to the point of excusing herself and fleeing the room if the slightest comment was made. And she'd shielded Annie from the truth, too. Rachel sidestepped, no matter what, the possibility of stirring up perplexing memories in both herself and her little girl. Emotionally wounded, Rachel was a bit *ab im Kopp*—off in the head. And though time seemed to have run out for Rachel's sight ever returning, Susanna hadn't given up hope of a full recovery. One way or the other.

Overall, her daughter was a joy to have around. In fact, inviting her and Annie to move in with them two years ago was the best thing Susanna and Ben could've done for their daughter, granddaughter, and for themselves. Rachel cheerfully pulled her weight with the housework, especially helping with the numerous loads of laundry. She was a good cook, too, and helpful in the vegetable and flower gardens close in toward the house. She was always more than happy to lend a hand; a diligent worker, no getting around it. But the spring in her step was long gone.

Rachel reminded them frequently to avoid the Crossroad, and Susanna understood, for she was loath to go near it as well. This meant they had to spend precious time driving horse and buggy out of the way, going west on Route 340—away from the accident site—then south on Lynwood Road to attend church and to visit several of Susanna's sisters, cousins, and Lavina Troyer, too, for quilting frolics and such.

Avoiding the Crossroad was one of the few things

Rachel requested. It made no sense, really, especially since she couldn't see much of anything. But they humored her—at least on that matter. Something else bothered Susanna to no end. It was Rachel's insistence that she attend her *own* church—the Amish Mennonite church she and Jacob had chosen—though there were times when it simply didn't suit. So more often than not, Rachel had to be content with Old Order preaching services at one aunt's house or another.

Despite the random inconveniences, Susanna had reconciled herself more and more to doing certain things Rachel's way. When all was said and done, wasn't it the least she and Benjamin could do for their disabled daughter?

"Mam?" Rachel's voice interrupted Susanna's brooding. "You're ever so quiet."

"Jah, I 'spect I am," she replied, wiping her hands on her apron. "I didn't mean to snap at you. Honest, I didn't."

Rachel fidgeted, gathering up the dinner plates. " 'Spose I had it comin', really."

Annie glanced up; her blue eyes blinked several times thoughtfully. Then she got up quickly, calling for Copper, who came bounding into the kitchen through the doggie opening in the screen door. The girl and the dog scampered outside.

"Don't go off too far now," Susanna warned. "Supper's almost ready."

"Ach, she needs to run a bit," Rachel said. "Annie's been cooped up all day."

"And what about *you*, Daughter?" Susanna stood at the back door, watching the early autumn haze as it settled over the apple orchard. "Why don'tcha go out and sit in the sun for a bit? Fresh air will do you gut."

Rachel sighed. "Maybe tomorrow."

Susanna turned, watching her daughter place freshly laundered cloth napkins, dinner plates, and the supper silverware on the wooden tray. Then, slowly, Rachel moved toward the dining room, shuffling her bare feet across the floor, feeling her way as she'd come to do.

Maybe tomorrow . . .

Susanna had tired of Rachel's *alt Leier*—same old story. Would tomorrow ever come? she wondered. And if so, what would it take to move Rachel past her complacency?

Somewhat annoyed, she opened the screen door and went out to sit on the flagstone patio in the waning sun, watching Annie and their lively pet run back and forth through the wide yard. They chased each other around and through the oval gazebo.

There was a hint of woodsmoke in the air, and Susanna relished the scent, breathing it in. A flock of birds flapped their wings high overhead, and she suspected they were making preliminary plans to head south.

She delighted in the hydrangeas just beginning to turn bright pink, spilling long and bushy into the yard beyond the house. Soon they'd bronze with age as September faded. The lawn was still green, but she could see it beginning to lose its lush color, leaning toward autumn dormancy. When had *that* happened? she wondered. The circle of seasons was evident all about her, an inkling of the fall brilliance—reds, oranges, and golds—to come.

Annie was smack-dab in her springtime, while Susanna and Benjamin were fully enjoying the early winter of their lives.

But Rachel . . . where was *she*? To look at her, you'd think she was older than all of them put together! Yet Susanna forced herself to dwell on the bright side and silently rejoiced that her widowed daughter possessed a resolute spirit. The girl was ingenious when it came to needlework, especially crocheting. Why, she'd designed the prettiest pattern for several of the bow-top canopy beds upstairs and seemed right joyful in making them. When the womenfolk gathered for apple picking or canning, Rachel put herself in the middle of things, always a smile on her face. It was at such times Susanna suspected the key to bringing Rachel out of her shell was keeping her hands busy. 'Least then her mind couldn't torment her so.

"Come along now, Annie," she called, chuckling at the girl's antics. So like her mother she was, playing and enjoying the out-of-doors. Or how her mother *used* to be, was more like it.

Rachel had always been the last one to come dragging into the house when the dinner bell was rung, back at the old homestead. As a girl, she'd rather have stayed outside, even all night long, than come inside to a hot house in summer, or, as she liked to say, to the *dunkel Haus*—dark house in winter. Young Rachel had decided that houses were dismal places of retreat compared to the shining meadows and ample pastureland surrounding the large farmhouse. Even now, Susanna surmised that Rachel missed the farm where she'd romped through the fields of her childhood, helping her older brothers and sisters work the soil and bring in the harvest.

Getting up, Susanna called to Annie again. "Bring Copper with you, please. Time to wash up for supper."

"Already 'tis?" Annie asked, eyes wide. "Seems like we just come out here."

"Jah, I 'spect it does." And she headed into the house.

Susanna found Benjamin washing up as she hurried into

the kitchen. "Smells gut, jah?" she said, greeting him.

"It's bound to be *appeditlich*—delicious—if *you're* doin' the cooking." His smile stretched across his tawny, wrinkled face. He wore his best white shirt and tan suspenders, all dressed up for supper. It was his gray hair that looked a bit oily, and she suspected he'd been out working all afternoon in his straw hat, tidying up the front lawn. The man never tired of odd jobs, whether it was around the B&B or over at the old homestead, helping his sons work the land.

"We're full-up in the guest quarters tonight," she told him, turning her attention to the meal at hand.

"Yes, and I do believe we've got ourselves a big-city reporter in residence." Benjamin reached for the towel and dried his hands.

"A reporter? *Here?* Are you sure?"

He smiled, slipping his arm around her waist. "Sure as the sugar maple turns crimson. I sniffed him a mile away. Philip Bradley's the name, and you best be watchin' what you say at supper, hear?"

Ben oughta know, she thought. He'd smelled a rat before, not from visitors up north or anywhere else for that matter. But she'd seen his God-given gift in action many a time. It was the gift of discernment, all right. He could pretty much tell who was who and what was what before anyone fessed up to much of anything. And Susanna, well, she liked it just fine that way. Jah, she'd be mighty careful what she said from now on.

'Twould never do to have some dark-headed English reporter snooping around here, living under their roof and writing stories that weren't one bit true—or slanted at best. Wouldn't do, a'tall.

They'd had more than their share of false reporting.

Amish were forever being featured in one newspaper or another, especially after that drug business broke last summer. But for the most part, far as she was concerned, the reporting was heavy on exaggeration and sensationalism. She'd never known a single Amish teenager doing drugs of any kind. *Net*—never! 'Least not in their church district. English newspapers were cooked up by many a misguided writer, hoping to turn a few heads and make a dollar. When it came right down to it, a body had to stick to what they believed—wrong or right. And that was that.

Eight

$\mathcal{P}$hilip stared at his laptop computer screen, scanning the description he'd written before supper. *Before* the cordial hostess—Mrs. Susanna Zook—had decided to give him a rather cold shoulder. At first he had just assumed that her detached manner during the meal was due to the fact that both she and her husband were busily engaged in conversation with a number of other guests, three couples from the Midwest who seemed rather ignorant of the Plain lifestyle and who fairly dominated the evening's chatter. This turn of events had suited him fine because he merely had to listen to the responses given by Susanna and Benjamin, though occasionally guarded, to learn tidbits of Amish tradition.

Interestingly, the most fascinating aspect of the evening had been the grand entrance made by Annie Yoder, introduced by Benjamin as their "littlest helper." She was as candid and bright as his own niece had been at the coy age. However, he did not hold out false hope of making friends with the Zooks' granddaughter. The B&B owners had become somewhat cautious around him, and the obvious shift in their demeanor had him utterly intrigued.

First thing tomorrow, he would wander down the road to the village shops—see if he could eavesdrop on some of the locals prior to his formal afternoon interviews. In leafing through the tourist handbook, he'd noticed that several

Bird-in-Hand stores—among them Fisher's Handmade Quilts and the Country Barn Quilts and Crafts—offered genuine Amish quilts, wall hangings, and other handcrafted items. Folks at country stores often stood around, conversing while they drank coffee or sipped apple cider. Most likely, there would be some Amish person he could connect with in the immediate area *before* his interview with Stephen Flory's contact, unless, of course, he was able to get things back on an even keel with Susanna Zook.

What *had* he said or done to make the Zooks so suspicious?

❖ ❖ ❖

"Ach, you're not sittin' very still," Rachel chided her daughter. She let her fingers run down the long, silky tresses, weaving Annie's hair back and forth, doing her best to make a smooth braid.

"It's awful hard to sit still, Mamma."

Rachel understood. "'Twas hard for me, too, at your age."

"It was?"

"Oh my, yes." She remembered the many times her mamma had asked her to stop *rutschich*—squirming. "That was long before you were born," Rachel added.

"How old were you when it started . . . the rutsching, I mean?"

She had to laugh. "Well, ya know, I was born with the wiggles most prob'ly. Was forever running through your *dawdi* Benjamin's farmland—makin' mazes in the cornfields an' all. Just ask him."

Annie must've moved again because Rachel lost hold of the braid. "Ach, where'd you go to?"

"I'm right here, Mamma. Right in front of you." There was a long pause, though Rachel heard Annie's short, breathy sighs. "How much of me can ya see just now?"

A pain stabbed her heart. "Why do ya ask?"

" 'Cause I wanna know."

Rachel didn't know how to begin to tell anyone the truth, let alone her own little girl. And her heart thumped against her rib cage, so hard she wondered if Annie might be able to see her apron puff out.

"Mamma? Won'tcha tell me what you see?"

She moaned, resisting the question, not wanting to say one word about her blindness. "I . . . it's not so easy to tell you what I see and what I don't," she began. "If I lift my hand up to your face, like this—" and here she reached out to find Annie's forehead, allowing her fingers to slip down over the warm cheeks and across to the familiar button nose—"if I do that, I can see you in my own way."

"But what if I got up real close to you, like this," said Annie. "*Then* could ya see my face without feeling it?"

Sadly, Rachel knew enough not to try. "Sometimes I see light flickers, but that's only on good days. It doesn't matter, really, how close you sit to me, Annie; I don't see any part of your face at all."

"What about my eyes, if I make them great big, like this?"

Rachel suspected what her daughter was doing. "Are your eyes as big as moons?" she asked, playing along.

"Jah, very big moons." Annie giggled.

"And are they big and beautiful *blue* moons?" she asked quickly, hoping to divert Annie's attention.

"How'd ya know, Mamma? Jah, they're blue!" Annie was in her lap now, hugging her neck. "Oh, Mamma, you *can* see me! You can!"

She waited for Annie to settle down a bit. "No, I really can't see your face. But I *do* know how beautiful and blue your eyes are. I saw you the night you were born, and I saw you every day of your life until . . ."

"Every day till what, Mamma? Till the accident?"

Rachel sucked in air suddenly, then coughed. Someone had reminded Annie about the Crossroad, about that horrible day. Surely they had, for her daughter, at only four years of age, would never have remembered without someone prompting her.

Who?

It was then that she actually tried to force herself to see, that very moment as she pulled her darling girl into her arms, holding her close. She tried so deliberately that it hurt, like knowing there was surely a light at the end of a long, long dark tunnel. Knowing this only because people told you it was there, and trying so hard to see it for yourself.

Leaning forward . . . straining, with Annie still tight in her embrace, Rachel strove to catch a glimpse of the minuscule, round opening—the light—at the end of the blackness, *her* blackness. At the end of the pain.

"Why can't you see, Mamma?"

"I . . . well . . ." She couldn't explain, not really. How could she make her daughter understand something so complicated?

"Mamma?"

She felt Annie's tears against her own face. Oh, her heart was going to break in two all over again if she didn't put a stop to this. "Now, ya mustn't be cryin' over nothing at all," she said, stroking the tiny head.

"I won't cry," Annie said, sniffling. "I promise I won't, Mamma, if *you* won't."

Again, the pain cut a blow to her heart. How did Annie know about Rachel's tears? Had she heard what her grandfather used to say, back before they'd come to live here? Was Benjamin still telling folk that his daughter had cried her eyes out—that's why she couldn't see? 'Course, no one in their Plain community really and truly believed what the English doctor had said—not anymore anyway. He'd said Rachel's sight would return quickly, but it hadn't. No amount of wishing or hoping could make it so.

"Will you promise, Mamma?" Annie said again.

"I can't promise you for sure, but I'll try at least."

"That's wonderful-gut. Because we've got us some pumpkins to pick tomorrow. Won'tcha come help me?" Annie wrapped her slender arms around Rachel and hugged her hard.

"Maybe I will," replied Rachel, hugging back. "Maybe tomorrow I will."

❖ ❖ ❖

Philip was contemplating his interview questions, crafting them wisely as his sister had recommended, even getting them down in longhand for a change. Stopping, he stared at the desk, tinkering with his pen. He noticed the many cubicles and cubbyholes, realizing that most men probably would not have concerned themselves over the size of a compartment to store paper clips, staples, and the like. But he was one to enjoy a systematic approach to order, and the current location of his computer work station and filing cabinets in his home office were not conducive to anything akin to organization.

In the process of opening and closing the various drawers and investigating the nooks in the magnificent desk, he acquired the notion that his system was too limited, at best.

Where can I locate such a desk? he wondered. Almost immediately he decided against inquiring of Susanna or Benjamin Zook. Perhaps someone at the Country Store might be able to direct him to an antique auction or estate sale. Yes, that's what he might do after his interviews tomorrow. The plan of action, though rather simple, gave him a surprising surge of energy. Not to say that he wasn't still thoroughly worn out, but the idea *was* a grand one.

Just as he thought he might head downstairs to have another look at the tourist guide before turning in for the night, he tugged on a rather flat, thin drawer. No more than two inches deep, it was ideal for fine stationery or a slim stack of computer paper.

The drawer was entirely stuck. He tried opening it again. It didn't move one iota. More struggling brought no result. The drawer was simply not going to budge.

"That's strange," he said aloud. Then, getting down on his knees, he peered under the desk, trying to see what was causing the drawer to malfunction, if anything.

The ceiling light, along with the several lamps on either side of the desk, cast a dense shadow on the underside of the desk. So much so that he got up and went over to the reading lamp on the table beside the bed and unplugged it. He carried it over and plugged it into the outlet near the desk, then removed the lampshade so that the light bulb was exposed. He felt like a Boy Scout—though he'd never been one—on an adventure of some sort.

Squatting down, he shone the light directly under the desk, into the inner recesses, hoping to see what was jamming the drawer. As he held the light steady, he spied something sticking out beneath a seam in the wood. He reached for it, holding the lamp in the other hand. Just what it was, he couldn't be sure. But he was determined to find out.

Reaching up, he made a jiggling motion, discovering that the item was heavier than typical writing paper, more like card stock. He peered closer, trying to see how to dislodge it.

Getting up, he placed the lamp carefully beside his computer, then began to work on the narrow drawer again, wiggling it from this angle. "Out with you," he grumbled impatiently, and carefully, little by little, he coaxed the drawer out of its too-snug spot.

Once free, the drawer was clearly empty. But it was within the far end of the slot that the problem lay. He reached his fingers into the narrow mouth and tugged.

The culprit proved to be a wrinkled plain postcard, slightly torn and yellowing around the edges. The stamp had begun to fade, but the postmark—May 17, 1962—was clear enough. So was the writing, though the message looked to be a foreign language. What it was he did not know, since they were words he'd never seen. Possibly German. Could it be that this was Pennsylvania Dutch, the language of most Old Order Amish?

Philip was curious, but he had more important work to accomplish here than obsessing over a crumpled postcard. "Ach, such awful important work," he said, mimicking some of the phraseology he'd heard repeatedly during supper.

Then an idea came to him, possibly just the thing to get

Susanna Zook talking again. He would produce the postcard tomorrow, sometime prior to breakfast, before the other guests came downstairs. Perhaps in a private encounter, she might even offer to decipher the message, though he would never be so forward as to ask.

More than likely, the postcard belonged to the Zooks. Something they might be quite glad he had uncovered, or perhaps it was worth nothing at all. Yet he wondered how long the card had been lodged in the drawer. Even more fascinating—how had it found its way into the dark confines of the old desk in the first place? In his line of work, he was constantly asking the "Five W's" of good reporting—Who? What? Why? Where? and When? *How* was never to be over-looked, of course.

Nine

*P*hilip was restless.

The night was exceptionally warm for mid-September, though too early to be classified as Indian summer, since the first frost had not yet occurred. He rolled out of bed to open the window, then switched on the ceiling fan, hoping the night breeze and the whirring sound might help him drift off again. Not accustomed to sleeping in total silence, he searched the room once again for a clock radio, anything for a little background noise—something to soothe his wakefulness.

There was not even an alarm clock, let alone a radio. And no TV. Such were the heralded benefits of a back-roads bed-and-breakfast—peace and tranquillity accompanied by nighttime silence, broken only by a multitude of night insects, including some loud crickets.

Philip lay on the bed, concentrating on the vigorous chirping outside the window. Listening to the rhythm in the crickets' song, he noticed after a while that the various cadence patterns gradually began to correspond with each other. He'd read of this phenomenon, kindred to clock pendulums on the same wall aligning themselves over a period of time.

For one ridiculous moment, he thought of Lauren Hale. How fortunate for him that they had parted ways. To think that he might have begun to match the ebb and flow of *her* spirit and general approach to life was appalling and made him roll out of bed again to shake himself. He should've known better than to get involved with a stubborn, self-absorbed young woman.

Thoughts of the ill-fated romance made him more unsettled than before, and he decided to turn on the light, thoroughly disgusted with his insomnia. Perhaps his body was too tired, too wound up to relax; that had occurred on any number of occasions in the past.

Pacing the floor, he caught a glimpse of the postcard on the right side of his laptop, where he'd placed it before retiring. He picked it up, studying the steady hand of the writer. The addressee was a Miss Adele Herr, and though the street number and name were illegibly smudged, the city and state—Reading, Pennsylvania—were remarkably clear. The message was signed simply, *Gabe.*

Post-office issued, the card seemed in fairly good shape, but then, it may have been kept from the light for who knows how long. Nevertheless, he sat at the desk and scrutinized the handwriting, the unfamiliar prose stirring his interest.

He leaned back in the chair, his long legs sprawled out before him, taking in the country-red apothecary chest on the opposite wall, the wide-plank pine floors scattered with braided oval rugs, and the tall highboy. Even the ceiling fan had the appearance of being bent with age. If he hadn't known better, he might've suspected that he'd been tricked somehow—transported back in time. He wondered if, on some subconscious level, the discovery of the postcard had indeed roused him from slumber—the soul-deep slumber of spirit that had marked him for too long, despite the frenetic rhythm of his days.

❖ ❖ ❖

Rachel turned in her sleep, aware that a window was being opened in one of the guest quarters at the far end of the house. In her drowsiness, she reached for her daughter, who often slept next to her these lonely nights. Annie had a small single bed across the room but didn't often start out the night sleeping there. Annie much preferred falling asleep next to her mother, and Rachel didn't mind at all.

"Annie?" she whispered, sitting up.

"I'm here, Mamma" came the reply from the foot of the bed. "It's too hot to sleep."

"Well, let's open the window, then."

"Open them *all* up," Annie suggested.

"Gut idea." Getting up, Rachel counted four short steps to the first window. In an instant Annie was next to her, pushing against the wooden panel, helpful as always. "There, that's better, ain't so?" she said, breathing in the clean night air.

They stood in the window, enjoying the breeze as it sifted through the screen and caressed their faces. "Sometime I wanna sleep outside all night long. Beside the creek, maybe," Annie said. "What do ya think of that?"

Rachel chuckled softly. "Well, I must admit that I had the same bee in my bonnet back when I was your age."

"So then you might let me fall asleep under the sky so I can listen to the hoot owls and the crickets and—"

"Careful not to raise your voice," she interrupted her

daughter. "We have guests in the house tonight."

"Sorry, Mamma. But we have guests in the house most *every* night, except come winter, ain't so?"

"Jah, and it's a wonderful-gut way for all of us to make a livin' these days. Besides that, we can be a blessing to tourists."

"Jah, the tourists," the girl whispered.

Rachel hoped her little one didn't resent the never-ending flow of B&B guests. "We have much to offer our English friends."

"'Tis what Dawdi Ben says, too." Annie reached for Rachel's hand and led her back to bed. "I'm gettin' sleepy now."

"*Gut Nacht*, dear. See you in the morning."

Annie was silent for a moment, then she said, "Will ya, Mamma, really? Will ya honestly *see* me? There ain't nothin' wrong with your eyes, is there?"

"Well, where'd you get a silly idea like that?"

"Joshua says."

She knew well and good young Joshua, Lizzy's middle son, had probably overheard some adult talk here and there. The boy was too rambunctious for his britches. "What else is Joshua saying?" she asked, nearly in a whisper.

Annie was suddenly quiet.

Rachel felt awkward, pushing for answers from one so young. "Annie? You all right?"

"I surely don't wanna tell a lie, Mamma."

"Well, then, we best drop the whole thing right now," she said, slipping into bed, leaving the sheet and coverlet off for now. 'Least till the breeze from the window cooled things off a bit.

But she was wide awake. Couldn't sleep a wink, even

long after Annie's breathing became slow and even. Poor, dear child . . . what she'd had to suffer. All because of an unfortunate accident that might easily have been avoided if they hadn't had to take the shortcut. *If only I hadn't slept through the alarm*, she thought.

Lying there in the stillness, Rachel realized that she'd never forgiven herself. She felt sadly responsible for Jacob's and Aaron's deaths, and the truth of it bewildered her daily. As for her inability to see, she had rather adapted to her level of blindness these two years, feeling her way around the boundaries of her familiar world—the realm of her lonely existence. Truth be told, she felt right safe in the co-coon she'd spun for herself, but it broke her heart not to see her only child growing up. There were times when she missed roamin' freely outdoors, taking long walks on de-serted roads, strollin' through orchards and meadows, seein' the new baby lambs in the spring. On occasion, she actually questioned her resolve not to visit Blue Johnny or other sympathy healers, her desire to see springin' up in her more and more these days.

A waft of cool air blew in the window, and as she lis-tened to the sounds of the night, she noticed that the crick-ets' chorus seemed noisier than usual. Had it not been for the fact that there were several roomers in the house, she might've sneaked downstairs and sat out on the back patio, inhaling the rich, spicy fragrance of the humid night. Re-cently, on two separate occasions—though Mam would've been downright surprised—Rachel had slipped out into the night, unable to sleep due to the warm temperatures. And missing Jacob. Tonight she might've risked doing so again, but Dat had warned that a New York reporter was snooping around—staying right here under their noses, of all things.

Fact was, Dat had gotten wind that a well-respected tour guide in Lancaster had made plans to take the big-city fella to have a confidential chat with a local Amishman, come tomorrow afternoon.

"Best be watchin' yourself . . . what you say, anyhow," Dat informed her before supper.

'Course she agreed to be cautious, though it wouldn't require much of a change on her part. Occasionally she helped out in the Gift Nook, their gift shop, an addition on the north side of the house. She preferred her role as the silent helper, and Dat and Mam pretty much allowed her to live her life that way. Looking after Annie was her one and only aim.

Turning in bed, she faced the window and wished she might dream of Jacob holding her or whispering adoring words in her ear. Jah, she would like that right nice. But her dreams weren't always romantic ones. Frequently, there were taunting nightmares in the middle of the night—dreadful visions of things that never, ever could be. Jumbled-up, hideous images that made no sense at all.

She knew that on the other side of those grisly pictures was her sight—her full and clear vision—but she was unwilling to allow herself to walk through the foggy maze to get to the sunlight.

Dozing off, she listened to the night sounds, and they mingled together with her thoughts till the crickets seemed to chirp in unison *Jacob . . . Jacob . . .*

Ten

❖ ❖ ❖

*P*hilip rushed through his usual early-morning routine—shaving, showering, dressing—eager to chat with either Susanna or Benjamin before breakfast. He tucked the postcard into his shirt pocket and headed downstairs.

"Good morning," he said, offering a broad smile as his hostess met him in the common room.

"Didja have a good night's sleep?" Susanna inquired, not waiting for his reply. Instead, she turned her attention to arranging some croissants and doughnuts on a tray.

"I slept quite well, thanks." He did not say that he'd lost several hours in the *middle* of his sleep, however.

She turned and glanced out the window. "Looks like it'll be a right nice day today."

"Yes." *Right nice indeed*, he thought, wondering if now was a good time to show Susanna the postcard he'd found buried deep inside the old desk.

"Will you be needing anything besides coffee just now?" she asked, clearly in a hurry to get back to the kitchen and breakfast preparations.

"Coffee's fine, thanks."

"Would there be anything else, then? There's sticky buns and things on the table." She gestured toward the tray behind him.

Before she bolted, Philip decided to plunge in. "I, uh,

found something stuck in the desk in my room." He reached into his pocket and pulled out the postcard. "This was caught behind one of the drawers."

She took the card, glancing at it casually. "Well, for goodness' sake." She pushed her glasses up, tilting her head back, and began to read. " 'My dearest Adele . . .' " Her voice trailed off, and though her lips continued to move silently, her eyes began to blink. "Oh . . . uh, that's all right. You'd better keep it." She pushed the postcard back into Philip's hand.

"Is something wrong?" he asked, concerned that her face had grown quite pale.

She shook her head back and forth, muttering something in what he guessed was Pennsylvania Dutch. Her voice had turned raspy. "You'll hafta excuse me. I've got sausage in the oven." And with that, she left the room.

He stood there, holding the innocuous postcard in his hand, and stared at the handwritten note. *My dearest Adele . . .* Why would a message that began so beautifully affect someone in such a strange manner? He really didn't know what to do with the postcard now that she had rejected it. But his curiosity was definitely heightened, and he decided the missive legitimately belonged to him since she'd actually invited him to keep it.

Hurrying back upstairs to his room, he copied the message as best he could, in case Susanna might have second thoughts. He wanted to know more; wanted to know what had disturbed her enough to stop reading and toss the postcard back in his face.

His mind was whirling, and he made a quick call on his cellular phone. "Stephen?" he said when his Mennonite contact answered. "Thought I'd let you know I'm in town."

"When did you get in?"

"Yesterday afternoon. I'm in Bird-in-Hand, at the Orchard Guest House B&B. Do you know the place?"

"Oh yes. Great spot to get away from it all, I hear."

His gaze dropped to the postcard. "Thought I'd check in, make sure we're still on for this afternoon."

Stephen chuckled. "I've got a live one for you. You're going to like Abram Beiler. He'll answer all your questions."

"Sounds good. Let's meet for lunch—on me."

"I can get away by twelve-thirty or so. You're not far from Plain and Fancy Farm, just down the road, east on Route 340. You'll see it on the left side—can't miss it—just before you get to Intercourse."

"Good enough." Then impatient to know, he said, "I was wondering if you happen to understand Pennsylvania Dutch?"

"Well, I don't speak the language, but Abram does. What do you need?"

He mentioned the postcard briefly.

"Sure, Abram will help you out. And if he can't, there are several translators here where I work."

"That's good to know. See you soon." Philip put the postcard and his own written copy of it in his briefcase, then went and stood in front of the window, looking out at the expanse of Amish farmland in the distant morning mist. Closer in, toward the area of the backyard, he noticed for the first time since he was a boy that there were water droplets shining atop the grass, some creating tiny rainbows in the early-morning light.

On a sudden impulse, he stooped down and got his nose up next to the screened-in open window, inhaling the pungent smells, a hint of spice in the air. His view encompassed the apple orchard, with a glimpse of the creek beyond. Mill Creek, it was called, according to his map. He would have to go exploring sometime before he checked out. His sister would be surprised to hear that he'd actually taken some time for himself on this trip.

Getting his fill, he left the room and stood out in the hallway, leaning his ear toward the stairway, listening for the other guests. It would be wise to wait until there were plenty of people gathering for breakfast before heading back downstairs.

He thought he probably looked quite peculiar standing there, eavesdropping that way, especially to the little Amish girl who came hurrying toward him.

"Hullo, mister."

"Hello, Annie."

Her eyes popped open wide. "How do you know my name?" she asked in an ecstatic whisper.

"Your grandmother told me, that's how," he whispered back, just as enthusiastically. "What do you think of that?" He had the urge to reach out and poke her arm playfully, but he resisted, lest he scare her off.

Her face was bright with a smile, and today she wore a tiny white head covering similar to Susanna's adult-sized one. "I never heard nobody talk like you do."

"Never met anyone from New York City, then, did you?"

She shook her head slowly, and just the way she did, Philip remembered her grandmother, Susanna, doing the same thing, the same way, after reading the postcard. "Are *you* from New York?" asked Annie, still grinning.

"Born and raised in the Big Apple. I'm what you call a city guy, but"—and here he squatted down, placing himself at eye level with the darling child—"I have to tell you a secret."

"A secret? I like secrets." Her light brown eyebrows rose higher.

"Then I'll tell you." He lowered his voice. "I'm not much for big cities. They're noisy and busy and—"

"Why'd you come here?" she interrupted. "To find bigger apples?"

He couldn't help himself—he laughed. Such an adorable child. He would have six or seven little girls just like this if ever he found the right woman to marry. "I came to meet *you*, Annie."

"You did?"

"Yes." He straightened now to his full height. "Would you like to go down to breakfast with me?"

"Okay, but I can't eat with you. You're a guest, and I live here all the time." She turned and bounced toward the stairs. "Just follow me, mister."

"My name is Philip," he said, jumping at the chance to introduce himself. Might be beneficial later.

"Mr. Philip," she replied. "Mamma would want me to call you *Mister* first."

"That's okay with me." And he followed her down the steps, congratulating himself on having made a new friend. A special little friend indeed!

❖ ❖ ❖

Rachel waited till after all the guests had cleared out of the breakfast area before asking Dat if she could talk to him. "It oughta be somewhere private," she said.

"Well, then, we'll walk outside. How's that?" Benjamin said, finding her walking cane.

She didn't have the energy to resist his suggestion. After all, it had been weeks since she'd ventured farther than a few short walks with Annie.

Dat guided her to the back door, and once they were outside, she brought up the topic that had troubled her. "I don't rightly know how to begin."

"It's not necessary to mince words with me, Rachel."

Fresh smells of autumn filled the air, and she remembered her promise to Annie to help gather pumpkins. "I oughta make this short," she continued. "But I'm thinkin' that besides young Joshua, someone might be giving Annie an earful—about certain things, you know?"

"Well, now, if you mean the accident, I think I know exactly what you're askin'."

For a fleeting moment, she wished she could see Dat's face, witness the way the smile lines had carved deep furrows at the corners of his mouth, see the sincerity and goodness in his eyes. Surely he had not been the one to tell Annie. Ach, surely not.

"She's still so young, ain't? And a mite small for her age, too," Rachel added.

"Jah, she's that. Still, it's time you sit her down and talk things out with her, tell how her father and brother died . . . from your point of view. Best not to keep her in the dark any longer."

She wondered if he'd said it that way—*in the dark*—to drive home a point. But she thought better of it. 'Twasn't her place to be questionin' her father. After all, she was under his protective covering and guidance as a single woman, in spite of the fact that she was raising a child.

"So *has* Annie overheard things from you and Mam?"

"Not overheard . . . outright *told* her," Dat replied, his voice stern yet soft. "If it makes you uneasy, then I 'spose you'd best be tellin' your daughter what *you* remember."

She sighed. "I don't remember anything. Not one thing." It was absolutely true, and with all her heart, she wished he hadn't questioned her. "In all of two years, nothin's changed, Dat."

"I don't doubt you. You've always been a woman of integrity, pleasing to the Lord. Bless you for that. But I beg to differ with you on Annie bein' talked to about the accident and all that it summons forth." Benjamin Zook had spoken, and there would be no pushing the issue. His word stood, and she resigned herself to respect and conform to his opinion.

They walked a bit farther, down the gravel footpath through the orchard. She breathed in the sweet aroma around her, felt the warmth of the sun on her face, and wondered why she didn't come outside more often.

Dat guided her, turning her around at the end of the walkway, and step by step they headed back to the yard and to the house. "It's gut to see ya come outside for a spell," he said. "The sun and air's gut for you."

"Mam and Annie are always saying the same thing."

"Well, it's high time you listened," he said, chortling.

"Jah, you're right about that." They laughed together, heading inside again. Rachel felt no animosity toward her father for bringing it up, but she wondered how to approach the subject of the accident with Annie. And when?

❖ ❖ ❖

Susanna was upstairs, stripping the sheets from the beds in the southeast room—Philip Bradley's room. She knew enough not to meddle in his business, wouldn't think of poking around in a paying guest's personal affairs. Still, she was mighty tempted to go a-fishin' in the dresser drawer, searchin' for that there postcard. Why on earth hadn't she taken it and ripped it up when she had the chance?

Ach, she'd behaved so . . . *ferhoodled*, her sisters would be sayin' if they knew what she'd done—and right there in front of that reporter-writer fella, no less. Benjamin would be terrible disappointed in her, too. Thing was, she had no plans to tell anyone of the postcard from that lunatic uncle of hers. Best if Gabe Esh had never been born Amish, let alone to be found writing such things. No wonder the Old Order had had to treat him like a shunned man—and this before he'd ever joined church, though at nearly thirty, his kin had perty much given up anyways. Well, she wasn't gonna let this keep on a-botherin' her all the live-long day.

Now . . . where would a big-city reporter put a thing like an old postcard? She honestly didn't want to go a-lookin' for it, but the more she thought of it, the more she knew she oughta at least try and retrieve it. And the sooner the better.

First place she looked was in the trash can near the desk, though she had no real hope of finding anything. Truly, by the curious look on Philip Bradley's face, she 'sposed he might just go off and ask someone to translate the message on the postcard for him. 'Course, then again, she easily could've misread his expression. She stood up and took a deep breath, deciding it was best to just forget the whole thing. Surely there was nothing to worry about anyhow.

Hastily, she put fresh sheets on the bed, dusted the furniture, and dry-mopped the floor. Rachel could finish up in the bathroom, replace the old soap and soiled towels with fresh, and wipe down the shower.

Her arms loaded up with sheets, she ran into Annie in the hall. "Mammi, Mammi, I know a secret!" the little girl said.

"Oh, is that right?" she muttered, hoping that whatever her granddaughter had to say wouldn't take too awful long.

"Mr. Philip wants to be a farmer, I think. He don't like city noises with big apples and he—"

"Who?"

"You know, that tall New York fella . . . with the funny-soundin' talk." Annie's face was alight with glee.

"You were talkin' to Philip Bradley?" she broke into the prattle.

"He's real nice, Mammi. Honest, he is."

She wondered what else *Mister* Philip had told the child. "Why don'tcha help me get these sheets downstairs," she said, wanting to change the subject.

Annie giggled, playing horsey with the tail end of one of the sheets. "I'll help you. Giddy-up!"

She didn't say it, but she wondered how long before one of them—either Benjamin or herself—would have to ask Annie not to talk so openly or get too chummy with the English guests that came their way. Especially those that came a-callin' from the newspapers and whatnot all.

Eleven

❖ ❖ ❖

*P*hilip spent part of an hour at the County Barn, which was in reality a renovated tobacco shed on an Amish farm. The place still had that faint, sweet pipe-smoking odor. He looked around for a while, paying more attention to various British tourists than to any one item in the entire shop.

Next, he stopped off at Fisher's Handmade Quilts and, for the first time, actually took notice of the intricate patterns and highly colorful pieces that went into making an Amish quilt. He thought again of Kari and felt bad that he had rejected his niece's plea to accompany him here. Sure, she and Janice would have had a good time—he would've seen to it—but he wondered how things might've turned out with them having to tag along to his interviews and all. Too late now.

The restaurant was humming with tourists. Philip registered his name with the hostess, waiting for Stephen Flory. He reached inside his sports jacket and felt the postcard there, while around him sightseers chattered about candle barns and basket lofts. The recent drug bust, involving two young Amishmen, seemed to be the biggest buzz on visitors' lips.

He had questioned Bob Snell, his editor, when given this

assignment, asking why a follow-up feature on the drug incident wouldn't be a good idea. "Amish family traditions—that's what I'm after," Bob had insisted.

So Philip's story was to be a "soft" spread, covering the customs and rituals of the American Old Order family unit. He liked the idea of focusing on Christmas and other holiday traditions, though he'd read that the Old Order bishops didn't encourage putting up trees or stringing up colored lights either inside or out, steering members away from worldly holiday merriment. In fact, the common practice of exchanging gifts was largely ignored in some church districts, except, of course, in the case of small children. Gift giving was especially impractical among families with many children.

He thought of Annie and wondered if she might tell him what gifts she had received for Christmas *last* year, though he couldn't count on having another opportunity to converse with her. Philip had noticed the guests at breakfast, all of them eager to hear more about Amish life. Some of them actually seemed interested in quitting their day jobs and moving to the community. One woman said she'd like to talk with an Amish elder about how to join the church.

He thought it a bit boorish of the woman, talking that way, though Susanna didn't seem flustered by it. In fact, she seemed genuinely interested in helping the woman understand the transition involved. "Going Plain ain't so easy for outsiders. Most *Englischers* who come our way, thinking they're ready to join church, last, oh, a couple of months, if that. Some fit in better than others, though, so it's hard to know for sure who'll keep their vow and who won't."

The thoroughly modern woman's spirits had not been dampened one iota by Susanna's comments, and he'd heard her tell another guest after breakfast that she was very serious about becoming Plain. "I can't wait for someone to teach me to quilt—that's going to be lots of fun."

Lots of fun . . .

He couldn't imagine the woman even remotely fitting into a work frolic, or so the Amish called their quilting bees. She had fake fingernails as long as any he'd seen, airbrushed hot pink and silver with gemstones glued to the tips. How did she expect to be able to produce the tiny stitches required to create the colorful, expensive quilts hanging in all the tourist traps around Lancaster? He wanted to ask her if she was willing to abandon her personal glamour—nails, lipstick, and dyed hair—for the good of the Amish community. However, he thought better of it and kept quiet. Yet he wondered about Susanna's comment—*Some outsiders last only a couple of months.*

What made the difference? Was it background that made it easier for some folk to "fit in better than others"? And what of the baptismal vow? Did modern folk just assume they could make a haphazard promise to God and the Amish church, only to break it if things didn't work out? Something akin to modern-day marriage vows, he supposed.

"Excuse me. Are you Philip Bradley?" A tall blond man in his mid-thirties approached him with a warm smile.

"Yes, I am. And you must be Stephen Flory."

They shook hands in the crowded entrance to the dining room. "A popular place," Philip commented, glancing around.

"You should see it in the summer. Lancaster is swarming with out-of-state folks. It's one of the top five tour-bus destinations. Isn't it amazing, the draw the Amish have?"

Philip nodded. "I read somewhere that one tourist actually thought the Amish were actors, hired by the county to pull in tourism dollars."

Stephen laughed. "You'd think folks would be more savvy. But then, if you've never seen the likes of horse-drawn buggies and mule-powered plowing, I guess a person might wonder."

Philip heard his name being paged, along with several others. "Our table's ready," he said, falling in step with the other man. "After that hearty breakfast Susanna Zook served this morning, I must confess I'm not very hungry."

"Susanna's an excellent cook, I hear."

"Aren't most Amishwomen?" Philip said, following the restaurant hostess into the large dining room.

After a light lunch and some preliminary talk—a few basic questions from Philip regarding the Amish—they rode in Stephen's car to New Holland, a seven-mile trip north of Intercourse.

"I wasn't sure what to expect when I arrived here," Philip admitted. "If it hadn't been for a quick phone chat with my sister, I'm afraid I would be even more ignorant of Amish ways. I thought I was coming to research a people who embraced a Quaker-like religion, but I'm finding out there is much more to them."

"They live out their faith daily," Stephen replied. "It's a lifestyle . . . a total culture. But they'd be the first to tell you they aren't perfect."

They pulled into a dirt lane and spotted a man who had to be Abram Beiler, sitting on the L-shaped front porch. A wide straw hat sat atop his hoary head, and he wore a black vest over a long-sleeved white shirt. His gray-white beard was long and untrimmed.

"Looks like Abram's ready for Sunday-go-to-meeting," Stephen commented, turning off the ignition and straightening his tie. He turned to Philip, lowering his voice. "Before we go in, you should know that Abram's straddling the fence between the Old Order and maybe Beachy Amish, I don't know. He and several other families are a little upset with their bishop and some of the preachers."

"Why is that?"

"Some problems in the church district," Stephen explained. "Half the community sides with the bishop's recent sanctioning of cell phones and pagers. The other half's rankled over it."

"Cell phones . . . are you kidding?"

Stephen shook his head. "They seem to be testing the waters, so to speak."

Philip had to admit he hadn't heard any of this, though he found it quite interesting. Rather humorous, too. "Does Abram own a cell phone?"

"Amish farmers aren't the ones using them. It's the woodworkers and blacksmiths, but especially the women who own craft and quilt shops. I have to tell you, Philip, the Plain community is changing by leaps and bounds."

"Oh" was all Philip said. Seemed to him that a farmer could benefit from a cell phone as well as anyone else.

Abram was coming down the front porch steps as they got out of the car. "*Wie geht's*, gentlemen. Name's Abram Beiler. I come from a long string of Beilers—even got me a cousin down in Hickory Hollow. A bishop, he is."

"Pleased to meet you, Abram," said Stephen, shaking the Amishman's hand. "I'm Stephen Flory, and here's Philip Bradley, the writer I told you about . . . from up north a piece."

"New York City, ain't?"

"That's right," Philip chimed in, extending his hand and receiving the man's strong grip in return. "Good to meet you, Abram. Nice of you to agree to talk with us."

"Ain't nothin' really. 'Tis always fun meeting up with interesting Englischers." He chuckled and motioned for them to follow him into the house.

The front room was as sparsely furnished as Philip's sister had said an Old Order Amish living room would be. Two hickory rockers sat side by side near the corner windows, as well as a tan couch with a purple and black afghan folded neatly over one arm. A number of multicolored rag rugs adorned the unstained pine floor, imparting a dry, silvery look. One especially large rug—a circular one in the middle of the long room—boasted nearly every color of the rainbow. There was a scenic calendar on the north wall, but no other decorations or pictures. On one small table in the corner, two kerosene lamps stood at perfect attention.

Abram promptly went to the kitchen and brought out a straight-backed cane chair for Philip. Stephen and Abram sat in the matching rockers.

"Ask away," said Abram, pulling on his scraggly beard. "You ain't the first fella with questions about us Amish folk."

"It's not always easy finding the right person to interview," Philip was quick to say.

"Jah, I 'spose that's true."

Philip began his conversation inquiring of daily family traditions, then worked his way to Christmas and Easter. He discovered, quite pleasantly, that there was another holiday observed by Lancaster County Amish—"Second Christmas" on December 26, a day set aside to visit with relatives and friends, offering yet another respite from work.

Abram was quick to point out that New Year's Day was little cause for much celebrating in Amish circles, albeit the People made note of the passing of another year. There was no special church meeting on New Year's Day, but "the young people sometimes use it as an excuse to have a school program," he added with a wry smile.

Irreconcilable differences in marriage were discussed next. "When a man and woman can't make things work out together, they might up an' separate," Abram explained, "and if they do, one or both will like as not leave the community. But those who do stay understand clearly that there'll be no remarryin'."

This led to a question-and-answer session on early-morning prayers, as well as lively talk around the table every night. "We all work together," Abram continued. "In the fields—plowin' and plantin', sowing and harvesting. In the barn—the milkin' and cleanin' up. But we play hard together, too. Games like volleyball and baseball are big around here. We'll often gather in the yard just to watch the sun go down of an evening. When everything's said and done, family's all we got."

"How many children do you and your wife have?" Philip asked.

"Fifteen—eight boys and seven girls—and that gives us eighty-five grandchildren, with plenty more on the way."

Stephen spoke up. "Enough to start your own church district?"

The threesome laughed at that, but Philip presumed Stephen's comment wasn't too far afield. He asked several more wrap-up questions, then glanced at his watch and was amazed to see that two hours had passed so quickly. The answers to his numerous questions had come so effortlessly, he was, in fact, astonished when he arrived at the end with such success. "I'm grateful for your time, Abram," he said, closing his notebook and feeling confident he had covered all the bases.

"If ya think of anything else, just come on out and see me. Gut enough?"

Philip nodded. "That's very kind of you." He could certainly see a resemblance between affable Abram Beiler and his own deceased grandpap. Miles apart in culture, however. "Oh, before I forget, I wonder if you might be able to translate something for me?"

"Why, sure—so long as it ain't French," said Abram with a snigger. "I know only two languages. One's the English I butcher daily, the other's Amish. How can I help ya?"

Philip pulled out the postcard and showed it to the old gentleman. "Any idea what this says?"

"Let's have a look-see." Abram took out a pair of reading glasses and slipped them on the tip of his nose. He began to read silently, his silver eyebrows rising over deep-set eyes. "My, my . . . I believe what you've got here is a love note, among other things." He smiled briefly, the wrinkles creasing hard around his eyes.

Philip had suspected as much, based on Susanna Zook's reading of the greeting.

Abram looked at the front of the postcard and leaned forward, eyeing the postmark through his reading glasses. A frown furrowed his brow, and he removed his glasses. "Well, *was der Dausich, Deixel!*—what the dickens! You know, it sure seems like I've heard tell of this fella. I think this here's that preacher-boy who caused such a stir years ago."

Philip was astounded that Abram seemed to know the writer.

"Jah," Abram was saying, "and the sign-off, 'Gabe,' matches up with Gabriel Esh, the young man I'm a-thinkin' of. Honestly, I believe he went by Gabe quite a lot, if I'm right about this."

"Do you know anything more about the man?"

"Well, I 'spose there's a way to double-check, but it sure seems like young Gabe died over a Memorial Day weekend. Most all of Lancaster County was whispering 'bout it." He nodded his head, touching the postmark with his pointer finger. "Jah, Gabe Esh died just two weeks after this here postcard was mailed, if I remember rightly."

"Gabe *died?*" Flabbergasted, Philip knew he'd have to follow up on this. First thing tomorrow, he'd make a trip to the library and look up the obituaries for deaths that had occurred the weekend of Memorial Day 1962.

Abram was rocking in his chair now, fidgeting with the card. "Somethin' seems mighty strange about this," he said, waving the postcard in the air.

"What's that?"

"Why on heaven's earth did Gabe Esh write a love note in Amish . . . to an English girl? Don't make any sense." Then a smile creased his ruddy face. "Unless, of course, 'twas a code of some kind."

"Maybe Gabe didn't want anyone to know what he'd written—at the postcard's final destination, that is," Stephen piped up.

Philip made a mental note of everything, thinking that this might be the seed for a much bigger story, not just a two-page soft spread. Perhaps even a lead story!

"Gabe's girlfriend surely could read Amish, if that's what you're thinkin'," Abram spoke up, grinning at Philip.

"Why, yes, as a matter of fact, I *was* wondering that!"

They had another hearty laugh, but because Philip sensed the Amishman's restlessness, he asked again for the translation. "I want to jot down the words as you read," he said, anxious to hear the message, more so now than before. Gabe Esh's postcard had become far more intriguing than anything he'd planned to write for the magazine. In fact, more fascinating than anything he'd come across in recent travels.

"Would you mind reading it to me slowly?" Philip said, his pen poised over his notepad.

Twelve

❖ ❖ ❖

Rachel walked hand in hand with Annie down the narrow road, enjoying the rumble of the pony cart just ahead. They had single-handedly filled a small wagon with small and medium-sized pumpkins. 'Course, Dat had come along later to help with loading up the biggest ones.

"I think Dawdi Ben's gonna beat us home," Annie said, giggling. "Let's run just a bit?"

"Oh, Annie, it's best that I walk."

"But Mammi says you used to run fast as the wind when you were little. Was that so long ago?"

Rachel had to chuckle at that. "Not so long ago, no, but . . ."

"C'mon, Mamma. Take my hand and skip just a little. Please?"

Skipping was safe enough. Sure, she could skip down Olde Mill Road this once with her daughter. "Keep holding my hand," she said, lifting the walking cane in the other.

"Are ya ready?" Annie asked.

"*Fix un faerdich*—all ready!" She moved awkwardly at first, trying to keep up with her energetic girl. Every so often the cane bumped the road, throwing her off balance, but she stayed upright. The jaunt took her back to the many foot races she'd enjoyed with her brothers and sisters out on the dusty mule roads that crisscrossed between Dat's cornfields, tobacco fields, and pastureland. Usually, she was the winner of such events, though occasionally her brother Noah might beat her by a hairsbreadth at their homemade finish line. Then it was up to Joseph or Matthew to intervene and decide once and for all who'd really and truly come in first.

Those free and easy days of youth were long past, and she felt some regret that there was no longer much fellowship between herself and a good many of her siblings and their spouses. Nowadays, she had more connection with her mother's sisters and cousins, and there was always Lavina Troyer, the garlic-lovin' distant cousin on Dat's side of the family. It was a regrettable situation all around, but many of Rachel's brothers and sisters had simply chosen to stay away. She sensed it was because she hadn't given in and gone to the powwow doctors, seeking help for her eye condition—or *mental* condition, as some had surely concluded.

In spite of all that, she'd preferred to let bygones be bygones, settling into her snug and happy life with Dat, Mam, and Annie, never thinking much ahead to the future. Or the past.

"Ach, I'm winded," she confessed at last, slowing down while Annie ran ahead. Rachel heard her daughter's bare feet smack against the pavement, distinguishing that sound from the gentle rumble of the pony cart. If someone had told her that one day her sense of hearing would be this acute, she might've laughed. Within just a few months of her eyes clouding up, after the accident, she'd been able to hear an owl calling to its mate and tell how far away the creature was. She could also make out the buggies going up and down Beechdale Road to the west of them—things nobody else could hear. Though she didn't take pride in her heightened hearing ability, she was ever thankful to God for allowing her this compensation.

"What'll we do with all those pumpkins?" Annie called, running back to her and tugging on her apron. "Can we set up a vegetable stand in front of the house? Can we, Mamma?"

Rachel was still catching her breath. "Sounds like fun, but we'll hafta see what Dawdi says. Don't wanna scare off any tourists, now do we?"

"Might bring *more* guests," Annie suggested. "And I'd tend the stand, 'cause I don't mind talkin' to Englischers one bit. Some of them are right nice."

"Like Mr. Philip, maybe?"

Annie giggled. "Mammi Susanna told you, didn't she? *That's* how you know!"

"Jah, I guess I should 'fess up and say that I heard 'bout your little chat with our guest. But you know what?"

"Let me guess," Annie squealed. "He's gonna move clear from New York and come here and farm."

"Well, now, that's what *you* told your grandmother is more like it." She knew it was true.

"Well, Mr. Philip said so . . . I think."

She figured Annie had completely misunderstood whatever conversation she'd had with the reporter man. More than likely, Mr. Bradley had said something more on the order of being tired of big-city living—something like that. The child was known to exaggerate now and then.

"Maybe it's time we had a little talk about your chats with the B&B guests," she said, walking faster again.

"Do I talk too much, Mamma?"

She didn't want to discourage Annie's friendly nature— wouldn't think of hindering her that way. Yet there was an unspoken line between the People and outsiders that should never be crossed. She understood this fully; so did everyone around here. But how on earth was she to make such things clear to an outgoing six-year-old?

"I'll try not to be such a *Blappermaul*—blabbermouth. I'm awful sorry, Mamma."

Rachel's heart ached for her little one. "No . . . no, you're not to blame, dear. You have a wonderful-gut neighborly way aboutcha. That part mustn't change . . . not ever. But I want you to think about not gettin' too thick—too overly friendly—with outsiders. Do ya understand?"

"Jah, I think so."

"Gut, then." They walked another quarter mile or so to the Orchard Guest House. There was a slight chill in the air, though still unseasonably warm for the fourteenth day of September. She heard a distant song sparrow warbling its tune near Mill Creek, and she reveled in the outing Annie had planned for her today. Because she'd enjoyed herself so much, she decided to go for a walk again. Tomorrow, prob'ly.

"We're home," Annie said, leading her around the back to the kitchen door where Copper greeted them with doggie licks and jumps and excited yips.

Mam had warm chocolate chip cookies waiting, and Rachel busied herself, pouring tall glasses of milk for everyone while Annie recounted all the happenings of the afternoon.

"I do believe some things are settled with Annie now," Rachel told Mam before supper.

"Oh?"

"On our walk home we had a nice chat about the English guests." She told Mam how nice the day had been, spending time outside.

"I see your cheeks ain't nearly so pale. You best get out and go walkin' again real soon."

She was glad she'd gone, mostly for Annie's sake. Mam would always be pushing for more from her. That's just how Susanna Zook was and always had been.

"We wanna sell some early pumpkins," Annie piped up. "Out on the front lawn."

"*We?*" Rachel laughed. "Don't you mean *you* want to?"

Annie was giggling, slurping her cocoa. "Well, what do ya say, Mammi Susanna? Isn't it a gut idea?"

"Ask Dawdi about it," said Mam.

Annie continued. "You mean you don't wanna clutter up the front yard?"

"That's not what I said," Mam retorted.

Rachel sensed what was coming. Her mother would require her to reprimand Annie—make a point of belittling the girl in front of her elders.

"I think it's high time for some rebuke" came the stiff words.

"Annie, please come with me," Rachel said, getting up and tapping her cane across the floor. "We best wash up now."

She and Annie headed off to the stairs, and Rachel used her cane and the railing to guide her, letting the child run free this time. And just for this moment, she wished the two of them had stayed longer out in the sunshine and the fresh air.

❖ ❖ ❖

Silently, Philip reread the postcard's translation as Stephen drove him back toward Bird-in-Hand.

> My *dearest Adele*,
> *What a joy to receive your letter! Yes, my feelings remain the same, even stronger, but I should be the one to bridge the gap between us and leave my Amish ways behind—for you, my "fancy" dear girl.*
> *God is ever so faithful. Pray for me as I continue to expose the kingdom of darkness.*
> *Soon we'll be together, my love.*
> *Gabe (Philippians 1:4–6)*

Philip wondered what the Scripture reference might be and asked Stephen if he knew offhand.

"Sure do. It's one of my favorites. Would you like me to quote it?"

Oddly enough, he did. "Please do."

" 'In all my prayers for all of you, I always pray with joy because of your partnership in the gospel from the first day until now, being confident of this, that he who began a good work in you will carry it on to completion until the day of Christ Jesus.' "

"Wow, what a mouthful," Philip said, wishing now he hadn't asked.

"Verses to base a life on," Stephen said, nodding. "Gabe Esh must certainly have been a man of faith."

Philip stared at the line that stirred his curiosity most. "What do you make of 'the kingdom of darkness'?"

"Not so hard to say, really. Could be a reference to some local powwow practices." Stephen made the turn into the parking lot where Philip's car had been parked. "It's not commonly known by outsiders, but we Mennonites know that there are hex doctors, even today, among the Amish and other conservative circles, too, though some criticize it."

"Is that something pertaining to Native Americans?"

"Sympathy healing or the German term *Brauche*, as powwow doctoring is often called, has no direct association to Indian folk medicine. Its origins can be traced back to Swiss and Austrian Anabaptists who later immigrated to America. But Plain folk weren't the only ones who got caught up in the healing arts. Pennsylvania Germans practiced it, too."

"So . . . are you thinking that Gabe Esh considered pow-wowing as part of the kingdom of darkness?" Philip's interest was clearly piqued.

"It's quite possible . . . but who's to know for certain?"

Philip was reluctant to go on, unwilling to wear out his welcome. "I've kept you much too long, but getting back to the powwow issue—we're not talking witchcraft here, are we? I mean, don't Amish folk subscribe to the Christian way? Don't they read the Bible, pray—the things most Protestants do?"

"Old Order Amish follow the *Ordnung*—a code of unwritten rules. That, I would say, is quite different from what you just described. In fact, powwow doctoring is a type of white witchcraft—conjuring—and I assure you the spirits invoked are not godly ones." He paused, then continued. "One thing's for sure—don't expect to find an Amishman willing to discuss any of this."

"I appreciate the warning," Philip said, extending his hand. "Again, thanks for everything."

Stephen shook his hand cordially. "You know where to reach me if you have further questions."

"I'll see that you get a copy of the story when it runs."

"Yes, do that." And Stephen was gone.

Philip located his rental car and drove west toward the turnoff to Beechdale Road. He thought back to his interview with Abram Beiler. The old farmer hadn't mentioned the Ordnung, hadn't said a word about rules either. But overall, Philip was pleased with the favorable reception from both Stephen and Abram.

It was the postcard's entire message that plagued his thoughts, not so much the mention of evil deeds—although that aspect was intriguing—but the endearing phrases. Gabe Esh must have loved Adele Herr beyond all reason to be willing to abandon his People for her. They must have been true soul-mates, though he despised the term so overused in recent years. Heart-mates . . . yes, that was better. The ill-fated lovers had apparently belonged together, culture clash or no, though Gabe's untimely death had kept them apart forever.

One thought nagged at him. *How could such a declaration of love have been buried in an old desk?* Something as compelling as an Amishman pledging to leave his People for his beloved—why was such a message not found among Miss Herr's most precious possessions—in a fragrant box with other love letters and notes? Surely Gabe's sweetheart would have treasured the postcard for a lifetime, possibly the last correspondence between them.

Soon we'll be together. . . .

The tender words haunted him as he drove back to Orchard Guest House and long into the night.

Thirteen

Susanna poured out her heart to Benjamin before retiring. "I shoulda had you look at that stubborn drawer in the antique desk upstairs a long time ago," she said, brushing her hair. "You know, the one we bought over to Emma's?"

Her husband grunted his answer from under the sheets. She knew better than to push the issue, late as it was. Benjamin's brain perty near shut down around eight-thirty every night. No gettin' around it. The man's body clock was set to wind down with the chickens, from all those years of farming. "Never mind, then," she whispered, about to outen the lantern light.

"What's that?" Ben asked, lifting his head off the pillow to stare at her.

"Ach, that writer fella you warned us about found an old postcard written by my scoundrel uncle."

"Gabriel Esh? You don't say."

"I saw the postcard with my own eyes."

"Your uncle Gabe, your mother's little brother?" Ben asked again, pulling himself up on his elbows. "Glad we had sense enough to disown him back when. It's a real shame, a blight on the whole family . . . and the community, too, the way he carried on."

"Lavina stuck up for him, remember?" Susanna sput-

131

tered. "The only one around these parts who did, that I know of."

"Lavina's a crazy one, she is," said Benjamin. "*Nadier-lich*—naïve as the day is long."

Surprised that Ben was coherent enough to pay any mind to her ramblings, Susanna seized on the opportunity. "Cousin Lavina has a right gentle way about her, though. Folks seems to know better than to meddle with her opinion. They just leave her be, really."

"Leave her be? The way most our grown children have turned a deaf ear toward Rachel, you mean?"

Her heart pricked at Benjamin's words. "What's important now is that postcard Gabe wrote—a love note to his English girlfriend. If that don't beat all."

"Well, what'd it say?"

"Don't have it no more."

"But you said you found it, didn'tcha?"

"Philip Bradley did," she insisted. "He brought it down and showed me this morning before breakfast, but I was so flustered when I saw it, I didn't wanna have nothin' to do with it, so I gave it back to him."

"You did *what?*" Ben's face had turned redder than any beet she'd ever peeled.

"I told him I had no use for it."

Ben shook his head. "Well, didja read any of it?"

"Mostly romantic prattle. I didn't care to read it really." She wasn't sure she should say more—especially the part where Gabe had asked Adele, his English sweetheart, to pray that he might uncover more of the sin and darkness in the community.

"That's all it was, then—just a love note?"

Ben knew her too well to let this drop. True, he wouldn't

go 'round tellin' folk that he'd smelled a rat in his own bedroom, but if she didn't come clean and confess everything,
he'd probably know anyways. Insight from God was right
strong in Ben. Everybody knew it was. One of the many old
"family" gifts Benjamin believed in.

"Well, jah, there was more," she said at last, a bit reluctant to own up. "Gabe wrote something about evil spirits at
work among the People. 'The kingdom of darkness,' I think
was how he put it."

Ben motioned for her to come to bed. "Aw, that's *alt*—
old news, Susie. Long ago dealt with. Nothin' to worry about
now, I'd say."

" 'Sposin' you're right." She knew she'd sleep ever so
much better now, just hearing her husband say that there
was no need to be concerned, this wonderful-gut man who
knew far more about the intangible things of life than most
anybody. If Ben Zook said it, most likely it was true.

❖ ❖ ❖

Philip stayed up late, writing the first draft of his Amish
family article on his laptop computer. Every detail, each cultural nuance that Abram Beiler had mentioned fit together
like a jigsaw puzzle, and when Philip was satisfied with the
initial draft, long past midnight, he decided this assignment
had been one of the easiest he'd ever undertaken. Quite possibly the most enjoyable in recent months.

But it was the message on the postcard that energized
him. Tomorrow morning he would drive downtown to Duke
Street, to the Lancaster County Library, and begin his research on Gabriel Esh's death. Perhaps someone in Bird-in-

Hand would know something of the man's life as well. After all, the postmark had originated there.

Young Annie crossed his mind, but he rejected the idea of pursuing a small girl with such serious questions. Surely Susanna Zook's young granddaughter would not have been told stories involving a preacher-man who'd planned to leave the Amish for a modern woman. Philip resolved to be more cautious around the Zooks, especially prudent with Annie—that is, if there was to be another encounter with the precocious child, though he had left some space in his article in case he was able to chat with her about Christmas gifts. Annie had an uncanny way about her, delightfully attractive. She was gifted in all the social graces, especially for one so young. And strikingly pretty, as beautiful as the woman whom he'd observed touching the child's cheek. Annie's mother, he was sure.

The more he pondered it, the more he realized he could not leave just yet. He would discuss with Susanna Zook the possibility of booking the room for a few more days. Yes, he would take care of that small matter tomorrow, immediately after breakfast.

❖ ❖ ❖

Rachel crept downstairs to the parlor, her tape recorder in hand. She'd waited till the house was quiet, until Annie had fallen asleep. A taped letter to her dear cousin was long overdue. Already two weeks had passed since she'd received Esther's ninety-minute cassette recording in the mail. How wonderful-gut it had been to hear from her. Working the land, sowing seed—and this with Esther side by side with

Levi and their children. She could just picture all of them out in the field with the mules, the smell of manure and soil mixed together, the sun shining down on their heads.

The scene in her mind made her awful lonesome for Jacob. She figured if he were alive today, she, Aaron, Annie, and the child she'd miscarried would be doing the selfsame chores together as a family . . . out in Ohio.

Closing the door to the small room, she located the electric outlet under the lamp table and plugged in the recorder. Then she felt for the masking tape where Mam had marked the Record button. She pushed it and sat on the floor next to the recorder, pulling her long bathrobe around her.

"Hullo, again, Esther," she began, holding the tiny microphone close to her lips. "It's been ever so long since I talked to you this way. I can't begin to tell you what a busy time we've had this fall, what with the steady stream of out-of-town tourists. But, then, you must surely have the same thing there in Holmes County, right?

"I haven't been too happy about certain things that I 'spect are goin' on behind my back. I wouldn't be surprised if Mam went to visit Blue Johnny last week. Maybe she even stood in for me, the way she used to have Elizabeth and Matthew do for ailing elderly folk now and then. Anyways, there was one day when she was gone for the longest time, and I honestly felt somethin' right peculiar come over me. But, of course, none of the powwow magic worked on me, because I have very little faith in it. I memorized the Bible verses in Jeremiah you read in your last tape to me. 'Blessed is the man that trusteth in the Lord, and whose hope the Lord is. For he shall be as a tree planted by the waters, and that spreadeth out her roots by the river, and shall not see when heat cometh, but her leaf shall be green.'

"Anyways, when Mamma finally did come home, she kept a-hummin' the same tune—sayin' the words over and over again. I never asked her about it, but I sure thought somethin' was up. Like maybe Blue Johnny gave her some charms to say around me.

"Oh, I wish you could come visit again. I wanna talk to you more about that article by Jacob Hershberger. You remember how we discussed it up one side and down the other, back when my Jacob was still alive? Well, I can't put my finger on it, really, but there seems to be something to what that Hershberger fella wrote so long ago. Seems to me he's right, though Dat would prob'ly make a big fuss if he knew I was talkin' to you about such things.

"Well, it's gettin' late, so I best sign off for now. Send me a tape back real soon, ya hear?

"I love you, Esther. Take gut care now, all right? Tell Levi and the children I said hullo, just don't let anyone else listen to this. And I promise to do the same when I hear next from you.

"Ach, I come near forgettin' to tell you that Annie and I spent the afternoon picking pumpkins over at the neighbors. They promised to give us whatever we picked, so we've got us a pony cart full. The pumpkins felt so smooth and round in my hands, I could almost *feel* the deep orange color, though I wouldn't say that to anyone but you, Esther. Certain folk 'round here might get the wrong idea and start thinkin' they oughta come to *me* for their amulets and charms. Honestly, I want nothin' to do with powwow doctoring. You know my heart in this.

"Well, back to the afternoon, which took me by surprise. I felt that I'd gone right back to our pumpkin-pickin' frolics when we were little girls. Oh, I wish you and Levi had never left here. Any chance of you returning to Lancaster County? Never mind, that's not fair to ask. Of course you wanna stay put there in Ohio. I'd give just about anything to have land . . . with Jacob and Aaron still alive to help farm it. But we all know that wasn't God's will.

"The Lord be with you, dear Esther. From your cousin in Pennsylvania."

Rachel pressed Stop and then ejected the tape from the recorder before unplugging it. She slipped the "letter-tape" into her bathrobe and carried the recorder upstairs.

Her fondest memories of Jacob made her cry, and when it was time for her bedtime prayers, she only had tears to say.

❖ ❖ ❖

Philip thought he heard talking in the room below him. He couldn't be sure if what he heard was a woman's voice or a child's, but something was going on downstairs in the parlor.

For a fleeting moment, he wondered how many secrets the walls of this house had witnessed. Were there others, like the mysterious postcard, hidden elsewhere? What about compartments in old furniture? He'd read once about a late–1700s Rhode Island desk and bookcase combination that had sliding panels, concealing six separate hiding places. He suspected that his brain was tired, thus the curious notions.

After turning out the light, he got into bed. A piece of the moon shone through some scraps of clouds, the faint light filtering in through the window. The crickets were more subdued tonight, making it possible to overhear, but not decipher, the soft words spoken in the room below. A woman was talking alone, to herself perhaps, Philip decided just as he fell asleep, though he was too drowsy to determine if the sounds were merely part of a dream or not.

❖ ❖ ❖

Susanna was altogether dumbstruck at the things her daughter was saying in the quietude of the parlor. She had been thirsty in the night and needed some water. Tiptoeing out to the kitchen, she'd heard Rachel's voice, of all things.

What in the world? she wondered, starting to open the door, then realized that Rachel was prob'ly up making a late-night recording to Esther.

Instead of interrupting, she leaned her ear against the door, listening to the most revealing one-sided conversation she'd ever heard tell. Jah, she knew of Rachel's and Esther's plan to send taped messages back and forth once a week. In fact, she'd encouraged the idea, thinking it would give Rachel someone to pour out her heart to, though she wished her daughter might share her thoughts with someone besides Esther. Someone like her own mother, although she wouldn't have admitted to being envious. Never!

But this . . . this idle rambling about Blue Johnny! How *could* Rachel have known where Susanna had gone last week? *Puh!* The girl must be a diviner, as receptive and open to intangible things as the water witchers and powwow doctors themselves. After all, her daughter had been just six, around Annie's age, the first time someone handed her a hazel twig—a dowsing fork—and, praise be, if it didn't start a-jerkin' like nobody's business, right there in Rachel's tiny hands. 'Course, then she was so awful young she couldn't be expected to go chasing after well water with other dowsers. Which was prob'ly just fine, what with past years of community strife over the use of black magic or hexing having finally died down.

Still, the more she thought about it, the more she suspected she was right about the *real* reason for Rachel's resistance to sympathy healers these many months. Nay, most all her life.

Susanna shivered with excitement. Could it be that her youngest daughter had been rejecting the inclinations in her own mind—the uncultivated giftings of a full-fledged powwow doctor—all along? Supernatural gifts were often passed from one generation to the next, and in spite of the folk who condemned powwowing practices, the age-old giftings continued to flourish through the blood lines, though kept hush-hush to outsiders. Mediumistic transference—from one powerful dowser or powwow doctor to a younger member of the community or family—was another way the "miracle" gifts were passed on.

Susanna wondered if Rachel had shied away from Blue Johnny out of bashfulness, though she didn't see why Rachel should be afraid, if she was. After all, it was considered a high compliment to be chosen, anybody knew that. If her guess was right, he'd had Rachel in mind all these years, wanting to bestow the full mediumistic transference to her.

Susanna nearly burst out laughing. Here was a young woman who'd willed herself not to see, of all things! Her highly sensitive, reserved Rachel—why in the world hadn't she thought of this before? Her very own daughter had all the makings of a *Brauchfraa*—powwow doctor—and to think that she was most standoffish around one of their best-known healers of all!

'Course, it would be prudent for Susanna not to be mistaken about any of this. She decided to get Benjamin's opinion on the matter. Ben would understand her suspicions, maybe even stamp his approval on them.

Tomorrow, just as soon as breakfast was served to the B&B guests, she would find out and settle the whole thing in her mind. Once and for all.

Fourteen

❖ ❖ ❖

Philip had often noticed during his years of research that librarians seemed to subscribe to a most gracious and accommodating code of behavior. More so than any other profession he could think of. "Why, certainly," they'd say. "I know well that particular book." Or . . . "Why, yes, I just spotted that reference for another library patron."

Patron? The word conjured up visions of the wealthy elderly who made huge annual donations to well-known organizations. Never anonymously, however.

Philip stood in line to request microfilm for the *Lancaster Intelligencer Journal*—for the last fifteen days of May 1962. Unwittingly, he made the comparison between the amicable qualities of most librarians and the lack of such traits of his former girlfriend. Not that Lauren held any residual influence over him. No, what their relationship had granted him—literally—was the realization that he was now able to describe in words the kind of woman he wanted to marry someday.

First and foremost, she must be a lady, someone mannerly and appreciative. He also did not think much of married women who felt they had to invent their husbands. He had decided the day after Lauren and he broke up that if ever he was to marry, the girl would have to be demure—a nice change. A young woman who allowed him to lead, though he was no tyrant. In the two years he'd spent dating Lauren, the role of leadership—something he believed a man and woman ought to share equally—had been totally usurped. Was it old-fashioned to long for sweet submission in a mate—and be willing to give it as well? His own mother's humble approach toward his father had worked beautifully for their marriage, and when asked to give their formula for a lifetime of happiness, they often referred to Bible verses, pointing to characteristics such as meekness—a give-and-take relationship. That, he would be quick to acknowledge, had never once occurred with his former girlfriend.

"How may I help you?" asked the librarian, bringing him back to the task at hand.

He made his request and waited, wondering where he might meet up with the sort of girl he'd decided he must have, or be content to remain a bachelor. Would she love books and research as much as he? Perhaps she might be a librarian or, at least, a library *patron*. He grinned at his own thoughts.

When the librarian had located the particular microfilm spool, she was all smiles. "Here we are." She handed it to him.

"Thank you," he said, his mind on the data he held in his hand. The mystery of the postcard had gripped him beyond belief.

The obituary stated that the twenty-seven-year-old man had died on Sunday, May 30, 1962, and been laid to rest in Reading, Pennsylvania, though his place of birth was listed as Bird-in-Hand. Why Reading and not Lancaster County, somewhere close to his family? Philip found it equally interesting that no services had been offered for the young Amishman. Why?

According to the obit, Gabe had been the only son born to John and Lydia Esh. His surviving sisters were many: Mary and Martha—twins—Nancy, Ruth, Katie, Naomi, and Rebekah. There was no way of knowing Gabe's birth order, though the thought of being the only brother of seven sisters made Philip break out in a sweat.

While there, he looked up the name *Herr* in the Reading phone book. To his amazement, he discovered page after page of Herrs. He decided that, if necessary, he would go to the trouble of driving to Reading at some point and put his investigative skills to the task. But first he wanted to drop in at the Old Village Store in Bird-in-Hand, nose around a bit, get acquainted with some of the local folk.

He left the library, briefcase in hand, and walked a block down sun-dappled cobblestone sidewalks to his rental car. Then, driving to King Street, he turned east and rode past long red-brick blocks, reminding him somewhat of the famous Beacon Hill row houses of Boston. He passed the Conestoga View County Home, then veering left, took Route 340, also known as the Old Philadelphia Pike.

The sun had climbed the sky while he was inside the library, turning hot enough for Philip to push the AC dash button. The day was as bright as any September day he recalled in recent years, and while driving along the busy road, he realized just how inspired he had become since arriving here a scant two days ago. He made a mental note to phone his sister and let her know that he had been surprisingly revitalized on this trip. He guessed what her response might be. She would say she wasn't surprised, that he'd needed to experience a simpler, less-harried pace. She might also encourage him to go a step further and get in touch with his Maker. After all, Pennsylvania had long been considered a "God-fearing" state, due to William Penn's influence, offering land to immigrants in search of religious freedom.

Glancing in the rearview mirror, he noticed a horse and carriage trailing behind him as he came up on the old, abandoned Lampeter Friends Meetinghouse. The horse and buggy followed him down the pike, past the Hand-in-Hand Fire Station on the left and the Greystone Manor B&B on the right, then under the railroad bridge. He definitely wanted to thank his editor for having shoved the Amish assignment down his throat. Yes, he would do just that the minute he stepped foot back in the magazine office.

Philip began to formulate a strategy for gathering answers to his growing list of questions. To start with, he hoped to meet with at least one of Gabe's seven sisters. Surely, out of all those Esh women, one would have settled in the Lancaster area.

The Old Village Store was coming up on the left-hand side of the road. The prominent sign out in front—complete with well pump adjacent to it—declared the date of establishment as 1890. The inverted U-shaped, barnlike buildings had intrigued him earlier this morning when he first drove past this stretch of road. A store with such origins might have some folk connected with it who'd known Gabe Esh or his family, someone who might be willing to direct him to the right people. Hopefully even one of the Esh sisters; perhaps one who may have had a soft spot in her heart for the young man for whom no one had cared to conduct even a memorial service.

❖ ❖ ❖

Susanna and her younger sister Leah were friends on two important levels. On the first and most significant, they were intimate sibling-friends; on the second, they were farmers' wives, or at least had been once. Now that Susanna was busy running an Amish B&B, she regretted not being able to get out to near as many quilting frolics.

On the first level, the sisters shared memories. They grew up learning the importance of patience and submission to God, the Amish church, and their elders. They sewed together, helped their mamma cook, made beds, mended their brothers' socks, swept the kitchen, hoed the vegetable and flower gardens, washed the clothes, raked the front and side yards, and put up as many canned goods as any other hardworking sibling team around. When they got married, nothing much changed. They still worked from dawn to sunset, never stopping to rest or think of themselves. It was always "put yourself before others"—their mother's motto for all her children, especially the girls. So they were prime examples of Mamma's strict upbringing.

On the second level, Susanna and Leah had given birth to a good percentage of their offspring in nearly the same months of the year, for all but two sons. (Rachel and Esther had come into the world on the exact same day, like twins carried by different mothers.) Now the two sisters enjoyed sharing stories or chatting over common gossip in each other's kitchens, usually with a cup of black coffee or iced tea, depending on the season. Or, here lately, they might slip off into town together, stop at the Bird-in-Hand Bakery, and secretly splurge on Grandma Smucker's giant cinnamon rolls, though they could've easily made some at home, had they cared to. The idea of getting out and away from what was forever expected of them was the main thing that compelled them out for a half hour here or there, especially now that most of their children were grown and gone. Leah's two youngest girls were courtin' age—Molly, seventeen, and Sadie Mae, nineteen—still living at home and anxiously awaiting the right carpenter's son or farmer's boy to ask them to "go for steady or so."

When Susanna and Leah weren't planning the next quilting or apple butter frolic, they were discussing their many grandchildren, commenting on whose offspring reminded them of which brother or sister. Or, in some cases, aunts or uncles.

But today Susanna had felt the need to make a quick run over to see Leah about something far removed from grandchildren and the like. "Somethin' I need to tell you," she'd said right out the minute her sister motioned her into the long, sunny kitchen.

"You feelin' all right?" Leah asked, her big brown eyes narrowing a bit as they met Susanna's.

"Never better." Susanna fanned herself with the flap of her long apron.

Leah pulled out a chair for her, and the two of them sat at the table with a tall glass of iced tea, eyeing each other and ready to giggle like schoolgirls. "This must be some juicy gossip I don't know about. I've never seen your face so flushed."

"Well, I wouldn't go so far as to say it's gossip, but what I have to tell you is mighty interesting, for sure and for certain."

Leah's eyes brightened. "I'm all ears."

"Will you hear me out before you say a word?"

Leah indicated that she would with a smile and a nod.

Then, taking a deep breath, Susanna began to relay the conversation she'd had with Benjamin, first thing after they were up and dressed, as she couldn't bear to wait till after the B&B guests had their turn at the breakfast table. "I coaxed Benjamin outside onto the back patio, and here's what I said to him. It's beyond me how I coulda missed somethin' this special all this time. 'Course he wanted to know exactly what I was thinking, but I hafta to tell ya, Leah, I think—and Ben agrees—that our Rachel is someone Blue Johnny's got his eyes on."

Leah's mouth dropped open. "But he's a man in his fifties, and he ain't even Amish, so how on earth's that gonna work out?"

Susanna laughed right out loud. "C'mon, now, think 'bout what I'm sayin' here. In no way am I referrin' to marriage. The man's old enough to be Rachel's father, for pity's sake! What I'm tryin' to tell ya is that I think she's gonna be our next powwow doctor."

"Rachel is?"

Susanna shared with her sister regarding the giftings she'd noticed in Rachel off and on her whole life. "Anyone who's as sensitive to things like she's always been—making herself blind and all—well, I'm tellin' ya, she's bound to be next. You just wait and see."

Leah shook her head, smiling. "And to think you're her mother and all."

"Oh, don't go giving honor where it ain't due. It's nothing I've done."

"You gave birth to her, didn'tcha?"

"And eleven others, but none of the rest showed any

signs of the abilities Rachel's got." Susanna stopped to sip some tea. "To tell you the truth, I'm a-thinkin' the healing gift must've skipped a generation—stopped with Uncle Gabe when he died. But to think now it's showin' up again, and right under my nose, for goodness' sake!"

"Well, what's Rachel think of all this?" Leah asked, tracing the pattern on the green-checkered oil cloth.

"The poor dear's fightin' her natural-born inclinations, rejecting the gifts like I've never seen the likes of it since—"

"Don't tell me!" Leah blurted.

"Jah, you know exactly who I'm talking 'bout. I'm afraid she's an awful lot like our uncle Gabriel, except he was far more outspoken and fired up. Bold to a fault—and look where it got him. Honest to goodness, Rachel would be right content to sit in the parlor and crochet afghans most every day if it wasn't for Annie. Someone besides me oughta tell her that courage ain't the lack of discouragement or fear but the might to push forward in spite of it."

"Ach, you're soundin' more like a sage than a guest-house owner." Leah laughed, her round cheeks turning pink. "Does Annie ever coax Rachel outdoors?"

"Jah, they were out pickin' pumpkins over at the neighbors' just yesterday."

Leah rose and freshened their drinks, then sat back down. "You don't think she's scared, do ya?"

Susanna was shocked that her sister would say such a thing. "Afraid of the transference or just accepting the whole idea of being a powwower?"

"Well, you know what folks were sayin' back when Gabe was preachin' all that about wickedness among the People—evil spirits in the community and all. I remember overhearing a lot of it from our parents, and honestly it makes a body think twice about some of what was going on back then . . . and still is."

Susanna huffed at her sister and tapped her fist on the table. "Now, you listen here and listen gut. There ain't no way on God's green earth that what the powwow doctors are doin' is wrong or comin' from the devil. They're helping folk, plain and simple, and that's just right fine with me." She went on to recite the healings of Bishop Seth's deaf great-grandson and Caleb Yoder's second-degree burns. Even Benjamin's driving horses had been cured of ulcers when the local veterinarian couldn't do anything. She knew she didn't have to, but she reminded her sister of Lizzy's bad rheumatism. "It's gone for gut now, ain't? So how could something like that be wrong?"

Leah nodded her head slowly, and Susanna felt it was time she oughta be leavin', now that things were back on somewhat of an even keel between them.

"Are you planning to go to Lavina's tomorrow?" Leah wanted to know. "Some of us are gettin' together to make applesauce, then put up some pickled beets. You could come after you serve breakfast to your guests."

Susanna headed for the back door. "I'll see if Rachel wants to."

"Tell her Molly and Sadie are goin'."

Calling her good-byes over her shoulder, Susanna wondered why Leah had mentioned her unmarried daughters— Molly and Sadie Mae. The younger girls, along with all the rest of Leah's daughters, not including Esther out in Ohio, had written Rachel off after the accident. Susanna figured she knew why, too. None of their Amish kinfolk honestly believed that Rachel's vision problems had anything to do with the English doctors' explanations. Some of them prob'ly thought she might be faking her blindness, yet if they lived with Rachel and saw how she shuffled through the house, reacting the way a truly blind person would, they'd know. Truth be told, she herself had tested Rachel of sorts, flicking dishrags at her every so often. But every single time Rachel never so much as blinked an eyelash. So Susanna was convinced that her daughter couldn't see much—knew it beyond a shadow of doubt. She just had no idea why her eyes hadn't cleared up long ago like the hospital doctor had said they would.

Well, for now she wasn't gonna fret over what Leah's grown children—or hers and Benjamin's for that matter— thought of Rachel. Leah was prob'ly laughing up a blue streak over Susanna's idea that Rachel had inherited miracle-working powers. She'd seen the skeptical gleam in her sister's eye. Leah would be tellin Molly and Sadie Mae 'bout it, too. "Why, Susanna's girl can't even make *herself* see, so how's she gonna heal anybody else?"

Jah, that's what Leah was saying about now. But Susanna didn't much care. Her sister and all the rest of her Esh relatives—Zooks, too—just might be in for a big surprise one day. Maybe sooner than anyone expected.

❖ ❖ ❖

Less than forty-eight hours earlier, on Monday, Philip had been going about his life—rushing here and there, gathering information for assignments, writing rough drafts, revising them, handing them off to his line editor—in general, eking out a living the only way he knew how. But here it was Wednesday, and too much had happened for him to merely fly home with his tidy and tight feature article in hand. He'd landed the perfect story, and if he could satisfy his reporter's curiosity and make everything fit, perhaps he would write a major spread—a human interest piece based on the postcard's message that would surpass anything he had yet contributed. That is, if he had any success in finding one Miss Adele Herr.

The postcard, after all, belonged to Gabe's sweetheart, wherever she might be. He would take some extra time— between assignments—to locate the lady.

He pulled into the designated parking area in front of the village store side of the complex of buildings and walked across to the hardware store. He noticed the large red pop machine standing to the left of the entrance and almost bought a can of soda, but he was distracted by a pay telephone with a phone book dangling on a chain on the opposite side of the door. On impulse he looked up the name *Herr* in the book, discovering there were almost as many listed here as in the Reading phone book. *Must be a popular German name*, he thought. Locating Adele Herr, especially if she had married, could take some time. While he had the book in his hands, he checked on the name *Esh* and discovered that *that* name was also common to the area.

Closing the book, he headed inside to find the most rustic setting he'd seen in years. The hardware shop was a typical country store, complete with wood-burning fireplace and bare wood floors. Every imaginable gadget was on display—an impressive array of items—from hand tools to shovels, nails, screws, and brackets of every conceivable size. Antique furniture, scattered around the store, caught his eye, and he wondered if a place like this might sell old writing desks, though he wouldn't have thought so. Not a hardware store. But as he strolled the aisles, he decided to inquire about antique furniture as a way of striking up a conversation with one of the clerks—if he could locate one.

"May I help you, sir?"

He turned to see a short little man with an eager smile. "Yes, I hope you can," Philip said. "I noticed your antiques . . . are any of them for sale?"

"I'm sorry, but no. They're just to give the old place some atmosphere, you know."

Philip glanced at the wide plank floors. *As if it needs atmosphere,* he thought, returning the man's smile.

They talked about the weather, how mild and warm it was for this late in the season—a real plus for the tourist business. "We have lots of tourist trade around here. This store's always busy in the summer and fall. Folks like to come to Lancaster to see the leaves turn colors, you know, especially on toward October."

Philip asked where he might find an antique desk. "Something on the order of a rolltop. Know of anything like that?"

The clerk scratched the back of his neck, wrinkling up his face. "Seems to me Emma had an old piece like that back a few years ago. Wouldn't have any idea who bought it, though. You could check with her about it."

"Emma, you say?"

"She's down just apiece, off the pike here"—he was pointing east—"then south on Harvest Road. You'll see her sign . . . says Emma's Antique Store."

"Thanks, I'll check there," said Philip. "By the way, you wouldn't happen to know of any Amish folk named Esh around here, would you? I'm looking for one of Gabriel Esh's sisters. I understand he had seven, two were twins. Ring a bell?"

The man grinned from ear to ear. "Asking for Plain folk named Esh is like lookin' for a needle in a haystack, so to say."

Philip nodded. "This man, Gabe Esh, was only twenty-seven when he died—nearly forty years ago. Supposedly, he was a renegade preacher." Philip was so eager it was all he could do to restrain the flood of questions he wished to ask.

The clerk held up his finger, glancing over his shoulder. "Hold on there, just a second. Let me ask someone who might know better about this."

Hope fading, Philip idly picked up a tiny gadget for curtain rods, hoping to blend in with the other customers. Still, dressed in slacks and sports coat, he looked every whit the part of a New York reporter. What *had* he been thinking to make himself so conspicuous?

When the clerk returned, he had a thin, gray-haired woman with him. She was cheerful enough—seemed to want to help, too. "Joe, here, tells me you're looking for the Esh sisters?"

"Why, yes, I am." Philip realized she was waiting for something more from him, some reason for her to offer information to a total stranger. "I'd like to talk with someone related to the late Gabriel Esh. Someone who might've known of his love interest, a Miss Adele Herr."

The woman's eyebrows arched over her inquisitive blue eyes. "Well, in that case, I suppose you should go on over to see Martha Stoltzfus. She runs a quilting barn down off Lynwood Road. There's a big white tourist sign out front. You can't miss it."

"This Martha Stoltzfus—is she Amish?"

"Old Order through and through. She's one of the twins, Gabe's youngest siblings, 'cept Mary's gone now, like all the others."

"Thanks for your help," he said. "I appreciate it very much."

"I'll call Martha and let her know you're coming. She doesn't take too well to non-Amish men, though. Just be sure and take a close look at those quilts of hers—some of the finest around Lancaster. And tell her Bertha Denlinger sent you."

He thanked both the woman and her short male side-kick and headed out the door, stopping to buy a can of soda on the front porch of the store. "Too easy," he said, pulling open the can and having a long swig in celebration.

When he returned to the car, he discovered that Stephen Flory had left a message on his cell phone's voice mail. "How goes the investigation?" The recording revealed a strong interest in Philip's work.

He phoned Stephen back before pulling out of the parking space. "I'm heading off later to an Amish quilt barn to chat with one of Gabe Esh's sisters."

"So . . . you're hot on his trail," Stephen remarked with a slight chuckle.

"After that puzzling postcard message, I had to know more of the story. I've arranged to keep my room at the B&B through Saturday."

"Sounds interesting, your visit with Gabe's sister. Maybe you can fill me in sometime." The man was more than eager to be included, and rightly so. After all, he had gone out of his way to introduce Philip to Abram Beiler yesterday afternoon—with the appropriate pay, of course—but the matter had become more than an extension of his job, it seemed. Stephen Flory was hooked.

But Philip preferred not to be put on the spot, having to invite Stephen along to meet Martha Esh Stoltzfus, though the man was cordial enough—and fine company. He just didn't see the need to alarm the Amishwoman needlessly with *two* strange men showing up at her place of business. That was one sensible excuse, at any rate. "I'll give you a complete report, if you'd like." It was his awkward, yet fastidious way of sidestepping the issue.

Stephen seemed reluctant to hang up, and when he pressed for more details, Philip finally mentioned having been to the library, "where I discovered some interesting facts."

Admitting that he, too, had read and copied the obituary that morning at his place of work, Stephen demonstrated far more than a passing interest in the story behind the postcard. "Turns out one of my colleagues knows something of Gabe Esh and his precarious relationship with his family and the Old Order community. From what my friend says, the young man was more than a rebel in the community. He was outcast among his people. They out-and-out shunned him . . . and he wasn't even a church member. How do you figure that?"

It was Philip's turn to be curious. "So you *do* have something on him?" he joked.

"Maybe we should pool our resources."

"Tomorrow . . . you name the place."

"The Bird-in-Hand Family Restaurant has a good menu. I'll meet you there for supper." So it was set. The two would attempt to piece together the puzzle of Gabriel Esh's life.

Meanwhile, Philip needed some fresh air and a change

of clothes—something casual that would give him the appearance of a relaxed sightseer instead of a journalist. He drove down the road, drinking his soda as he headed back toward the turnoff to Beechdale Road. Noticing how clear and blue the sky was, he thought it a good idea to get out and enjoy the morning. Susanna had kindly suggested the walking path through the orchard a number of times since he'd checked in. Now would be as good a time as any.

Pulling into the lane at the Orchard Guest House, he parked the rental car on the far north side, in front of the Gift Nook just off the main house. He wondered if the boutique had been a *Dawdi Haus* at one time—an addition built to house aging Amish grandparents, so he'd learned.

He turned off the ignition and shed his sports coat, heading around the side of the house, past lavender and rose-pink asters standing sentry along a floor of old bricks. He was able to put a name to the large flowers because he'd heard his grandmother mention their names more than once as a boy. "Asters are as showy as can be," she would say of her favorite annuals.

Philip paused to take in the well-manicured back lawn, noticing an antique-style wooden wheelbarrow overflowing with red geraniums and white nasturtiums. His gaze lingered on an oval gazebo with its crested roof and vines trailing up its lathed posts in the front. Something out of *Better Homes and Gardens.*

Beyond the gazebo, east of the yard, the gravel footpath beckoned to him by way of colorful pots of hybrid fuchsias—deep pinks, reds, and purples—their bright heads nodding in a row. He strolled past a white resin birdbath and decided he wouldn't take time to change clothes before his walk. The breezes were warm and tantalizing, and he knew from having stared out the second-story bedroom window that far beyond the orchard a creek awaited him. He wanted to sit beside its banks, the way he and Grandpap had often sat when he was a young boy. Wanted to contemplate the remarkable morning, to collect his thoughts before the visit with Gabe's sister.

❖ ❖ ❖

Just southeast of the B&B, farmers were cutting tobacco. Rachel didn't have to see it to know. The smell was fondly familiar, pungent with memories of playing near the tobacco shed with Esther while their fathers and brothers worked hard to cut and store the moneymaking crop come September and October every year.

She wanted to go walking out to Mill Creek while Mam was out visiting Aunt Leah. The creek, which ran diagonally across her father's property, was running full due to recent rains, Dat had said at breakfast. She had never ventured so far on the property and decided today was the day for some adventure.

"Wanna go for a gut long walk?" she asked Annie, finding her cane in the umbrella stand just inside the back door.

"Mamma? Are ya sure?"

"I'm sure."

"But you usually say you'd rather stay inside."

"I know, but it's high time I got out more," she admitted. "Besides it's a perfect day for a walk, ain't so?"

"Can we take Copper along?" Annie asked, scurrying about.

"Not such a rowdy dog. He might lead us astray." She

laughed but meant every word.

She heard Annie's feet slide against the floor. "You can't be comin' along with us this time," Annie was telling the dog. "You best wait till Mammi Susanna gets back. Maybe then I'll take ya for a walk."

"That shouldn't be too long now," added Rachel. "So are we ready?"

They headed outside, past the flagstone patio, making their way through the wide backyard toward the direction of the orchard. The grass felt cool on her bare feet, and she thrilled to the buzzing of bees and the intermittent chirping of birds, some close in trees, others farther away. "Tell me what you see, Annie."

"Well, there's hardly any clouds . . . except for one tiny little one at two o'clock."

Rachel chuckled at her daughter's use of the traditional time positioning to describe the cloud's location. "Tell me what it looks like. Is it a double dip of ice cream or puffs of cotton batting?"

Annie was laughing now. "It's none of those things, Mamma. It's like an upside-down tooth. Just like the tiny little tooth I lost last month. Remember?"

"Jah, I remember." She thought about Annie's tooth, how easily it had come out while Annie bit into a Macintosh apple—their very own. "Now, what else do you see?"

"Birds. There's a robin over near the creek. Oh, we hafta be quiet . . . I think he's taking an air bath." She was silent, then—"Jah, that's what he's doing, picking away at his feathers."

"That's how they clean themselves," Rachel said, recalling her own fascination with birds, especially baby birds in the spring.

"Hold my hand tight now, Mamma. We're gonna cross the footbridge."

"Is the bridge very plain?" she asked.

"Not so plain, really. There's a nice wide place to walk. It's all wooden, not painted any color—just the wood color, you know. But the best part of all is two people can walk side-by-side on this little bridge."

Rachel's heart sang as she tapped her cane with one hand and gripped Annie's hand with the other. "Can we stop in the middle?"

"Two more steps to go . . . there." Annie led her to the wooden railing.

"Tell me about the creek. What's it look like today? What color is it?" Rachel leaned on the railing, then placed her hand on her daughter's back, feeling the restless muscles between the child's shoulder blades.

"It's blue from the sky and brown from the dead leaves on either side—and it's purple, too, all mixed up together. And there's dancing pennies on the water, just a-floatin' downstream. Oh, Mamma, we'd have lotsa money if I could take a bucket down there and dip it up."

"The pennies are really the sunshine twinkling on the creek, ain't so?" Rachel said.

"No . . . no. You mustn't spoil the picture." Annie threw her arms around her mother. "There's pennies in there, Mamma. You should see 'em."

"Jah, pennies . . ." Rachel smiled. "I don't know 'bout you today." They stood there silently, listening to all the sounds around them.

"Think of the prettiest place you ever saw before you couldn't see anymore," Annie whispered.

"I've got a right gut place in mind." Rachel thought of

the time she and Esther had gone wading in the Atlantic Ocean.

"Tell me about it," Annie said, giggling. "I wanna know."

Rachel described the cold sting of the water on her bare feet, the foamy white edges of the tide as it rolled up toward her and Esther, splashing over their ankles. "It was prob'ly the pertiest place in the whole world."

"I wanna go to the shore someday. Do you think we could?"

"Maybe . . ." She had no idea when that might be—if ever again—but she didn't want to discourage her little one. The girl was filled up with a love for God's creation.

"Now it's your turn. Tell me about the pertiest place you've ever seen." She tickled Annie's neck.

But Annie stiffened just then. "Ach, there's someone sittin' over yonder," she said softly. "Oh, never mind, it's just that tall Mr. Philip. He's over there near the creek bank, throwing twigs into the water." Before Rachel could tell her daughter not to call to him, Annie did just that. "Hullo, there, Mr. Philip!"

"Hi again, Annie. It's a beautiful day, isn't it?"

The man's voice sounded altogether kind, not what Rachel had expected from a fancy reporter-writer. And snoop. Still, she felt terribly unsettled being out here, so far from the house, with Annie calling attention to them like this.

"It's a right nice day, all right," Annie replied.

Rachel held her breath, hoping the man wouldn't answer her this time. "Let's head back to the house," she whispered to Annie.

"Take my hand, Mamma."

All the way back, on the dirt path through the orchard, Rachel felt uneasy. She wanted to be left alone with Annie on this, her first visit to Mill Creek and the footbridge.

Left alone . . .

The motto of the past two years.

To get her mind off herself, she thought of the blue and purple creek with its dancing pennies. Annie was cute that way, describing things in such a fresh, interesting manner.

"Denki, Annie," she said, almost without thinking.

"For what?"

"For going with me on our beautiful walk. I enjoyed the creek pennies, especially."

"Me too, Mamma. Maybe I'll go back and dip up some of them. Then you'll believe they're for real."

"Promise me you won't go back there alone," Rachel blurted.

"I won't go by myself. I'll take Copper with me, if Mammi Susanna says it's all right."

Rachel guessed they'd be puttin' lunch together here before long. That would keep the girl from running back to the footbridge . . . and to Mr. Philip. Why on earth did she have to be so downright gabby with strangers? Rachel bit her lip but didn't say a word. She figured she'd said enough already.

All the way back through the apple trees, Rachel heard the clear song of the brook. She felt the warm, dry dirt under her feet and was ever so thankful for the day.

❖ ❖ ❖

He was crouched along the bank of the creek, tossing

pieces of sticks into the stream, when he first noticed Annie with the young woman. They were leaning on the footbridge railing, peering into the water below. The girl was talking about the brook, it seemed, pointing and laughing.

The woman, whom he was increasingly sure was Annie's mother, placed her hand gently on the child's back, eyes closed as she faced the sky. The sun on the water made tiny round jewels of light, and he noticed it especially because Annie was gesturing toward it.

Yet his eyes were drawn back to the beautiful woman, her face still raised to the heavens. In spite of her gray dress and black apron, he found her breathtaking, and he might've continued to stare if it hadn't been for Annie's enthusiastic greeting.

Only after he had called back to her did Philip begin to understand why the child seemed to stand so close to the woman, why Annie took the hesitant woman's hand and guided her safely, step by step, away from the bridge and back to the orchard path.

Annie's mother was *blind*. The realization struck him hard, and he shrank from it, thinking he must be mistaken, wanting to be wrong for Annie's sake. For her mother's.

Long after they'd gone, he sat beside Mill Creek, beholding brown clumps of earth as they curled around the mossy banks. He watched with pleasure the delicate shadows made by lofty maples, their yellow-green leaves trembling in a soft flurry of air, and he gazed at silver sunbeams falling atop a riffle of water on smooth gray rocks—seeing with new eyes.

❖ ❖ ❖

Susanna picked up the reins and called, "*Hott rum!*" instructing the horse to move out to the right. The path that led home was a straight strip ahead with a yellow do-not-pass line running down the middle. Stretching out flat and narrow, the road skirted the edge of the white fence that ran along Gibbons Road, where a red Amish schoolhouse stood, facing east. She relived bygone memories of having dropped off two or three of their sons at a similar one-room school on raw, wintry days while riding along with Benjamin and the boys in their horse-drawn sleigh. Oh, so many years ago.

Roadside flower beds of orange, yellow, and red blossomed as edging along rows of cabbage or sweet corn, the typical Amish way to fancy up property borders. The bishops had no say in how a farmer's wife "dressed" her flower gardens—couldn't keep nature from shouting with color. Susanna smiled to herself, privy to the unspoken reason why many of her Amish neighbors chose such a profuse variety of hues. Some of the crimsons, yellows, and oranges clashed—colors they were forbidden to wear, all of them.

Her thoughts roamed back to her conversation with Leah, then back to Rachel. How could she get her timid daughter to see the light about Blue Johnny? She could smooth the way and talk to Bishop Seth Fisher or one of their preachers about it maybe. But, no, it'd be best coming from Benjamin, though she knew he wouldn't be one for taking sides. The man was easily persuaded when it came to his blind daughter, though he wouldn't think of letting his partiality show, 'specially in front of his other adult children. Susanna suspected he'd had a favorite these many years. As for Annie, well, there was no getting 'round it, the child was a favorite of them both, even though Susanna wished she could do something about Rachel's unwise, forbearing approach with the little girl.

Making the turn onto Olde Mill Road, she waved and called a greeting to Rebekah Zook, both her neighbor and cousin by marriage, on her husband's side. "Another nice day, ain't so?"

Rebekah looked up from her yellow spider mums and waved. "We could use some rain one of these days."

"Jah, rain," Susanna agreed, craning her neck to peer at the blue sky out of the buggy.

The mare bobbed her head, pulling the carriage toward home. Susanna settled back in the carriage, thinking more about Rachel, ever so glad she'd taken the time to stop by and see Leah.

For better or worse.

Fifteen

❖ ❖ ❖

*T*he Quilt Barn was filled with handmade goods. King-and queen-sized bed quilts hung from the rafters, smaller wall-hangings and samplers hung on wooden stands, and table runners of every color and shade were displayed on a number of tables, along with place mats, napkins, and pot-holders.

One wall hanging especially caught Philip's eye. It was the King James Version of one of the Scripture verses from Gabe's postcard: *He which hath begun a good work in you will perform it until the day of Jesus Christ.*

Philip didn't give it a second thought and went in search of something authentically Amish to take back to his sister and niece. He was playing tourist, hoping to ease his way into a chat with the owner. A bright-colored quilted apron seemed to have Janice's name on it, and he carried it over his arm, heading for the next section of goods. He had to look longer to find something he thought Kari might like, finally settling on a faceless Amish doll, though he couldn't be sure that Kari, knowing how she liked to embroider, might not end up making cross-stitched eyes, nose, and mouth on the doll dressed in the traditional cape dress and apron.

When he went to pay for the items, he introduced him-self to the elderly woman behind the counter. "I'm the man

Bertha Denlinger sent over . . . from the hardware store," he said, offering the woman a hearty smile.

"She called me not long ago."

He waited for her to say that she was indeed Martha Stoltzfus, but she leaned hard on her cane while adding up the amounts on a small calculator. "That'll be forty-two dollars and fifty-five cents."

He pulled out his wallet and paid with a fifty-dollar bill, hoping to buy some time with the woman while she made change. "Bertha Denlinger said you might be able to help me locate someone"—he paused—"if you're Martha Esh Stoltzfus, that is."

She didn't blink an eye, just looked him straight in the face and said, "Bertha should learn to speak for herself."

"I see," he said, not sure how to proceed. "Well, if it's not a good time, I can certainly come back."

"Come . . . go, do as you please, but I'm tellin' ya right now, there's nothing more to be said about my dead brother and that wicked woman of his."

He chose to ignore her terse remark. "How can I get in touch with Adele Herr? I have something important that belongs to her."

She snorted. "That woman dropped out of the picture a long time ago. Last I heard, she's dead."

"Are you sure about that?" He wished the question hadn't come out sounding so brash.

"She hasn't been heard of since her father died of a heart attack."

"Her father?"

"Jah, a Baptist minister up in Reading."

"Would you happen to know when Adele passed away?" he asked, softening his approach.

"Couldn't say." She clammed up after that, sitting down behind the counter, still leaning on her cane, her long blue dress nearly touching the floor.

"Uh, this may be a strange question, but why wasn't your brother buried in Lancaster? Why Reading?" It was an assertive question, no getting around it, but he felt it might be his last stab.

"Now, you listen here." She'd lowered her voice, teetering forward on her chair. "We don't make a habit of speakin' much 'bout shunned folk—dead or alive—around here, so it'd be best now for you to be goin'."

She doesn't take too well to non-Amish men. . . .

"I'm sorry to have upset you, Mrs. Stoltzfus." His attempt was met with utter silence, and for the old woman's sake, he was glad the other customers were not within earshot.

❖ ❖ ❖

Rachel helped Mam clear away the lunch dishes. "I can look after the Gift Nook tonight, if you want," she offered.

"You sure?"

Rachel heard the surprise in her mother's voice. "Jah, and Annie can help me with prices and things. We'll do that for you; give you some rest for a change."

"That's right nice of you, Rachel. I think I could use a bit of peace and quiet tonight. S'been quite a morning."

"We had a busy morning, too," Annie piped up.

"Well, what're ya waitin' for? Let's hear all about it," Mam said across the table.

"To start with, Mamma and me stripped down all the

beds upstairs. We dusted and mopped and cleaned the bathrooms. Then we went walkin' . . . clean out to the end of the footpath, to the mill bridge."

"Is that so?" Mam seemed pleased.

"Jah, and we saw pennies—lotsa them!"

"I think ya best tell Mammi Susanna whatcha *really* saw today, Annie," Rachel cut in just then.

"It was pennies! Hundreds of tiny pennies a-skippin' down the creek."

Rachel waited for her darling child to 'fess up, though she wouldn't have pushed for an end to this fantasy. Not yet anyways. Annie was having too much fun.

"Let me guess," Susanna said. "Was it very sunny out?"

"Jah," Annie replied.

"And was it about noon, when the sun's straight up in the sky?"

"Jah."

"Then, I do believe what you saw out there in the creek was the sunlight dancing on the water. Am I right?" Mam's voice wasn't the least bit harsh, and for that Rachel was thankful.

She could just imagine her daughter nodding her little head ever so slowly, head tilted down a bit, and big blue eyes looking up as innocently as she ever had back when she was only four years old. Annie was a dilly, she was.

"How'dja know that, Mammi? And you weren't even there," said Annie, as serious as anything.

"Oh, I've lived many a year if I've lived a day, so you ain't tellin' me anything new. There's nothin' new under the sun, I tell you."

Rachel was perty sure her little one was thinking Mammi Susanna might be wrong about that. That those shiny, bright pennies were as new as new could be. 'Course, if you'd never seen such a thing as glory-lights on a brook as it flowed joyously downstream, you just might be thinking the same thing.

❖ ❖ ❖

Emma's Antique Shop was a thing of beauty. Well organized and attractive, the place was an antique shopper's paradise. Even the smallest items such as dinnerware, tea sets, and odd dishes had been carefully arranged for display. On one wall, there were decorative plates with tiny crack lines indicating age as well as character. Stacked up in a corner hutch, odds and ends of turn-of-the-century yellowware caught his eye. The pieces reminded Philip of Grandma Bradley's old set, the same grandmother who sang to her African violets to make them grow. There was also an abundant assortment of sea green apothecary bottles, he noticed, and he was reaching for one of them when a cheerful voice rang out, "Let me know if I can help you find something."

He turned toward the register, searching for a face to match the engaging female voice. "I'm looking for a rolltop desk," he said, wondering where Emma might be.

Slowly, a young Mennonite woman emerged from behind the long counter. She wore a print dress in a tiny floral pattern, high at the throat and sleeves with lace trim at the wrists. Her prayer veiling was different from the formal caps he'd seen on older women. Shaped more like a bandanna, only white and edged with lace, it hung down gracefully in back. "Oh my," she said, rolling up a dust cloth. "Someone oughta clean under there once in a while." She broke into a smile then, catching his gaze. "It's a desk you want? Now, let me see." She glanced around the large room. "I know I've got one coming in next week. Would you care to see it then?"

"Well, I'm from out of town, but I thought if you had something available, I'd take a look."

"I'm sorry about that," she said, coming out into the aisle. "What was it you were looking for exactly?"

He described to her the old desk in the bedroom at the Orchard Guest House. "It's magnificent."

Emma's eyes lit up. "I know that desk! I sold it to Susanna Zook myself."

He was surprised at the coincidence, and this on the heels of having just encountered the most discouraging Martha Stoltzfus. "I've hoped to find a desk similar to it ever since I first laid eyes on it. Wouldn't it be nice if it had a twin somewhere?"

"Maybe somewhere in England there's another one just like it, though I doubt it." She was grinning, nodding her head. "No . . . no, that desk was one of a kind, let me tell you."

A light switched on in his brain, and he knew he had to stick his neck out about the desk's origins. "Would you happen to know where it came from . . . I mean, before you acquired it?"

"As a matter of fact, I stumbled across it in a run-down secondhand store in downtown Reading, of all things. Not a soul there seemed to have any idea how old it was, and let me tell you, it was in sad shape when I bought it for a little bit of nothing. Now, don't you tell any of this to Susanna Zook, you hear?"

Philip nodded his promise, delighted to meet someone so cordial and willing to chat.

"Before that, a lady in the store seemed to think Bishop Seth's nephew by marriage had it holed up in a shed somewhere, waiting to be hauled off. And before that, I honestly don't know."

Philip had to ask. "Who's Bishop Seth?"

"Oh, I almost forgot you're not from around here." She took a slight step backward before continuing. "Seth Fisher is the oldest Amish bishop living in Lancaster County. Last I heard, he was ninety-three. They call him the 'anointed one'—guess that's what his first name means. Anyway, it's hard to believe it, but most of his wife's family—her brothers and sisters, at least—were never even Amish, never joined church, I mean. Now, isn't that something?"

Philip nodded.

The woman continued. "From what I know, Seth Fisher's wife's nephew, who had the desk, was a Baptist minister, of all things. I've forgotten the man's name, but I think he pastored a church up in Reading somewhere. Anyway, that's about all I know of Susanna Zook's desk."

Philip's head was spinning with more information than he might've hoped for. "Do you have a business card?" he asked, out of the blue, thinking that he might actually call the friendly woman and see if he couldn't purchase an old desk from her sometime. If not next week, another time. And he told her so.

"Oh my, yes." She turned back to the counter. "I've got plenty here. How many do you want?"

"One is fine," he said and thanked her for her help, though he did not reveal just *how* much help the woman had been.

❖ ❖ ❖

Rachel tapped her cane across the hardwood floor in the common area of the B&B, following Annie. "We're gonna have fun tonight," she said, feeling her way to the Gift Nook. "We could sell some of those creek pennies of yours maybe, in the gift shop, ya know."

"Ach, Mamma, you're pokin' fun!"

Laughing, Rachel unlocked the door and right away smelled the scented candles and other fragrances, a mishmash of odors, though she detected peach and strawberry real strong.

"What's on sale tonight?" Annie asked, standing beside her behind the small counter.

"Nothin's on sale, but everything's *for* sale!"

"Oh, I get it," replied her daughter. "Jah, I like that."

Rachel could hear Annie's pencil making circles on a pad of paper. "What's that you're drawing?" she asked.

"Can ya guess?"

"Maybe it's pennies? From the creek?"

Annie laughed. "Not that again, Mamma." She quieted down quickly as a customer walked in. The footsteps were heavy, more like a man's tread.

"Well, it's you again, Annie" came the man's voice. "We seem to keep running into each other, don't we?"

Rachel recognized the mellow voice and felt herself stiffen. Feeling awful shy, she wondered if other guests had come in, too, or if the man was by himself.

"I don't mind it one bit, Mr. Philip. You can talk to me anytime ya want."

"That's nice to know. Thank you, Annie."

"We have all sorts of souvenirs in here," the girl said, "case you wanna take somethin' back to New York."

"Annie dear," whispered Rachel. She truly wished her daughter might remember the things they'd discussed on the way home from pumpkin-pickin' yesterday.

"I almost forgot, Mr. Philip. I'm not 'sposed to be talkin' so awful much. My mamma says so."

Ach, Annie, must ya go on so? thought Rachel, not only feeling shy but terribly awkward now as well.

"And is this your mother?" the man asked.

"Jah, she's Mamma." The next thing Rachel knew, Annie's hand was on hers, pulling on it to shake with Philip Bradley. "Mr. Philip wants to meet you, Mamma. He's real nice, so it's all right if I talk to him this much, jah?"

Rachel smiled at her little chatterbox. "Hullo, Mr. Bradley," she said, feeling the warmth of his handshake before releasing it quickly.

"Please, call me Philip. Mr. Bradley is much too formal for my taste."

"See, Mamma, I told you he was real nice."

She honestly wished Annie would stop talking altogether, though she wouldn't have embarrassed her daughter for anything. "There's lots of handmade items in the shop," she managed to say, hoping Mr. Bradley wasn't looking at her but had turned to see what was available maybe.

"Yes, I noticed," he replied. "And who's responsible for making these lovely things?"

"Oh, Mamma makes most everything in here," Annie volunteered. "She can crochet as gut as anybody 'round Lancaster."

"I believe that must be true" came the courteous response.

Rachel hadn't realized she'd been clenching her hands during the conversation with Philip Bradley and Annie—a three-way chat to be sure. She willed herself to relax. *There's no reason to be so tense*, she decided, though she wondered how long the man would stay in the tiny shop just talking and not looking.

"Do you wanna buy something for your wife or children?" asked Annie.

"That's very nice of you to ask, but I'm not married."

"Oh," said Annie, "that's too bad."

"Well, I don't mind being single. It's not such a bad thing." He was silent for a moment. Then—"I wonder if you might be able to tell me something, Annie? Something about how you celebrate Christmas. That is, if it's all right with your mother."

"Is it, Mamma?"

Rachel had no idea what on earth the man might want to be asking about Christmas, so she didn't know if it was all right or not.

But before she could speak, the young man said, "I'm working on a story for a magazine about Amish family traditions, and I have only one question to finish the story. Do you mind if I ask Annie what she received for Christmas last year?"

Rachel almost laughed out of pure relief. This wasn't going to be so hard after all. "Well, I guess so. If Annie can remember."

" 'Course I remember, Mamma. I got this right here in my hand—a great big pad of rainbow papers and a set of colored pencils. *Des is ewwe es Allerbescht.*"

Rachel knew Annie had been right surprised to get the thick pad of paper, but she really didn't expect her to say what she did just now. Especially not in front of an En-glischer, for goodness' sake!

"What's *des is ewwe* . . . mean?" asked the man.

"Oh, I'm awful sorry, Mr. Philip. I just said, 'This is the best of all,' " Annie explained.

"I'll write that into my article, if you don't mind," he said with a quiet laugh. "And I think I'll have one of these crocheted angels to take home with me . . . uh, Mrs. . . . ."

Rachel thought he was waiting for her to say her name, to introduce herself, but surely she must be mistaken. Quickly as it had come, she dismissed the silly thought.

"It's five dollars and fifty cents," Annie said, helping the way she usually did.

"And I'm giving you a ten-dollar bill," Philip said.

He knows I can't see, Rachel thought, opening the register and making the correct change. The idea that he might have observed her and Annie this morning out at the creek made her feel even more uncomfortable. She handed the money to Annie to give to Philip Bradley, then felt for the box of tissue paper under the counter and began to wrap the crocheted angel.

"Do you sew, too, Annie?" Philip asked.

"A little bit."

"I saw some quilts today over at Martha Stoltzfus's quilt-ing barn."

"Jah, I've been there. Mamma and Mammi Susanna go there sometimes to make big quilts for the tourists."

"I think my niece would be a good quilter, too," he said. "She likes needlework."

"What's her name?" asked Annie.

"Kari, and she wanted to come with me to visit Lancaster. I know she would like you and your mother . . . if she had."

"Oh, bring her along next time maybe."

He chuckled. "You know what? I believe Kari would enjoy that very much."

Rachel heard several more guests wander into the shop just then and she breathed a sigh of relief. The conversation with Annie and the Englischer had gone on much too long.

"I'll see ya tomorrow," Annie said, and Rachel assumed that Philip Bradley had waved or made a motion toward the door.

"It was wonderful to see you again, Annie and . . ."

Rachel held her breath. He *was* waiting for her to mention her name!

"Mamma's name is Rachel," Annie filled in the silence.

"Very nice to meet you, Rachel."

And with that, he was gone.

Sixteen

❖ ❖ ❖

$\mathcal{P}$hilip thought he'd like to go to Reading and locate the cemetery where Gabe Esh was buried, but before heading out the next morning, he happened to notice Susanna changing the table runner in the dining room. The house was almost too quiet, so he assumed that most of the guests had already checked out, though he heard the soft *clink* of silverware in the kitchen.

Tentatively, he stepped into the large room where a long pine farm table, stained ruby red, was surrounded by his favorite style of antique chair—the comb-back Windsor. On the wall opposite low, deep-silled windows, a tall, slant-backed cupboard, housing a set of white china, graced the space.

"Excuse me, Susanna," he said, getting her attention. "I don't mean to bother you, but I'm curious about a particular man, Gabe Esh, who wrote the postcard—the one I showed you yesterday. Would you happen to know if his fiancée is still alive?"

Her face went ashen at the mention of the card. "I . . . uh, I don't have any idea what happened. . . ." She caught her breath and tried to continue. "His fiancée, you say?"

"Yes—Adele Herr. Do you know what may have become of her?"

Susanna shook her head repeatedly. "Honestly, I wish

177

you'd never found that . . . that horrid thing," she was saying, her face turning from white to pink. "I wish you'd just leave things be. It's none of your business, really it ain't."

"Please forgive me. I didn't intend to upset you this way."

She pulled a chair out and had to sit down. "It's not the kind of thing you wanna delve into, Mr. Bradley, and I'm sorry that I didn't come across that postcard myself. Seems to me I oughta be askin' you for it back." Her final sentence had turned into a bit of muttering, but Philip had heard nevertheless.

"I'm just trying to put some pieces together, that's all. I wouldn't think of causing trouble," he assured her.

There was a sudden commotion behind Susanna— young Annie, coming into the common area from the kitchen, carrying an armful of soiled cloth napkins, place mats, and dish towels. "Mammi Susanna, I think I need some help," the child said, about to drop the load.

"Here, let *me* help you," he said, taking the pile from her. "Just head me in the right direction."

"That would be around the corner, down the hall, and down the cellar steps," Susanna said rather tersely. "And I must say, since we bought this house, I've never, ever allowed a guest to help thisaway."

He heard the edginess in her voice and knew she was more upset over the postcard questions than his assistance with Annie's load of dirty towels. Yet she followed him down the hall and on down the cellar steps, with little Annie close behind.

In the end it was Rachel's daughter who saved the day, diverting Susanna's attention away from Philip's questions. "Mamma needs ya just now."

Susanna responded by showing him where to put the laundry items. "Thanks for helpin' my granddaughter out," she said, heading for the stairs.

Philip knew the woman expected him to follow, and follow he did, up the stairs and into the hallway. When he came to the second flight of stairs, he turned and made his departure to the southeast guest room.

❖ ❖ ❖

Susanna's reaction to the boarder's questions had flustered her no end. Even worse, Rachel must've overheard part of the conversation in the dining room, and now that Susanna was in the kitchen, Rachel wanted to know how Mr. Philip Bradley knew about her great-uncle.

"I couldn't believe my ears—I honestly thought I heard him askin' about your uncle, Gabriel Esh," said Rachel, frowning.

"Jah, you heard right, but you also must've heard me say that it's not nobody's business what went on back forty years ago. That includes you, my dear. Besides, it ain't right to be talkin' so awful much about a dead man under the shunning."

"Why *was* your uncle shunned, Mam?" Rachel seemed to be looking right at her, and even though Susanna knew her daughter couldn't make out her face or her frame, she almost wondered now as she stood there if the young woman's sight had suddenly returned. *Himmel*, there was almost a bold look on her daughter's face, and it got her thinking how to smooth this whole ridiculous dialogue over, bring it to a quick end.

"No need us wastin' precious time talking 'bout what's over and done with," she said softly, hoping her tone might quell the matter. She surely didn't want to open that can of worms.

Rachel stood near the sink, the breakfast silverware in her hand. Susanna fully expected her to turn back to the task of drying the knives, forks, and spoons, but Rachel shuffled past her, without reaching for her cane, sliding her bare feet along the floor, the utensils and dish towel still in her hands. "Where're you going, Daughter?"

When there was no reply, she decided to let things drop. No way, nohow, did she ever want Rachel to inquire about Gabe Esh again. Not the way her daughter seemed so hesitant toward the area healers. Not the way she'd wavered about Blue Johnny these many years.

❖ ❖ ❖

Rachel sat on the deacon's bench in the entryway, waiting for the New York man to come downstairs. She didn't rightly know how she would find her voice and ask the stranger what she wanted to know. It was a hard thing to cross the unspoken line the People had drawn between themselves and outsiders. Yet all her life she had wished for someone to talk to her about the mysterious great-uncle on her mother's side. But just about the time she'd get up a speckle of pluck to ask, the wind was knocked out of her courage.

The last time she'd almost stuck her neck out and asked about Gabe Esh was the day she'd ridden along to town with Dat, nearly a month ago. They'd been talking about this and that, most anything that came to mind; her father had spilled the beans and said he'd purchased a set of Bible tapes for her to listen to. "Don't be tellin' anyone 'bout it, though," he'd said.

She'd come that close to blurting her question out. In all her days, she'd never known or heard of a person being shunned for no gut cause. Surely there must be some important reason why.

Another time she thought of asking someone like her cousin Esther to write a letter to Bishop Glick—Esther's husband's grandfather—since she figured the bishop would surely know about Gabe's shunning, but she didn't want to step on Esther's toes, using her that way. If Bishop Glick was the sort of man her Jacob had been, she might've felt she could speak to him privately—in the presence of his wife, of course—but the bishop was rather reserved, not someone you could just walk up to after a preachin' service and ask a question like that. Bishop Glick was as reticent, folks said, as she herself was. Still, Rachel wondered what things he might know—what others in the community knew but weren't saying.

"Good morning, Rachel." Hearing her name spoken by a man jolted her out of her musing.

"Oh, hullo," she said, almost forgetting why she'd sat here so close to the front door.

"Have a nice day, and tell Annie I said good-bye."

Philip's kind voice encouraged her to reply. "Are you leaving?" she said, then realized what he meant, that he was saying 'good-bye' just for the day.

"No . . . no." He laughed, and she felt her cheeks heat at her blunder. "I'm paid through until Saturday. Can't let a terrific room like that slip through my fingers."

She didn't quite know how to respond to that, but she was surprised that she was able to get any words out at all. Here she was talking to the sophisticated New York guest. "May I . . . I mean, would it be all right . . . if I ask you a question?"

"You certainly may. What is it, Rachel?"

She was taken a little by surprise, the way he said her name—kind and gentle-like. "I heard you talking to my mother about Gabe Esh a little while ago."

"Yes?"

"How did you know him?"

"Well, I didn't know him at all. I found an old postcard in the desk upstairs . . . in my room, which he wrote forty years ago."

"A postcard . . . from Gabe Esh? Who was he writing to?"

"Here, let me show it to you. Maybe *you'll* know more about this. It's written in Pennsylvania Dutch, but I'll read the translation to you."

Slowly, he began. Rachel was silent, listening intently. "Oh my, what a mysterious and beautiful message," she said when he finished.

"Do you know who Adele Herr was?"

She shook her head. "Sorry, I've never heard of her. But I, too, am curious . . . been wanting to know more about my great-uncle . . . for many years now."

"Gabe was your great-uncle?"

"Jah, on Mam's side of the family."

"I didn't know."

"Well, what did my mother say about her?"

He was silent, and she wondered why. Then he said softly, "Your mother seemed quite troubled by this, so per-

haps you should speak to *her*. I don't want to cause problems."

She was quite taken aback by his sincerity. "Thank you,
Mr. Bradley. That is very kind."

"Philip—remember? I don't quite know how to react to
anything more formal."

He'd said precisely the same thing last evening, and she
felt foolish about having forgotten. "I apologize, Philip," she
said, enjoying the sound of his name.

"That's quite all right. And, if it should work out for me
to relay to you any information I might uncover today—
about your uncle—I will certainly do that."

"Denki," she said, almost without thinking. "Thank you
very much."

"Well, it's another warm day. Maybe you and Annie will
go for another walk."

"Oh, I don't know about that. We'll be makin' applesauce and picklin' beets today," she said, aware that the
silverware and dish towel were still in her hands. "There
may not be much time for walkin'."

"Well, then, good-bye," he said and was out the door
before she realized that she'd talked nearly a blue streak to
a stranger. And an Englischer at that.

Rachel was standing at the back door, waiting for Annie
to fill Copper's water dish outside. She heard Mam scurrying
about the kitchen, straightening things up before they
headed off to Lavina's.

"I don't know what you were thinkin', talking to Philip
Bradley thataway, Rachel. It was like you were just tarryin'
there for him to come downstairs."

She wondered how much her mother had overheard,

though she didn't think it was much to worry about. "He seems nice enough" was all she said.

"He's a snoop, and he's got his gall nosin' into our family business."

Rachel said nothing, knowing from past experience it was best not to egg Mamma on. Susanna hadn't heard everything Philip had said, though now to think of it, Rachel could scarcely believe the conversation had taken place at all. What *had* come over her to speak to a stranger like that? She'd told him something she'd never told a soul on earth except Cousin Esther, for goodness' sake! So now Mr. Philip Bradley knew just how curious she was about Gabe Esh, and that she had been all her life.

On the buggy ride to Lavina's, she second-guessed herself, worrying that she'd made a mistake talking to a stranger. One thing was sure—he had the nicest-sounding voice she thought she'd ever heard. And wonder of wonders, he was on his way to dig up information about Gabriel Esh. And Adele Herr.

Adele Herr ain't Amish, she thought.

Could it be true that Gabriel Esh had had an English sweetheart, like the postcard seemed to indicate? Was *that* the reason for his shunning?

❖ ❖ ❖

Philip took Interstate 176 to Reading, eager to get there as soon as possible. He wanted to have plenty of time to locate Gabe's grave marker, if there was one, before heading back to Lancaster in order to meet Stephen Flory for supper at the Bird-in-Hand Family Restaurant. He also wanted to do some checking, see if anyone in the area might have known Adele or knew the date of her passing. Ultimately, if need be, he could search back microfilms for a death notice, but he much preferred the human connection. The tenderness with which the postcard's message had been written and the fact that the postcard itself had been entrusted to him were, perhaps, the driving forces behind his desire, spurring him on to locate both Gabe's final resting place and Adele herself, though he feared the lady might also be deceased.

Between Plowville and Green Hills he wiled away the miles, talking to his sister on his cell phone. "Thought I'd check in and let you know your brother's still alive and kicking."

"How's the article coming?" asked Janice.

"Nearly finished."

"You're always in a rush, aren't you, looking ahead to the next project? Never take a minute to sigh."

"Not this time. I'm actually thinking of joining up with the Amish." He laughed. "So . . . how would you and Kari like to come help me run a bed-and-breakfast in Pennsylvania?"

"In Amish country?" She was hooting. "What would Ken say?"

"Just get him here, then we'll tell him. I'm not kidding—it's beautiful."

"Hey, you're sounding like your old self. What's happened? Did you meet a girl?"

He snorted. "Like I need one more failed relationship."

"Don't get sarcastic with me. You just sound so good . . . well rested or something."

"I like that—the rested part."

"Kari misses you," said Janice. "Maybe you can give her a call when you get home tomorrow."

"Didn't I tell you? I'm staying till Saturday . . . rescheduled my flight and everything."

"How come?"

"I'm on a fast track to solving an old, old mystery. What do you think of that?"

"Doesn't sound like you, Phil. What's going on?"

"Hey, that's interesting—you're starting to sound worried, more like the old Janice."

"You're bad," she said. "What are you *really* doing there?"

"No joking, I'm playing detective with a forty-year-old postcard as my guide, and if you don't think this is fascinating, you'll just have to wait and read the book."

"Are you sure you're all right, Phil? You didn't just say you're planning to write a book, did you? You can't sit still long enough to tie your shoes. What is it . . . a novel?"

"I'm toying with the idea, that's all." He wouldn't let her get the best of him.

They talked for a few more minutes, then he hung up to look at the map, glad that Janice hadn't chosen this phone chat to lecture him about slowing down, getting married, joining a church.

His mind wandered back to the peculiar scene in the entryway of Zooks' Orchard Guest House. Annie's beautiful, blind mother had clearly been waiting for him, sitting there on an old deacon's bench just to the right of the front door. It struck him as odd even now—that she had wanted to ask about Gabe Esh—and the way she had brought up the subject almost seemed as if her mother's uncle had been kept a deep, dark secret. Martha Stoltzfus had also given the same impression.

Something had startled him about seeing Rachel sitting in the foyer, holding silverware in one hand and a white dish towel in the other, so quiet and still—the way he'd seen her in the parlor with Annie that first day. He'd initially shrugged it off, thinking she may have been merely resting, not waiting to speak to him at all. He hadn't known why a thought like that might cross his mind. Rachel, after all, had not a single reason to speak to him. She was Amish, and from everything he'd gleaned of Plain women, they didn't go out of their way to talk to outsiders.

So he'd just assumed she was catching her breath. Nothing more. He also had the feeling that Susanna Zook took advantage of her daughter and any and all help she could get around the place. Husband Benjamin included. The man was constantly weeding the garden or trimming the lawn, working the acreage just as he surely must have worked his farm for many years. Farming was probably in the retired man's blood—couldn't help but be—and Philip had an inkling he knew what that might feel like, though he'd never had a real chance at plowing or planting sunup to sundown. He would have been happy to have the experience of such a day, though; had even attempted to keep up with his grandpap several summers in a row at the Vermont cottage, there being a good amount of land behind the house.

The Amish B&B family—the Zooks and their daughter and granddaughter—certainly made up a unique nucleus of people. Three generations under one roof. He didn't know why it bothered him that Rachel was blind. Perhaps it was because her daughter was so vivacious and alive, so outgoing. And where was Rachel's husband? Dead? Divorced?

Hardly, according to Abram Beiler, who had said all the area bishops spoke out severely against divorce. "We turn lemons into lemonade, but no divorcing 'round here," Abram had said during the interview.

Philip hadn't realized it until just this moment, but he was indeed interested in knowing more about the entire Zook family. Only two days remained. Could he tend to Gabe Esh and Adele Herr *and* learn more about the Zooks in such a short time?

❖ ❖ ❖

"Mmm, delicious," Rachel said, smelling bushels of tart Macintosh apples as they walked through the screened-in porch at Lavina's. The fresh apple smell covered Lavina's usual garlic-ridden kitchen odor.

"We're here—anybody home?" called Mam, guiding Rachel inside.

"Hullo . . . hullo! Smell them apples, Rachel? I'm tellin' ya they're the best apples this year, ain't?" Lavina said as Rachel, Annie, and Mam made their way to the kitchen.

"It's a gut day for making applesauce, too," Mam chimed in. "Not so warm as it's been."

"How's Annie?" Lavina asked.

"Wonderful-gut!" replied Annie herself. "And I brought some extra raw sugar. In case we run out."

Annie's enthused response was met with laughter, and by that Rachel knew that most of the group had assembled. She didn't hold out any hope of hearing a "hullo" from either Molly or Sadie Mae, even though Mam had informed her of Leah's comment—that the girls were coming.

Rachel was just content to be around Lavina again. It had been a gut long time since she'd worked in the dear woman's kitchen, soakin' up some of the older women's unique perspectives on life, love, and family, among other things.

"Here, Mamma, can you hold this for me?" It was Annie pushing the bag of sugar into Rachel's hand. Applesauce, the way they made it, needed a good dose of sugar to mix with the delicious tartness of the Macintosh. Nothin' like home-made applesauce, especially made at Lavina's house. 'Course, her father's cousin was no ordinary woman. Something didn't seem quite right about her, though it had never bothered Rachel a bit. Spending time with her all day—canning or quilting—was always pleasant. Lavina had a sweet, giving spirit, and that's what came shining through, when all was said and done.

Rachel had overheard talk of a mental condition, when first she'd come to make apple butter in late October, years ago. She was only thirteen when one of her cousins remarked that Lavina was one of "God's special children," as if she were a product of a marriage of first cousins, but that wasn't the case. Rachel didn't understand the label at that time—not where Lavina was concerned—because she'd never had reason to think there was anything wrong with her father's cousin before then. Sure, Lavina had never married, but that didn't mean there was something amiss with her mind.

Rachel set about washing a bushel basketful of apples, helping several others while Mam, Aunt Leah, Molly, and Sadie Mae began pulling out stems and quartering the clean ones, preparing to boil them, skin and all. She felt she understood Lavina a lot better these days. Certain of the

People had called *her* mental, too, and all because of her reluctance to go to the powwow doctors. She knew what they said behind her back. She may be blind, but she wasn't stupid.

They were boiling the apples, a whole batch of them at once, when Lavina let slip the most peculiar thing. She said it loud enough so everyone heard. "Martha Stoltzfus had herself an English visitor yesterday afternoon, and you'll never guess who that stranger was asking 'bout."

"Who?" Leah spoke up.

"Gabriel Esh, of all people," Lavina replied. "Nobody's had the grit to bring up his name in nigh onto forty years."

Rachel perked up her ears. "Who was the stranger?" she said so softly she didn't expect to be heard.

"Some fella named Philip Bradley is what I heard," Lavina replied. "And I got it straight from Martha's mouth—hers and Bertha Denlinger's—ya know, up at the hardware store."

They all knew. Lavina didn't have to say where Bertha was workin' these days. Fact was, the women—both Martha and Bertha—had a negative outlook on life, far as Rachel was concerned. Neither one of them ever seemed to look on the bright side of things. Not anything; not ever.

Most amazing was how Mamma kept mum during all the talk at Lavina's. Rachel was mighty sure if she hadn't witnessed it for herself—if she hadn't been present to know how tight-lipped Mam was being about their New York B&B guest—well, she might not have believed it. Truth was, Mam prob'ly wouldn't be volunteering one thing, wouldn't want the women to know her guest was nosing around, stirring up something that was best left alone.

But, then again, maybe it would turn out that it was a

right gut thing that Philip Bradley had found that postcard and poked around after all.

'Course, all that remained to be seen. . . .

❖ ❖ ❖

The stone wall surrounding the Reading cemetery reminded Philip of a cemetery he'd visited in England many months before. It was the old-world setting he recalled—ancient trees with gnarled roots extended and exposed, leaf-filtered sunlight, and the overall serenity of gravestones. Weathered granite markers commingled with tall, stately headstones—some with angels, some with crosses. The day had been much different, however, with drizzle and fog, not like the sunny Pennsylvania morning he was presently enjoying, with temperatures high in the sixties.

He parked the car and got out, not knowing where to begin his actual search. He could walk down each row of markers, he supposed, but that could take all day. Then he spied the groundskeeper, a tall, thin, older gentleman, edging a circular section of lawn just below the crest of a hill.

Eager to make contact with him, Philip quickened his pace. "Excuse me, sir."

The old man stopped his work and leaned on a medium-sized headstone, mopping his brow. "Hello," he replied.

Philip said, "I wonder if you might be able to help me locate the marker for a Gabriel Esh."

"Gabriel . . . like the angel?"

Nodding, Philip realized he hadn't thought of the name being linked to the heavenly host. "According to an old obituary, he's buried in this cemetery."

The man's face was tired and drawn. "Yes, I know who you're talking about. He's buried seven rows over, in that direction." He pointed to the north. "It's quite peculiar, really, when you think of it."

"What's that?"

"For all the years I've worked here, except the last two, Gabriel's burial plot was covered with flowers, dozens of them . . . every year on his birthday."

"January seventh," Philip said, remembering the birth date on the obit.

"That's right, in the dead of winter. I tell you it was the strangest thing to be out here plowing snow off the walkways, and there'd be all those flowers, piled up on the grave—like the first crocus of spring when it pushes up through the ice and cold." He was nodding his head. "The oddest thing you'd ever want to see, but it wasn't my imagination. Those flowers kept coming every year like clockwork, and then, one year, they stopped."

"Any idea who was sending them?"

"All I know is, it was the same florist bringing them. A person in my business doesn't overlook something like that."

The old gentleman seemed glad to tell the name of the florist, and Philip jotted it down, thanking the man for the information. He hurried back to the car and drove several miles, following the gardener's specific directions.

The flower shop was tiny, crowded with white flower-filled buckets. Philip made his way through the maze, heading for the woman behind the cash register.

Except for one shopper, the place was empty. The customer's transaction took a few minutes and was done. When the florist offered to assist him, Philip found himself studying the woman, ticking off questions in his head. *Could she have been the one taking flowers to Gabe's grave? What could she tell him about the sender?*

"How may I help you, sir?" the middle-aged woman asked.

"I'm here not to purchase flowers but to ask about someone who must have been one of your faithful customers. I'm interested in knowing the name of a particular sender of large amounts of flowers. Every year, for a number of years . . . always on January seventh."

The woman pushed her long brown hair back away from her face. "Well, I'm the new owner here. I've only worked the shop about two and a half years, so I'm probably not the person to help you."

"Are you saying you have no records for someone purchasing flowers every January? For a Gabriel Esh's grave?"

Her face brightened with recognition. "You know, that name sounds very familiar to me. If I remember correctly, the sender was a woman. . . ."

Philip had to know. "Is there any way to check on that customer? Is the former owner of this shop in the area?"

"I'm really terribly sorry. If my memory serves me well, I believe the sender was ill . . . no, possibly deceased. Yes, I believe she passed away around the time the flowers stopped being ordered."

He felt the air go out of his chest and could not speak for the blow. With a wave of his hand, he gestured his thanks and found his way out of the shop, back to his car.

So Adele Herr was dead after all. She must have passed away the year the flowers ceased coming, just as grouchy Miss Martha Stoltzfus had said. But he hadn't paid attention. He'd pushed ahead, determined to find Adele Herr at all costs. And here, to think she'd died two years or so ago.

I should be the one to leave . . . my Amish ways behind. . . .

The poignant message, though safely tucked away, continued to trouble Philip. He would not have the pleasure of meeting Gabe's beloved, would not experience the joy of returning the postcard to its rightful owner.

He drove through the outskirts of Reading and made the turn onto the southbound ramp, heading back to the interstate. It was then, as he settled in for the drive to Lancaster, that he was struck with a sorrowful thought. Was it possible, could it be that Adele had breathed her last without ever laying eyes on the postcard?

Seventeen

❖ ❖ ❖

$\mathcal{I}$t had been coming on toward midafternoon, and the sky was beginning to cloud up like it might rain any minute. Susanna hoped they could get home before a gully-washer descended—them without umbrellas and all.

"Smells like rain's comin'," Annie said from the back-seat of the carriage.

"Jah, and it's a gut thing, too. It's been almost too warm for this time of year, ain't?" Rachel observed.

Susanna breathed in the damp smell a-stirrin' in the air, thinking that now might be the right time to talk to Rachel about her God-given gifts. She'd had a chance to mention it briefly to Benjamin, getting his word on the situation, and he'd given her the go-ahead. "Tell her just to be open, if nothin' else," he'd said. "She oughta at least think on the idea of receivin' the healing gift from Blue Johnny, if that's what he's got in mind."

So she humored her daughter a bit. "I'd hafta agree with you on the weather these past few weeks. A body hates to see it frost too early in the season, but I'm ready for a little nip in the air myself."

They rode along quietly after that, Susanna hoping Annie might nod off and give the women a chance to talk heart-to-heart. A number of years had passed since such a thing had happened between them—back before Rachel had married Jacob Yoder and joined up with the Beachy church. It wasn't that she and her youngest daughter didn't have much to say to each other; 'twasn't that at all. There was far more to it, and she 'sposed it had a lot to do with Rachel having been so close to her husband, Jacob Yoder. 'Course, she wouldn't be one to fault the couple for having had such a bond. But it did seem mighty unusual to have a relationship like that with a man.

As for her and Benjamin, their marriage was right suitable. Ben was a gut provider, no question about that, all the years of farming an' all. But to share her heart and soul with him would seem unnatural somehow; the furthest thing from her mind. How much easier to confide in another woman—an aunt or close female cousin—someone who truly understood how you felt, how you thought.

A light rain began to fall, coming down like a mist and without a smidgen of wind. The moisture made the vegetation along the road look greener. The leaves on the maple trees, too.

Susanna glanced over her shoulder at Annie, who had fallen asleep, sure enough. It was high time to forge ahead, and she did, opened her mouth up and got the words said right out. "Rachel, I know you may be opposed to what I wanna say, but I feel I should say it anyhow."

Rachel didn't move or speak, so Susanna continued. "When you were just a girl, I recognized some real special things in you, Daughter. Gifts from the almighty God, I'd say. But I wasn't the only one who noticed. Our bishop did, too, and so did the faith healers around here, 'specially after you held that water-witching stick and it came alive in your little hands. Remember that?"

Rachel winced. "Mamma, you're gonna talk about Blue

Johnny. I know that's what you're workin' up to."

Susanna wasn't too surprised to hear Rachel speak up so; the young woman had been throwin' out her opinion quite freely here lately. "Blue Johnny's only the half of it," Susanna went on. "There's so much more for you to consider than whether or not you should go to him about your sight. To begin with, I'm a-thinkin' Blue Johnny has his eye on you, Rachel. I think he has you in mind to pass his healing powers to."

Rachel frowned. "Do ya really *think* so?"

"Jah . . . I do."

Her daughter was quiet for a spell. Then, "I never told you this, but Cousin Esther says powwowing is wrong—black as sin. She and Levi believe the angel of the Lord is siftin' through families, showing certain ones 'bout sins of their ancestors. They're even willin' to be the only ones in the family who repent and renounce those sins. And Esther says if they hafta stand alone in this, they will."

"Well, I'll be," Susanna muttered, figuring now was as gut a time to shut her mouth as any. But she sure didn't like hearing that Esther and Levi Glick, way out there in Ohio, were the ones filling her girl's head with this nonsense. What was the matter with them? Maybe somebody from the church here oughta set 'em straight, and if no one was up to the task, she wouldn't think twice about volunteering.

"Esther wants to be pure and spotless before the Lord, wants to clean house in her heart, with God's help." Rachel seemed too talkative all of a sudden. "Clear back through the generations of her and Levi's families, they wanna tidy up spiritually, so to speak."

"Well, that's *their* business, I'd hafta say. Just you remember that the gift transference from one healer to another is a sacred honor. You oughta know that by now. There's nothin' a bit sinful 'bout it, neither."

"But Esther says—"

"Your cousin's wrong," Susanna cut in. *Esther this and Esther that . . .* What on earth would Leah think of all this! Honestly, she hadn't heard any such blather since her preacher-uncle was alive and causin' an uproar amongst the People. "Seems you oughta be takin' a closer look at yourself, Daughter."

"What're you sayin'?"

She sighed. "If you ask me, it's your inclination toward the powwow gift that's makin' you blind."

Rachel gasped. "How can you say such a thing?"

"I've hit the nail on the head, and you know it."

Looking as if she might cry, Rachel confessed, "I'm all mixed up 'bout bein' tried for with Blue Johnny, really I am. Esther believes one thing; you say something else altogether. I just don't know what to think anymore."

Susanna felt her chest tighten, and she picked up the reins. Best they be gettin' on home. She didn't know how much more of this she could stand to hear.

Lord o' mercy, she thought. It was downright uncanny the way Rachel was spoutin' off Esther's heretical quibble— sounded like Gabriel Esh all over again, back from the dead.

❖ ❖ ❖

Benjamin sat all of them down in the upstairs sitting room, Annie included, and read from the Bible. " 'These six things doth the Lord hate; yea, seven are an abomination unto him: a proud look, a lying tongue, and hands that shed

innocent blood, a heart that deviseth wicked imagina-
tions...' " He paused for emphasis, then continued on,
" '... feet that be swift in running to mischief, a false witness
that speaketh lies, and he that soweth discord among breth-
ren.' "

Rachel was perty sure Mam had filled Dat in on the comments Esther had made about powwowing and the evil
thereof, thus the reason for the impromptu Bible-reading
session. And the tone of reproof in Dat's voice.

"Can we hear the story of Samuel, when God calls to
him in the temple?" Annie piped up.

"Jah, gut idea," Susanna said.

Rachel was silent, sitting next to Annie. *It's your inclination toward the powwow gift that's making you blind. . . ."*

Mamma was wrong about what she'd said in the buggy,
coming home from Lavina's! The more Rachel thought
about it, the more Mam's statement upset her. She felt
downright fatigued after spouting off so much in the buggy,
defending her cousin thataway. Jah, she felt nearly as
drained as she had after holding that dowsing fork in her
little hands, twenty-one years ago.

And here Dat had just read a passage in Proverbs—
nothin' whatsoever pertaining to Esther's and Levi's desire
to forsake and repent of the past sins of their family. She
truly felt she had been wrongly reprimanded, treated as a
child. A *Sindhaft*—sinful child.

An astonishing thought crossed her mind: Had Gabriel
Esh felt the selfsame way back long before she was ever born?
He'd been shunned . . . but for what reason? For speaking
out against sin? She had no way of knowing for sure, except
for the hints Philip Bradley had dropped this morning on
his way out the door.

While Dat read the Bible, she pondered these things silently.

❖ ❖ ❖

"The Reading trip turned out to be a waste of time," Philip told Stephen Flory as the two men opened their supper menus. "Except for meeting an elderly gentleman in the graveyard."

"What do you mean?" Stephen blinked with anticipation.

"The groundskeeper had an interesting tidbit about Gabe Esh. Said flowers had been delivered and put on Gabe's grave every year on the man's birthday by the same florist shop."

"January seventh?"

Philip smiled his answer. "Too bad I didn't come to Pennsylvania and find the postcard two years ago."

"Why's that?"

"The flowers stopped coming about then."

Stephen leaned back in the booth, his arms crossed over his chest. "Let me guess—you traced the flowers to the florist and found nothing."

"I found something, but not what I wanted to hear." He inhaled deeply. "Adele Herr passed away a while back, it seems." He explained that both Gabe's sister and the florist had indicated they were aware of Miss Herr's death. "It's a closed door, I'm sorry to say. And I wonder if for some reason Adele never received the postcard in the first place."

"Let's double-check her obituary. Reading, right?"

Philip hadn't thought of doing that. "Sure, let's find out

when and where she died." He took a drink of his water. "By the way, didn't you say you had something, from someone at your work?"

Stephen nodded slowly. "I don't know how it would be possible to track this down, knowing how tight-lipped the Amish are, but my colleague's friend seems to think that Gabe Esh was disowned by his father."

"For what reason?"

"Something to do with his resistance to a powerful bishop, though I don't know who."

"What kind of father would renounce his only son?" Philip asked, closing his menu.

"Your guess is as good as mine," Stephen said, his face solemn.

The waitress came to take their orders. Afterward, Philip was preoccupied with the unknown circumstances surrounding the postcard and its message. More than ever, he was determined to get to the root of the story.

❖ ❖ ❖

Susanna brought the mail inside, eyeing a tape mailer from Ohio. She assumed the package was another one of those spoken "letters" her niece and Rachel had been sending back and forth. She thought of listening to the tape first, before giving it to her daughter, but didn't dwell on that notion, knowing she wouldn't be able to live with herself for doing such a thing.

"Here's something for you." She placed the small package in Rachel's hand.

"From Esther?"

"Must be. The postmark's Ohio."

Rachel's face burst into a rainbow of a smile, and Susanna knew something was up. 'Course, then again, maybe not. Maybe the two women were just eager to correspond. It was just the idea of Esther reading all those Bible passages to Rachel that got her goat. Certain sections of Scripture were sanctioned by their bishop for use in personal reading and meditation. Seemed to her Rachel and Esther—Levi, too—had launched off on their own private exploration of God's Word. Didn't seem right, really. Too much like the Mennonites' way, but she wasn't about to consider that just now. She had enough problems of her own to take on the world, the flesh, and the devil.

❖ ❖ ❖

Rachel decided to wait till later to listen to Esther's tape recording. She couldn't tell for sure, but it seemed Mam might be too interested in what it had to say. She'd had enough of a run-in with her mother and felt a bit hemmed in. So she decided to wait for sleep to fall over the house before ever listening to Esther's tape-letter.

She had an idea that it was time to talk with Annie about some personal things. *Other* things besides the fact that the child was too friendly with strangers; it seemed to her that Annie hadn't made any big mistake by talking to the New York City writer. No, Philip Bradley came across as right trustworthy. 'Course, you could never be too sure of that, 'specially with outsiders.

What she needed to bring herself to do was tell Annie the things Rachel remembered about Jacob and Aaron.

About their life together before the accident, because evidently there was really nothing else she could add to what Dat had already told his little granddaughter. It appeared to be no secret that Dat and Mam had taken it upon themselves to bring up the subject of the accident with Annie.

So tonight, just as soon as the supper dishes were washed and cleared away, she would sit down with her little daughter and share with her the recollections of the wonderful-gut days. Days marked with laughter and sunshine, sounds of woodworking comin' from the barn, and smells of sawdust on the floor. Playful bickering between brother and sister, and the life-giving movement within Rachel's womb.

Jah, the best days of her life . . . gone forever.

❖ ❖ ❖

The drive to the Reading cemetery had been for the express purpose of locating Gabe Esh's tombstone, and Philip had ignored it altogether, he realized as he drove the short distance back to the Orchard Guest House B&B. There he had stood just seven rows of markers away from the Amishman's grave. Yet he'd turned on his heels to follow the interesting but dead-end lead to the florist shop.

Why he hadn't taken time to stop and pay his respects at the cemetery was beyond him. Now as he thought about it, he concluded that he had made an error in judgment, though at the time, it seemed the right thing to do—chasing after the unknown person responsible for yearly outpourings of love.

He wouldn't beat himself up over it, and he dismissed it as he pulled into the B&B driveway, noticing an abundance of cars. *The place is booked solid*, he thought, getting out of the car and wondering what he would do tomorrow to kill some time. Perhaps a bit of sightseeing was in order. No, what he really wanted to do was pitch hay with some Amishmen. Get a feel for more things Amish.

As for tonight, he would take a fresh look at his article before retiring. With the inclusion of Annie's Christmas tablet and colored pencils, and the addition of a strong yet heartwarming wrap-up, he was actually finished with the piece. He would email it to Bob first thing in the morning.

Heading to his room, he greeted Susanna, who forced a smile and nodded. *What a difference*, he thought, remembering the uncommon cordiality at the outset, followed by the more frosty treatment just hours after his arrival.

He wouldn't let it get the best of him. The thing he most wanted to do in the time remaining was to show continued kindness to Rachel—that is, if he should meet up with her again—and to be attentive to the little girl. He felt the child had been sorely cheated by fate. No father—at least no mention of one—a blind mother, and an overbearing grandmother. Annie's grandfather seemed disconnected to the family, though he assumed well his patriarchal position. Philip couldn't imagine the man going fishing with Annie—if Amish children even did such things with their elders. No, Benjamin Zook took more of a passive role with his exuberant grandchild, letting the women in Annie's life have the say-so. Yet the child displayed a sense of security and happiness. It made no sense, but then, life was rather senseless most of the time, he conceded.

❖ ❖ ❖

Rachel stayed put in her bedroom till after Annie was sound asleep. She got down on her hands and knees and rummaged around, trying to locate the electrical outlet near the bed, hoping she wouldn't cause too much noise and alert Mam. She didn't want Susanna to know she was still up, not this late, and she wanted complete privacy in listening to Esther's tape.

As it turned out, there had been no time to talk heart-to-heart with her little one as she'd planned. Mam had requested another round of Bible reading after supper. Dat had obliged, though it was apparent by the monotone that his heart wasn't much in it. Mam's doing, for sure.

Once Annie was bathed and dressed in her nightgown, it was too late to get such a serious talk started. Too late for a little girl to drift off to dreamland, thinking of the daddy she'd lost to death and the bright-eyed older brother no longer alive to tease or play with her.

So their talk would wait till tomorrow, after breakfast prob'ly. That's what Rachel decided and felt better about it. She hoped and prayed the dear Lord would guide her words, help her say the things that truly should be said, according to Dat and Mam anyways.

Sliding the volume down all the way to the lowest setting, she pushed the tape into the recorder and began to listen for the soft voice of her cousin.

Dearest Rachel,

I couldn't wait a minute longer for a letter from you, so I'm starting this tape now. It's Monday night, September thirteenth, and the house is as quiet as it ever gets around here, I 'spose. I trust everything's all right there with you, that you're healthy and Annie's well, too. Guess you're busy during the fall tourist season, and we are, too, but in a different way. I've put up more applesauce than ever; pickles, corn, succotash, and more chowchow, too.

Levi's been visiting with our preacher quite a lot this week. God continues to show us individually—and in the church body here—the importance of identifying generational sins and repenting of them. More and more, different ones in our church district are coming forward to confess patterns of family sins. What a joy to know that our prayers and testimony of faith are making a difference.

How're Susanna and Benjamin? We're praying for your parents more than ever, that the Lord will work in their hearts through His Word and through the nudging of the Holy Spirit, and that old Bishop Seth will wake up to the truths of the Gospel. We must pray that the Lord will plant a hunger in him for God's Word, then he could encourage the People to search out the Scriptures. It's not so far-fetched, really. We've been hearing of a real stirring—jah, a breakout of revival—amongst Plain circles in many areas. So we can pray and know our prayers are more powerful than anything we might do or say.

It's gettin' awful late now. I hear Levi a-snorin' so loud he's gonna shake the bed frame loose. That actually happened once. You should've seen the look on his face when he woke up with the mattress sliding toward the floor! It was a right funny sight to behold.

James, Ada, Mary, and Elijah are growin' like weeds—I can hardly keep them in clothes. I'm not complainin', but it keeps a body goin' in circles, trying to keep up with all the sewin' and whatnot all.

Before I sign off, I want to leave you with a verse from Second Corinthians, chapter two, verse fourteen. Here it is: "Now thanks be unto God, which always causeth us to triumph in Christ, and maketh manifest the savour of his knowledge by us in every place. For we are unto God a sweet savour of Christ, in them that are saved, and in them that perish. . . ."

That part about us being a sweet savour or fragrance to God is so encouraging to me . . . and you, too, ain't? I'll be sendin' you another preachin' tape from our pastor's sermon soon.

Well, I need my sleep for tomorrow's work. Blessings to you, dear cousin. And just as soon as you can, please send me a tape back. Give your darling girl a big hug from Cousin Esther.

Rachel turned off the recorder and hid the tape under her pillow. It was a wonderful-gut feeling to know that Esther, too, would prob'ly be listening to a tape tomorrow—the one Rachel had made for her two nights ago.

As she climbed into bed, she remembered the cutting, cruel thing Mam had said to her—about her special giftings being the reason Rachel was blind. And she wondered what Esther would think if she told her.

To soothe herself, she thought of the beautiful verse her cousin had quoted on the tape recording. *For we are unto God a sweet savour of Christ. . . .*

The words comforted her as she plumped her pillow and lay down. The day had been as trying as any recently, and the Scripture from Esther was just what she needed to think on as she entrusted her sleep, and her dreams, to God.

Eighteen

❖ ❖ ❖

On another day the early-morning landscape might have had a mark of lackluster, but in the predawn hour, Philip found himself seized by the awakening countryside. He walked west to Gibbons Road, then south to Beechdale, toward an iron-gated entrance to Beechdale Farm, relishing the quietude, the peace of his surroundings. What he wouldn't give to bottle up the tranquil setting and carry it back with him to New York.

Standing along the road in the midst of daybreak gold, he considered his life as one might at the conclusion of it. Where had he been heading these twenty-seven years? Would the path he was treading lead him out of his feature writer's cubicle to a senior staff writer's office? Was *that* what he wanted? What of the fading thrill of the chase—the journalistic hunt—the lonely hours and days of writing one assigned article, followed by yet another? How could such a life be Frost's road "less traveled by" that truly "made all the difference"?

The sun inched past the horizon, casting lengthy shadows over the fence palings, spilling them across the road. He longed for a stroll down one of the wagon paths he'd spied earlier, especially one bordered by identical cornfields on either side. Not willing to trespass, he continued walking south on Beechdale Road, toward Highway 340 and the village shops of Bird-in-Hand. No real direction to his journey. No viable reason to be out and roaming this early, except that he had awakened hours before his usual "rise and shine." Not having had adequate exercise in the past days, he'd slipped out of the house before the slightest indication of life was in evidence, meaning Susanna Zook had not made her presence known at the hour of his departure.

Stopping again, he propped his foot on the lower rung of a roadside fence, aware of the heavy dew on grass, foliage, and rust-red marigolds. He contemplated the hustle and flurry awaiting him at the magazine upon his return. Normally after finishing an assignment he would look ahead, ready to embark on the next. But over the past months his passion had waned to the point that he had mentioned to his mother that he might be considering a career change.

"At *your* age?" she'd replied, indicating with a grin that he was much too young to be disillusioned with his work.

"It's a mad chase all the time. Maybe it's just me. . . ."

"And maybe it's the *city* that doesn't agree with you. Lots of folk don't handle commotion well. Manhattan might not be your cup of tea, Phil."

Mom knew him about as well as anyone. She was right on, several counts' worth. He wasn't happiest among the glitz and the hubbub of big city life. "What would it be like to have a truck farm somewhere?" he'd blurted.

His mother's eyes lit up. "Now that would make your grandpap smile."

Shaking his head, he changed the subject to an upcoming European trip. "Pipe dreams."

"You must be having one of those days, right?"

Indeed, he'd confessed to having had a frustrating week in general. Not often he admitted something like that to her.

Dad, maybe. Never Mom. Didn't need to; she always knew.

A lone horse and buggy came up behind him, the spirited mare stepping out smartly as it pulled a gray boxlike carriage on its tall, oversized wheels, *clip-clop*ping toward the intersection of Beechdale and Route 340. It stopped, then crept out, clattering onto the main highway.

He'd never contemplated what it would be like to ride in an Amish buggy or any carriage, for that matter. The pace was problematic, he decided. Except, of course, if he'd never experienced the power and speed of a car. Yet Abram Beiler had said the Amish liked the *inconvenience* of horse and buggy travel because it let them "stop and smell the roses" of life, allowed them to feel the pith and the rhythm of their unsophisticated, sylvan reality.

His cell phone rang just then, interrupting the repose. "Phil Bradley here."

"Sorry I'm calling so early." It was Janice.

"It's not early here," he joked. "I've been up for two hours."

"Everything all right?" Naturally, she would assume something was wrong.

"I'm out on a ramble across a deserted byway and a wooded bower and—"

"Phil, you sound strange. You sure you're okay?"

"I'm okay if you're okay."

"No, seriously, I need to know when you're due in tomorrow."

"I'll have to let you know. My flight information's back at the B&B."

"So . . . you really are out on a walk this early."

"Ramble."

"Whatever."

He didn't think he could do justice, describing the sky just now. "I wish you could see the sun coming up. This place is nearly as captivating as Vermont, I guess."

"You're way out there, aren't you?" she remarked with a laugh. "Okay, I'll wait for your call later. But don't forget, unless, of course, you'd rather take a cab into the city."

"I vote for the welcoming committee. How is Kari doing?"

"Just waking up. I'll tell her you said hi."

"Yes, do that."

"Well, I'd better get busy here. Enjoy your last day in the bush."

"Don't worry. I'll talk to you later, sis."

He clicked off the phone and planted himself in the grassy eaves between the road and a potato field, staring through distant black trees as the sun made its glimmering ascent. Never had he witnessed a more awe-inspiring sight as this. Never had he felt so unsettled, glimpsing the panorama of his life.

❖ ❖ ❖

Susanna made note of Philip Bradley's absence at the table. The man was clearly sleeping in, and she wasn't about to take breakfast up to a lazy man. He'd just have to miss out.

"After bit, Dat and I have to make a quick run over to Smoketown," she informed Rachel. "But we won't be gone for long, I don't expect."

"Annie and I will be all right here. Take your time, Mam."

"I won't leave you with all the dishes, and I'll help strip down the beds before we go."

"That's fine, and I'll wash down all the showers while you're gone," Rachel said, gathering up two plates of eggs and bacon, one for herself and one for Annie. She picked up the heavy tray and started to shuffle toward the parlor. "You know where to find us."

"Wait . . . let me do that for you." Susanna intervened, taking the long wooden tray from Rachel, carrying it into the parlor room, where Annie was already drinking a glass of milk, a white ring above her lip. "There you are, girlie. How wouldja like some bacon and eggs with your glass of milk?"

Annie nodded, pulling her chair up to the sofa table she and Rachel always used for their private meals. "Can I take Copper out for a little walk after breakfast?"

"Don't see why not," Susanna replied, glancing at Rachel. "S'okay with you, Daughter?"

"If you stay away from the creek, Annie. You know what Dawdi Ben says about that. There's a couple hornets' nests down there, remember?"

"Jah, I remember. I spied 'em one day when Joshua came to visit."

Susanna said, "Well, just so you obey your mamma. Copper's leash is hanging out on the back hook, you know."

"Denki, Mammi! I'll take gut care of your doggie, I will."

She set the eggs and bacon and the smaller plates piled high with toast on the table, then removed the tray and headed for the kitchen. "Annie's gonna have herself a nice morning," she told Ben as he came through the kitchen on his way outside.

"A gut day to be outside," Ben called over his shoulder to her.

"Jah, a right gut day to be alive," she whispered, hurrying around to finish up the breakfast for the guests. She hadn't given Esther Glick's tape a second thought. Not till just now, and she didn't rightly know why. Maybe it was Rachel's somewhat subdued manner in the parlor. Maybe it was nothing, really.

❖ ❖ ❖

"Annie, honey," Rachel began hesitantly, when they were alone, "I wanna tell you what I remember about your father and brother."

The parlor was quiet, though she could hear Annie's soft breathing. "Dawdi Ben and Mammi Susanna already said how they died. Car hit 'em . . .'cause the horse got spooked."

"I didn't wanna talk about the accident so much as I thought we could share our favorite memories about Dat and Aaron." She felt a lump in her throat and was afraid she might lose control.

Annie was silent.

"You all right, honey?"

There were sniffles just then. "I don't remember anything," said Annie. "I tried plenty of times to think what my brother and Dat looked like, but it's all fuzzy in my head."

Like my eyes, thought Rachel.

"Well, then, let me tell you about the things I remember.

Our wonderful, happy days together . . . all of us." She told of long walks on summer afternoons, of taking the pony cart and filling it with hay on a sweet September night, and watching the lightning bugs dance up and down all over the meadow. "Dat loved nature, and Aaron, too. We were gonna buy us a big farm in Ohio, near where Esther and Levi live."

"We were? I didn't ever know that."

"Your father wanted to have dairy cows just like my brothers Noah and Joseph do."

"You mean over at Dawdi Ben's old place?"

"That's right. But we're here now—you and me—with your grandparents, and God's takin' care of us."

"And we're helpin' lots of tourists have a place to sleep at night, ain't so, Mamma?"

"Jah, we are that." She hoped this little talk with Annie might satisfy her father's request. "Is there anything you want to ask me?"

"Why'd you go blind, Mamma?" came the sincere words. "Dawdi Ben says you weren't even in the buggy when the car hit us, so how'd you get blind?"

"Oh, honey, I wish I could tell you."

"But you don't remember—that's what Dawdi says. You can't remember nothin' much about that day."

"I know *one* thing," she was able to say. "I'm ever so thankful that you weren't hurt too awful bad, that you were safe. God protected you . . . for me."

Annie's little arms slipped around her neck. "Oh, Mamma."

Rachel felt Annie's warm tears on her face. "I'm so sorry, little one . . . so very sorry. I should've never brought this up."

Annie whimpered against her neck, not saying anything. All the while, Rachel held her precious girl in her arms, rocking her and humming a hymn.

❖ ❖ ❖

After Annie had calmed down some, Rachel stood at the kitchen counter with Esther's tape, preparing to roll out dough for piecrusts, which Mam had prepared before leaving the house. Annie, bound and determined to take Copper for a short walk, had left not but five minutes before. Rachel figured she oughta keep her hands busy awhile; keep her mind busy, too, by listening again to her cousin's encouraging tape recording while she rolled out the dough.

The talk with Annie had upset them both, though she hadn't cried the way her darling girl had. What *was* she thinking, rehashing those things with one so young? She wouldn't harbor bitterness toward Dat for prompting such a conversation, no. She'd forgive him for bringing it up in the first place, for pushing her beyond her better judgment.

Just then, she heard pounding noises in the cellar. Sounded like something amiss with the washing machine, and she hurried down to check.

❖ ❖ ❖

He had done a lot of walking in his day, but never so far on an empty stomach. Upon his return to the guesthouse, Philip was glad to find a few sticky buns left on the corner table in the common area. Susanna hadn't forgotten him, even though she seemed to be distancing herself from him.

He stood in the front window, looking out while he devoured the fat, juicy pastry, licking his fingers clean when he was finished.

Only his rental car remained in the designated parking area, and he assumed he must be the only guest still around. The house seemed devoid of sound, too quiet, as he made his way upstairs to his room. Where was everyone?

He was surprised to see his room already clean, the bed made and towels freshened. "No time wasted around here," he muttered, heading for the closet. The postcard lay hidden in Philip's briefcase, and though he had uncovered only a few links to Gabe and Adele, he found it impossible to dismiss the young Amishman's urgent message. In his hands he held the final remnant to a long-ago love story, compelling and heartrending. One that he might never fully know. The realization struck him anew.

Sitting at the desk, he relocated the narrow drawer—the one that had been stuck—where he'd first discovered the postcard. Mentally, he ticked off a summary of the facts: Emma, at the antique shop, had acquired the desk two years ago, followed by the new owner, Susanna Zook. Evidently, the postcard had been placed inside the desk at some point prior to Emma's discovering the piece at the secondhand store in Reading—before Susanna ever laid eyes on it. Which meant the postcard must have managed to arrive safely in Reading at its intended destination. *Then why had Adele discarded such a message?* The question burned into his brain.

Philip wished he could offer the postcard as a remembrance to someone close to Adele Herr. Someone who might have loved her as a sister or dear friend. Surely, there was someone alive who had been devoted to the woman.

He went to brush his teeth; he had to get the sugary residue from the sticky bun out of his mouth. After doing so, he connected his cell phone and emailed the Amish family article to his editor in New York. He shut down his laptop, thinking that somehow or other he'd like to give Rachel a report of his trip to Reading, if that was even possible without Susanna overhearing. He went to the wall of built-in bookcases, scanning the choices and deciding on an old classic. He was just getting comfortable when he heard the sound of high-pitched barking. The commotion persisted until he was drawn to the window to see what was causing a dog to carry on so.

Below him on the patio, Rachel was floundering with her cane, trying to find her way while bumping into one flower pot after another. "Annie!" she called again and again.

He rushed downstairs, and when he burst out the back door and caught up with Rachel, he saw that she was weeping. "Annie!" she called pitifully. "Annie, where are you?"

But there was no answer, only the frenzied barking in the distance.

"Rachel, it's me, Philip Bradley," he said calmly, so as not to startle her. "What's happening?"

She was pushing her feet through the lawn, her cane swinging back and forth. "Annie went walking the dog . . . she hasn't come home for the longest time. Now Copper's barking out by the creek, and I'm terribly frightened."

"I'll look for Annie. Will you wait here?" he said, concerned that Rachel might stumble and fall.

"Please, bring her home to me." Her face was streaked with tears.

"I'll find her." He turned and ran toward the dog's yelping, through the apple trees, past the gravel walkway, over the footbridge, and to the opposite side of the creek. "Annie!" he called. Behind him he could still hear Rachel's distressed cries for her daughter.

The little girl sat in a heap of crumpled leaves on the bank of Mill Creek, her long rose-colored dress soiled, her white head covering in her hand. The dog was crouched near her, howling till his bark was nearly ragged.

"Annie, are you all right?" Philip hurried over to her, noticing a reddish swelling on her face.

"Oh, Mr. Philip, I got stinged so awful bad."

He saw that she had been crying and was rubbing her cheek where the swelling had extended past the wound itself. Searching for a stinger and finding none, he suspected that Annie had been stung by a wasp.

"I didn't . . . disobey Mamma, Mr. Philip . . . honest, I didn't. Copper got away from me, and I had to . . . run and catch him." She was wheezing now, and he recognized the dangerous asthmatic symptoms. His niece, Kari, often had such flare-ups, but this was different. Annie must be suffering from an allergic reaction.

"Ach, my head hurts, too," the little girl cried.

"Let's get you home. Your mamma's worried about you." He was concerned about her labored breathing and gathered the child into his arms. Dashing over the footbridge and through the orchard, he kept saying, "I'll take care of you, Annie. Don't cry, honey."

The braids that wound around her head began to fall loose as he ran with her toward the house. The dog nipped at his heels behind him, barking incessantly.

When he was within yards of the house, he caught sight

of the girl's mother. "Quick, Rachel, hold on to my arm," he called, hurrying over to her. "Annie's been stung. Let's get you both inside."

When Rachel and Annie were safely in the kitchen, Rachel leaned down to listen to her daughter's breathing.

"Does Annie have asthma?" Philip asked, still holding the child with Rachel hovering near.

"No . . . not asthma," Rachel whispered.

"Is she allergic to wasps or bees, that you know of?"

"This has never happened before." Rachel stroked Annie's face, letting go of Philip's arm.

"She needs a doctor right away, unless you have an inhaler, something to open an airway." The child was starting to go limp in his arms. "Where's the nearest hospital?"

"I'll call 9-1-1," Rachel said, her hand shaking as she reached for the phone.

"There's no time for that. You'll have to trust me. I can get Annie to a hospital faster than waiting for an ambulance."

Rachel grimaced. "The Community Hospital is the closest one."

Philip lost no time in getting Annie and her mother into his rental car. Nor could he spare a moment to consider Rachel's possible aversion to riding in a modern-day conveyance rather than the familiar horse and buggy.

On the way, Rachel whispered to the child in her first language, kissing her forehead every so often. She sat in the backseat, cradling Annie in her arms.

Philip pushed the speed limit where there was less traffic, hoping a policeman might spot him and escort them to the emergency room. He sensed a dire urgency as he stole glances at Rachel and her child in the rearview mirror.

Annie's continual struggle to breathe worried him so much he dialed 9-1-1 on his cell phone and alerted the hospital that they were on their way.

The closer they came to the downtown area, the more congested the traffic became, slowing their pace. For the first time in many years, he found himself praying under his breath.

Nineteen

❖ ❖ ❖

*W*ith great apprehension, Philip made himself pick up a sports magazine and thumb through it, impatient for some word—anything—on Annie's condition. He glanced up now and then to watch people coming and going. People watching. It was one of his favorite pastimes, though under the circumstances, he would much rather have been in an airport or any other public place. Hospitals made him nervous.

How was Annie doing now? The little child had looked absolutely miserable there by the creek bank when first he'd found her. And her breathing was terribly wispy, threadlike, continuing to be so as he carried her into the emergency room entrance not twenty minutes ago.

And what of Susanna Zook and her husband? Had both of them left the house? It seemed a bit strange that they would leave their blind daughter home alone with the rambunctious child, but then he didn't know their routine well enough to cast blame. The truth was, a little girl's life was hanging in the balance even as he sat here in the ER waiting room. He wished he could do something to guarantee that young Annie would survive the ordeal, come out of it unscathed. But it was difficult to erase the visions of her gasping for air, her tiny lungs giving out no matter how fast he had been willing to speed down the streets of Lancaster.

It was while he was recalling the morning's chaos that he realized he didn't know Rachel's last name. Couldn't be the same as her parents, or could it? She must surely have been married at one time or other. He took out his pen and a small tablet—the one he carried with him everywhere—and began jotting down all the things he *did* know about Rachel, though for no special reason. Instead of doodling like some folk, he often wrote lists of words, characteristics of people, or one-word descriptions of places. Though he had never actually put pen to paper and attempted to write a novel, he'd toyed with the idea often enough. And he had dozens of such character and setting lists in a file at home just waiting for the moment when he might actually get serious about fiction writing. If ever.

❖ ❖ ❖

Rachel trembled inwardly as she held Annie's limp hand in the emergency room. A number of nurses and the ER doctor surrounded them, administering the initial treatment—a shot of epinephrine, a muscle relaxant to aid in opening airways, and a bronchodilator, a fancy name for an inhaler, Rachel was told.

She imagined the doctor listening with a stethoscope to Annie's lungs, to make sure the constricted airways were beginning to open, though she continued to hear her daughter's raspy breathing.

"Is Annie gonna be all right?" she asked, her own chest feeling somewhat tight.

"The doctor wants to observe Annie for several hours, just to make sure she's clear before we release her," one nurse said. "You got her here just in time."

"Has Annie ever had a reaction like this from a sting?" the doctor inquired.

"Never before."

"If she is ever stung again, the second reaction is often more severe than the first. I'd recommend an epi-kit to keep with Annie wherever she goes."

"What's that . . . an epi-kit?"

"It's a wallet-sized case with a spring-loaded syringe similar to the shot we just gave your daughter. If Annie should ever experience similar symptoms, she or you can easily poke it into her thigh, or most any place on her body—even through her clothes. It could save her life," said the doctor with an ominous note of warning in his voice. "You can get one from your family doctor."

"I'd be interested in having something like that handy," Rachel said, wishing they *had* a family physician who was a real medical doctor.

Later, when she sensed she was alone with Annie, she leaned down and put her ear against the small chest. The crackling in Annie's lungs was beginning to subside.

"Can I sit up now, Mamma? I feel ever so much better."

"Why don't we wait till the doctor comes back." She cupped Annie's cheeks in her hands. "I'm so glad the Lord was with us."

"I feel awful jittery, Mamma."

"Jah, you're much better, but try to sit still so you won't fall off the examining table."

When the nurse came back, Rachel asked about Annie's sudden surge of energy. "She seems terribly restless."

"It's quite normal for her to feel a bit hyper, just until some of the adrenaline wears off."

Over a period of two and a half hours, there was repeated checking on the part of various nurses. Later, the doctor returned to discuss the benefits of allergen solutions or vaccines "to prevent a similar situation from occurring in the future. Hyposensitization is a long-term treatment by which an allergen is injected into the patient at regular intervals, at ever larger doses," he explained. "The body builds up a tolerance over time—three to five years in the case of wasp and bee stings. You may want to consider the desensitization route where Annie's concerned, especially if she plays outside a lot, or more specifically, in the vicinity of a creek, where bees and wasps tend to gather."

"I'll talk it over with my parents," Rachel replied.

"Well, I think Annie's ready to go home. She may seem tired after the shot wears off. Have her take it easy today," he suggested, then paused a moment. "Excuse me, I don't mean to be forward, but you look very familiar to me. Have you ever been treated at this hospital?"

"Well, yes . . . two years ago I had a miscarriage."

"I thought I remembered you and your family . . . yes, I remember quite clearly now." He was silent again. Then, "How is it that you are still blind, Mrs. Yoder?"

"On my best days I see shadows, but other than that, I don't see much of anything."

"But your vision . . . how can this be?"

She told him that she'd consulted a specialist. "He said my brain was recording images, yet I don't see them."

"Have you had any treatment?"

"What do you mean?" She'd heard there were professionals who offered hypnosis and other forms of psychotherapy. Such things didn't interest her—sounded like hocus-pocus to her, and there was far too much of that going on already.

"Would you like a referral for a psychiatrist friend of mine? I think he could help you."

Suddenly, she felt coerced—put on the spot—though she supposed she ought to be open to a truly medical remedy since she wasn't too sure about the alternative doctoring in the community. "I . . . uh, hadn't thought about it really."

"Well, here's my card if you should decide to try it."

She felt the business card against her hand and accepted it with her feeble thanks.

❖ ❖ ❖

When Susanna and Benjamin returned home, Susanna spied the flour and the rolling pin on the kitchen table, wondering where Rachel could be. She checked the upstairs rooms, then the parlor again. Searching the cellar, as well, she called for Rachel and Annie, who was apt to come flying through the house most any time now. "Rachel . . . Annie . . . are you here? Where are you?"

When there was no reply, she rushed back to the kitchen, only to see Benjamin outside with the dog. "The dog's here, at least."

"Any sign of Rachel or Annie?"

"I checked the footpath . . . nothing."

Unwilling to entertain panic-ridden thoughts, she spun in circles as she stood on the flagstone patio. "Well, it looks like Rachel or *somebody* was rolling out a couple o' pies, so where on earth could they be?"

"Gone for a walk maybe?" came Ben's reply. "I wouldn't be too worried."

"With dough spread out all over the table? I don't believe Rachel would do such a thing—leave the kitchen in such a mess."

"Well, you know how Annie is. She's been coaxin' her mamma out in the sunshine these past few days."

"But Rachel would've made her wait a bit—till the pies were filled and in the oven at least." Susanna felt mighty uneasy and ran back inside. That's when she happened to notice that Philip Bradley's car was no longer parked out front. "Himmel, he didn't kidnap 'em, did he?" she muttered, knowing she best not tell Ben what she was thinking just now.

When the phone rang, Susanna was out of breath. "Zooks' Orchard Guest House. Susanna Zook speaking."

"Mamma! I'm ever so happy you're home."

"Rachel, where are you?"

"At the hospital. Annie had a horrid wasp sting, and Philip Bradley drove us to town."

"Philip Brad—"

"It's all right, Mam. Annie's breathing is much, much better now. The color's come back in her cheeks, too. . . . But we nearly lost her."

Susanna put her hand to her forehead. "My, oh my, you gave us a fright, leavin' the house thataway. We hardly knew what to think, Dat and I."

"Annie's gonna be all right—that's what matters," Rachel said. "We have so much to thank the Lord for."

Gathering her wits, Susanna offered to have Benjamin call a Mennonite van driver. "We'll come get you."

"No . . . no, that's all right, really. Mr. Bradley's here with us. He'll bring us home when it's time."

Mr. Bradley this, and Philip Bradley that. . . . Thank goodness the man was checking out tomorrow!

❖ ❖ ❖

Once Annie was stabilized and given the okay to leave, Philip guided Rachel to the accounting window. There, he learned of Rachel's last name for the first time. Yoder. So—she was Rachel Yoder. He found himself wanting very much to remember.

She requested that the bill for treatment be mailed to Benjamin Zook. "Annie and I live with my father," she said, explaining that she had rushed out the door without money, not even a purse. "We don't carry medical insurance. It's *das alt Gebrauch*—the Old Way of doing things."

No insurance? Philip was stunned. How risky, especially raising an adventuresome child like Annie. Upon further investigation, he discovered that Amish folk didn't buy insurance of most *any* kind. They took care of each other through individual donations and the Amish Aid Society, a fund set up primarily for the purpose of aiding their farmers in the case of losses due to lightning, storms, or fires.

In the frenzy of leaving the house to get Annie to the ER, Rachel had evidently forgotten to bring along her cane as well. Now both Annie and Philip walked on either side of her, guiding her safely out to the car. What an odd-looking trio they must appear to be to anyone observing—Philip wearing modern attire, Rachel in her mourning dress—black apron and white prayer veiling—and young Annie still wearing the smudged rose-colored dress.

"I think you best be thankin' Mr. Bradley for savin' your life," Rachel said as they walked.

"*Philip*," he reminded her. "Call me Philip."

"Ach, I forgot already."

He laughed softly, thinking about her obvious hesitation with his first name. "Does a guy named 'Mr. Bradley' sound like someone who goes around saving little girls from wasp stings?"

Annie peeked around her mother's long dress at him, grinning. "You're funny, Mr. Philip. I like you. I wish you would stay 'round longer."

"Maybe I'll have to come back and visit again, how's that?"

She seemed satisfied with the idea, bobbing her little head up and down. Annie had a peachy glow about her now, probably from the adrenaline in the shot. Her hair had been neatly rebraided and wound around her head while in the emergency room. Rachel's doing, he assumed.

After they were settled in the car and heading back toward Bird-in-Hand, he heard Rachel tell Annie, "Never since the accident have I been so frightened as today."

"You mean since Dat and Aaron died?" Annie replied, next to Rachel in the backseat.

"Jah, since then."

Philip was stunned and spoke up, "Someone in your family was killed?"

"A car hit our market wagon, and my father and brother died," Annie said. "I was only four, so I don't much remember. But I broke my arm."

Unbelievable! To think that Rachel's husband and child had died so horribly. No wonder the young woman continued to wear her drab mourning clothes. How had Rachel and Annie been spared such an accident? He'd seen an Amish buggy up close enough to touch on his early-morning walk. The thought of a car ramming into a fragile rig like that, why, there was no way a person could survive an impact involving three tons—

"If anything had happened to you today," Rachel was saying to her little girl, "I could never have forgiven myself. Never."

"But it wasn't your fault I got stung by that mean old hornet," Annie insisted. "And Dawdi Ben says it ain't your fault about the accident at the Crossroad, neither."

Now it was Rachel who was silent, and Philip drove for several minutes without glancing once in his rearview mirror.

The sun bore down on the hood of the car as Philip drove Rachel and Annie Yoder back to Bird-in-Hand, to their home at Orchard Guest House. He thought of another Orchard House, though not an inn open to overnight guests. It was the Massachusetts home of Louisa May Alcott, a favorite author of his niece. He had taken Kari, along with her parents, on a tour of the old place on the outskirts of Concord. Set back in the woods, off a narrow, tree-lined road, stood the big brown house where the classic novel *Little Women* had been penned in 1868.

The call from Stephen Flory to his cell phone came quite unexpectedly as Philip was approaching Smoketown. "I think you're going to be very interested in something, Philip."

"What's up?"

"Believe it or not, a woman in Reading—residing in a

nursing home—is willing to tell you what she knows of Gabe Esh and Adele Herr."

"You're kidding."

"The ailing woman's name is Lily, in case you wish to pursue the lead."

"Do I ever!" He thought Rachel might be fascinated to hear this. "Sounds too good to be true."

"The connection came from a very reliable source right there in the Bird-in-Hand community—a friend-of-a-friend sort of thing—so you can believe it."

"Thanks, Stephen. I'll call you later, okay?"

"By the way, I'm still checking on that obit for you," Stephen added. "If Adele Herr died anywhere in Pennsylvania, I should be able to track down the death notice."

"Maybe this Lily in Reading can fill me in. Thanks."

"Give me a call when you can. I'll have more details for you."

Philip wondered how Susanna Zook would react when he asked to rebook his room. Again. As for juggling his flight schedule—that is *if* the Reading visit forced him to extend his stay—he might decide to take the Amtrak back to New York. At any rate, he'd have to give Bob Snell another call. Janice too.

"I may have some interesting news for you about your mother's uncle by this evening," he told Rachel, glancing over his shoulder.

"What do you mean?" she asked a bit hesitantly.

"A friend of mine put his feelers out and has a lead on someone who seems to know the woman Gabe wanted to marry. Looks like I'll be heading back to Reading this afternoon, hopefully."

Rachel was quiet. He wondered if she might have inquired more were it not for Annie seated next to her, looking wide-eyed. And now quite bushy-tailed.

"Sometime I'd like to tell you what I discovered in Reading . . . at a cemetery there," he said discreetly, even though Annie was hardly paying attention to the conversation.

Back at the Amish inn, Philip phoned his editor and left a message on his office phone. Next, he called Janice, who offered to pray for him while he was having some much needed "R 'n R." Downstairs, he waited for three other guests to complete the check-out process, expedited efficiently by Susanna Zook.

"I don't suppose it would be possible to lengthen my stay," he said as he paid his bill in full.

Susanna shook her head stiffly. "We're sold out up through the next full month." She flipped through a black leather notebook. "Sorry."

She offered not a word about his having befriended her daughter and granddaughter. No show of gratitude, though Philip wasn't looking for it. Still, he thought she seemed rather pleased that her B&B was fully booked—that there was not even a square inch left for one Philip Bradley.

He returned to his upstairs quarters to pack his bag. Finished with that small chore, he closed his laptop and carried his personal belongings to the front door, not bothering to call a good-bye to either Rachel or Annie, though he would have liked to, providing Susanna hadn't been hovering there, waiting for him to exit. She was so eager to see him out, in fact, she opened the door as if shooing out a nasty fly.

Outside, Benjamin was stooped over in the hot sun, weeding a long bed of low-growing cushion mums of red, yellow, and bronze. He looked up from his crouched position and nodded. "Didja enjoy your stay with us, Mr. Bradley?" the man asked, scratching his beard.

"Very much, sir. Have a nice day."

"And the same to you" came the tentative reply.

Philip proceeded quickly to his car, eager to phone Stephen Flory for more details regarding Lily, the friend of Adele Herr. Before pulling out of the driveway, he chatted by cell phone with Stephen about the location of Fairview Nursing Home and whom to contact once he arrived there. Also the phone number. "Any suggestions on a place to stay around here? Or maybe even Reading, if need be. I've been booted out."

"No kidding." Stephen seemed amused.

"It seems Benjamin and Susanna Zook were more than eager to have me vacate the premises."

"And why is that?"

He chuckled. "It's a mystery, unless they were put out with me for saving their granddaughter's life."

"Excuse me?"

"Never mind. Not important."

Stephen had a suggestion. "Why don't you come stay with us? We have a spare room in our basement. Think it over and let me know."

"Thanks, I appreciate the offer," said Philip. "I'll see what I can do about getting in to see Lily this afternoon."

"Better call ahead . . . find out the visiting hours."

"I'll do that and get back with you about the invitation. I just might take you up on it."

"Very good."

They hung up, and Philip immediately dialed the phone number for the Fairview Nursing Home in Reading. He had a good feeling about this visit.

Part Three

Love is intensity, that second in which the doors of time and space open just a crack. . . .

Octavio Paz

And it shall come to pass, that before they call, I will answer; and while they are yet speaking, I will hear.

Isaiah 65:24, KJV

Twenty

❖ ❖ ❖

The middle-aged receptionist greeted him warmly, almost too enthusiastically, as if she encountered few opportunities to welcome visitors.

"I've come to see Lily," he told the woman with red, shoulder-length hair. "My name's Philip Bradley."

"Ah yes." She pushed up her glasses. "And how is it you're related to our Lily?"

"No relation. I'm a friend of a friend, you could say." He thought about it, wanting to be absolutely truthful. "Actually, I have in my possession an old postcard that belonged to someone I understand Lily—your patient—knew well." He reached into his sports coat pocket, displaying the pictureless card and the English translation stuck to the front with a Post-it note.

The redheaded woman accepted it, glancing at the postcard briefly. "I'll give this to her and see if she's still up to having a visitor." She stood up then, and he saw that she was a short woman. Possibly only five feet tall or less. Shorter than his niece. "Can you wait here for just a moment?"

"I'd be glad to." He chose a comfortable chair in the small, fern-filled sitting area and found himself browsing through several magazines and waiting once again.

The receptionist returned sooner than he expected. "I'm

237

afraid Lily's not feeling well after all. She's simply not her best today, though she had agreed to see you. Perhaps another time."

His heart sank. "Tell her I hope she's better very soon."

The petite woman walked to the door with him. "Again, it's a shame you made the trip for nothing."

"No . . . no, I understand." Before leaving, he wrote his cell phone number on one of his business cards. "You can reach me at this number anytime." So determined was he to meet with Adele's friend, he had already made up his mind to be available for her. No matter what time of day— or night—Lily might be able to see him.

❖ ❖ ❖

Rachel and Mam made chowchow together after slipping three apple pies into the oven. "Annie's her happy self again," Rachel commented. "I can't begin to say how awful worried I was."

Susanna didn't reply but continued chopping cauliflower and celery to add to a large bowl of cut green and yellow beans, sliced cucumbers, lima beans, diced carrots, and corn. The ingredients would be cooked till tender, then salted and drained. Next came chopping and more salt for the green tomatoes and the red and yellow peppers. A syrup made from vinegar, sugar, celery seed, mustard seed, and other spices was brought to a rolling boil and mixed with the many vegetables. Rachel especially liked to add onion to their chowchow.

"I guess Annie will be stayin' far away from them hornets' nests from now on," Mam blurted. "A hard lesson to learn, to be sure."

"Jah, but she says she wasn't disobedient. Copper just got away."

"Still, she oughta be punished for it."

Rachel didn't have the heart to consider such a thing, not after her little one's suffering already today. "In case she ever gets stung again, I wanna get her an epi-kit."

"A what?"

Rachel explained what the doctor had said at the hospital. "It could be the difference between life and death."

"That's real silly, 'specially when Blue Johnny can do the same thing, prob'ly. And you could, too, if you stopped bein' so stubborn about receiving the blessing."

Rachel chose to ignore the comment. "If you'd heard Annie wheezin' and all—why, it was downright frightening." She paused, thinking she shouldn't say much more about this. "One of the nurses said we got Annie to the hospital just in time. Honestly, I don't know what we would've done if Philip hadn't helped us."

Again, Susanna clammed up.

Rachel hadn't found conversation with Mam to be very agreeable; she was a woman who fought against most everything a person had to say, it seemed. So when Mam was silent, there was usually an important reason for it. But just now, Rachel had no idea at all what was causing her mother to be so upset at Philip Bradley. None whatsoever.

"Philip Bradley's making another trip to Reading," she ventured, changing the subject, hoping Mam might not fly off the handle.

"What the world for?"

"Something about a cemetery up there . . . and a woman

in a nursing home who knew Adele Herr."

Mam nearly choked, carrying on so bad Rachel ran some water into the sink and filled up a glass real quick.

"Are you all right?"

"I'll be right fine when Mr. Bradley's long gone, that's what!"

Rachel was shocked. What had caused this hostility toward the kind and gentle young man?

❖ ❖ ❖

Philip attended church on Sunday with Stephen and his wife, Deborah. The interior of the meetinghouse was marked by stark simplicity: a small, raised platform with center pulpit, windows of clear glass, and modest light fixtures overhead. There were long wooden pews occupied by Mennonite worshipers—women and small children on the left side; men and older boys on the right. Most every woman wore a head covering of some kind or other. Some of the men wore plain black coats with no lapels, and collars similar to a liturgical collar.

So Stephen Flory was a Bible-believing, conservative Mennonite. Philip should have suspected as much, given the warm hospitality and congenial spirit exhibited by both Stephen and his wife. He took the knowledge of it in his stride. After all, the man had generously opened his home to this virtual stranger. "Stay as long as you like," he'd said upon Philip's arrival back from Reading. "We're always glad to have guests around here."

Deborah, a pleasantly plump brunette, had agreed, nodding her head and smiling her welcome. "We don't always get folk in from New York City."

He returned her smile, thinking he must be quite a spectacle here. It was as if Lancaster County residents didn't often get to see someone from the Big Apple. Glad to have the company, especially in view of the easy camaraderie between himself and Stephen, he was more than happy to go along with their church plans.

It was the pastor's sermon that caught him off guard. A message about the role of the Christian in spiritual warfare. When Philip inquired of the Scripture references later with Stephen, he was told that the pastor was well versed in intercession. "He's new here, but he's on fire. Wants to see us move forward in what we believe to be the end times before Jesus returns for His church."

Philip hadn't heard anything so straightforward, not even during his churchgoing days as a boy. But he was polite and listened. It was the least he could do for his host and hostess.

After church, he was treated to a superb dinner in the Flory home: roast beef, mashed potatoes and gravy, green beans, corn on the cob, coleslaw, Jell-O salad, and angel food cake. Table conversation centered around small talk mostly, but an occasional comment was made about the young, new pastor.

Just as he leaned back, realizing that he had enjoyed Deborah Flory's cooking entirely too much, Philip's cell phone jingled. He excused himself and took the call in the living room. "Hello?"

"Philip Bradley, please."

"This is he."

"I'm the receptionist at the Fairview Nursing Home in

Reading. Lily is asking for you. Would it be convenient for you to come see her today?"

"Why yes, I can leave here within the hour."

"She says, 'The sooner the better.' "

"Very good. Tell her it will be 'sooner.' " He didn't think to ask if the woman would mind if he made a tape recording of his visit. He was·thinking of Rachel just then, knowing that the young blind woman might enjoy hearing Lily's answers to his many questions. He would wait until he got there to ask permission.

Meanwhile, he thanked Deborah for the delicious dinner. "I'll treat the two of you to a meal before I leave."

"It's a deal." Stephen nodded, beaming. "Have a safe drive and a pleasant afternoon."

"Hopefully, Lily won't turn me away this time." He meant it as a joke, but he was more than ready for the solution to the postcard's mystery, hoping Lily might clear up a number of things for him. For Rachel, too.

❖ ❖ ❖

Rachel sat close to Annie on the preaching bench at Lavina's. It was the older woman's turn to have service at her house. The second sermon seemed ever so long—longer than usual—but maybe, Rachel thought, it was because she had other things on her mind. Things like wanting to sing praises to God for giving her Annie back to her, for sparing her little one's life. She wished it might've been possible for her to attend her Beachy church this morning, but Dat said they were runnin' late—his pat excuse, it seemed—and she went along with it. Still, she daydreamed about the more evangelical service going on up the road apiece.

Letting her mind wander, she thought about Mam's un-friendly comments toward Philip Bradley. She didn't know why it bothered her so that her mother didn't think kindly on the man who'd saved Annie's life. From everything she knew of him, Philip was good-hearted and trustworthy. It seemed there was a strong undertow of ill will toward their former guest. Maybe it was best he left when he did, but she wondered how she was ever to hear what he'd discovered in the cemetery in Reading. And what of the possibility of Philip talking to a woman who knew Gabe's English sweet-heart? She wished she might be told something, if not from Mam and Dat, then Philip Bradley.

She dismissed those thoughts in time for the benedic-tion, followed by Lavina's brothers and other men rearrang-ing the benches in the front room, making ready for the common meal.

As much as she loved the People here, she missed the fellowship of those friends and relatives at her own Beachy church. And she missed Esther on this day particularly, anx-ious to answer her cousin's recent tape with one of her own.

It was Lavina's strange remark to her that got Rachel thinking more about Philip Bradley and the "lead" on Adele Herr he supposedly had uncovered in Reading. "Someone's soon gonna hear the truth 'bout Gabe Esh," Lavina whis-pered in passing as she carried a stack of plastic plates across the kitchen.

There wasn't any question in Rachel's mind that Lavina was the one whispering because she recognized the familiar smell of garlic on her breath. What was going on that the older woman seemed to know—about Philip Bradley's plan to go to Reading? Or did she?

Rachel was downright befuddled; she couldn't quite put two and two together.

❖ ❖ ❖

By the time Philip made the turn into the long, wide driveway leading to the Fairview Nursing Home, the digital clock on the dash glowed three-fifty. He hoped the ailing woman might be well enough to see him this time. Parking the car, he reached for his briefcase, where he kept his portable tape recorder. If all went well, he'd soon have Lily on tape, answering his questions about Gabe Esh's life and the story embracing the postcard. Such a format was ideal for a blind woman, though he knew his visit here was more to satisfy his own curiosity than to present a tape to Benjamin and Susanna Zook's daughter.

"Oh, good, you're here," said the same receptionist, looking up, her green eyes smiling. "Lily's waiting for you."

"Thank you." He followed the slight woman down a long, narrow hall with private rooms on either side. An occasional wheelchair was parked next to the wall, but he saw no children or families and wondered how a sickly, elderly person might feel, banished to such a place.

The woman stopped at a doorway marked Rm. 147. "I'll be happy to introduce you."

"I'd appreciate that," he said, waiting for her to enter the sunny room.

A woman with pure white hair and round, rosy cheeks sat propped up with a myriad of pillows in a hospital-style bed. She wore a blue satiny bed jacket that brought out the azure in her eyes. Behind her, on the wall, a large bulletin board was filled with birthday cards.

Cheerfully, the receptionist announced his entry. "The young man I told you about is here to see you, Lily. His name is Philip Bradley."

"It's very nice to meet you, Lily." He offered his hand, and the delicate flower of a soul offered hers.

"Your name is Philip?" came the fragile voice.

"Yes."

"Please, pull up a chair and make yourself at home."

"Thank you."

When he was settled, she said, "Can you tell me where you found this postcard?" She held it in her thin, wrinkled hands.

"I certainly can. While I was staying at an Amish bed-and-breakfast in Lancaster this week, I discovered it caught under a drawer in an antique rolltop desk . . . in my room."

"Antique rolltop, you say?"

"I was told it dates back to the 1890s. A beautiful cherry-wood finish."

She was quiet for the longest time, only her eyes blinking, as if assimilating the information he'd offered. "Adele's mother once owned a desk like that," she said softly.

"Then you knew her well?"

A smile crossed her face. "Ah yes."

He was hesitant to spoil the moment by asking if he could tape-record their visit, but he mustered up enough professional oomph to do so. "I hope you won't mind."

"It's all right, I guess." She sighed, and Philip noticed dark circles under her eyes. "Perhaps it *is* time someone heard Adele's story."

"Most likely, someone besides myself will listen to this

tape," he explained. "Rachel, the grand-niece of Gabe Esh
. . . her mother's uncle."

Lily tilted her head and stared at the window. "I knew
a girl named Rachel once. She was a sweet little thing—an
Amish girl—one of Adele's students at the one-room school
where she substitute taught one year. But then, there were
many Plain girls named Rachel in Lancaster County—probably still are."

He switched on the Record button just as Lily mentioned the Amish schoolhouse. "Do you mind if I state the
date of our conversation before you begin?"

Offering a slight smile, she agreed. "Are you sure you're
not a newspaper reporter, Mr. Bradley?"

He'd come too far and too often for this meeting to fall
through the cracks. "One thing I'm *not* is a newspaperman."
He was glad that he could honestly say so, though writing
for a magazine hardly exempted him from the category.

"So, Mr. Bradley, what is it you would like to know about
Adele?" she asked.

The question took him by surprise. "There is much
about Gabe's situation I don't understand. An Amish farmer
told me he died soon after writing the postcard, yet Gabe
was buried *here* instead of Lancaster. That seems very strange
to me, given the circumstances."

"Yes, I suppose it does."

"I'm also curious to know why the man was shunned by
the Amish community when, according to various folk in
Bird-in-Hand, he never joined the Amish church." He
stopped, thinking he might have thrown out too many questions at once. "Maybe we should start with how *you* came
to know Adele Herr."

The white-haired woman looked toward the window

and seemed to lose herself there. "Adele and I were . . . quite close at one time."

He settled back in his chair, eager for the answers. "Then you must have known Gabe Esh as well?"

She nodded, closing her eyes for a moment, still clutching the postcard. "If it's Gabe you're interested in," she said, opening her eyes with a smile, "then perhaps I should take you back to the very beginning. . . ."

Twenty-One

❖ ❖ ❖

The day Gabriel Esh was born, a fierce snowstorm with up to forty-mile-an-hour winds swept through Bird-in-Hand. John and Lydia Esh had been blessed, at long last, with their first son. His seven older sisters were in attendance at the home birth, in one way or another. The older girls boiled water and ran errands for the midwife; the younger girls played checkers near the wood stove in the kitchen.

Shouts of "It's a boy!" rang through the farmhouse. The eldest dashed outside in knee-deep snow to ring the bell, announcing the news as a strong wind blew the message through the Amish community.

It didn't take long for his parents to see that Gabriel was an unusually sensitive child. Not the sort of rough-and-tumble son John Esh had long wished for, and not much good on the farm, he was so slight.

Along about his seventh birthday, things began to change for the quiet, blond-haired boy. He'd gone out with three of his older cousins—much older, in their teens—and was tramping around between the rows of corn at the far end of Bishop Seth Fisher's cornfield when he felt a peculiar burning sensation in his hands and a mighty downward pull, enough to halt him in his tracks. He battled against the unseen force that seemed to come from the ground beneath him.

Painstakingly, he was able to battle against it, moving his hands, palms flat out in front of him, while the other boys ran ahead. The hot tingling continued until young Gabe thought his hands might be reacting to a low-voltage current somewhere in the ground. He hadn't ever watched a man go dowsing for water across a field, but he'd heard enough stories about it, growing up in Lancaster County. Folks called dowsers did this sort of thing all the time, deciding where to drill for water or locating minerals, hidden treasures, and lost objects like keys and other things. But from the stories he'd heard, it was usually older men or women who were the ones out water-witching, not young boys half scared of their own voices.

When his cousins realized Gabe wasn't trailing along behind them, one of the boys came back for him. Seeing Gabe's hands trembling to beat the band, the boy shouted to the others. "Come, see this! Looks like we got ourselves a new little water-witcher in the family."

Gabe didn't like what he was feeling. The electricity flying through his hands made him think he might be close to being electrocuted. He clapped his hands, trying desperately to make them stop twitching. At last, he folded them as if in prayer, pulling them close to his chest, and stepped back. He stared in awe at the ground, knowing it belonged to Bishop Seth. "*Vas in der Welt?*—what in all the world?" he whispered.

"There's gotta be a water vein below us," Jeremiah, the oldest cousin, said. "We best mark the spot and tell the bishop."

"He'll be right happy to hear 'bout this," said his brother with glee.

The boys, all three of them, started laughing and hooting, jumping up and down, and getting right rowdy about the find. "Maybe there's a gold mine under our feet," said one. "If there is, we'll be richer 'n snot."

Then Jeremiah quit leaping long enough to say, "Wait a minute. Bishop Fisher's lookin' for someone to pass the pow-wowing gift on to, ain't so?"

"I heard Pop say he's a-huntin' for a young woman for the transference. It's been ever so long since we had *die Brauchfraa*—a lady powwow doctor—'round these parts. That's prob'ly why."

"No . . . no, it don't matter, just so long as the person's got a trace of the gift already. And lookee here who it is!" He was pointing to Gabe and laughing.

Soon all the boys were gathering around him, pretending to be sick or faint, begging him to chant or make up a charm over them.

Gabe ignored them, letting his hands drop to his sides. He shook them hard, feeling all wrung out—like he needed to lie down. "I'm goin' home now," he muttered.

"Oh no, you ain't. We're takin' you to see the bishop."

Gabe started running, fast as his little legs would take him, straight through the cornfield and down the dirt lane to his dawdi's side of the house.

He had outrun Jeremiah and the others that day, but it was just the beginning of folks taking notice of him. Word spread quick as lightning about the "wee dowser" in their midst, and Gabe couldn't go anywhere—school or church— without somebody comin' up to him and makin' over him, like he was special or something. Maybe it was because the bishop got a well driller to come out and sink a shaft in the corner of his cornfield. Lo and behold, if he didn't discover a water vein at twenty-five feet!

Seven years later, around the time Gabe turned fourteen, Preacher King took him aside, came right into the schoolhouse and escorted him outdoors. "Bishop Fisher wants to have a word with you, son."

"Me?"

Preacher looked over his shoulder comically. "Well, he sure ain't askin' for *me*."

Gabe ran his fingers up and down his suspenders, then took off his straw hat and looked it over good. "I didn't break the Ordnung, did I?" He shouldn't have let the tears well up in his eyes, this close to being a young man and all, but he was mighty worried he'd gotten himself into some trouble. Random transgressions happened all too often in the community, seemed to him—folks making a mistake about the width of a hat brim or the kind of hobbies they might choose.

"Best be gettin' yourself up to the bishop's and find out," said Preacher King. "But I'd say it's nothin' to fret over."

Preacher's laughter and the urgent, ominous look in his eyes made Gabe feel uneasy. He'd overheard some of the Mennonite teenagers talking disapprovingly about powwow doctors, that they were conjurers or hex doctors, but he'd never witnessed the "evil eye" as some of them cautioned. That day he felt something keeping him back, telling him *not* to go see the bishop, something as powerful as the pulling force in his hands the day he'd walked in that water-rich cornfield. Yet there was a fight raging inside him—another voice just as strong, nagging him to get going, urging him to obey the man of God.

"I don't know what's-a-matter with me," he told Lavina Troyer, a tall and skinny blond girl in the eighth grade. "I feel God callin' me to somethin'—I just don't know what. But everyone says I have this here gift, and if that's true, I should obey and see the bishop 'bout it, right?"

Lavina stared a hole clean through him. "This may sound like tomfoolery, but do you ever pray 'bout things before you just up and do 'em?"

It was the single most absurd thing he'd ever heard, but then most folk he knew figured there was something worse than wrong with Lavina. She struggled hard with book learning at school; most everywhere else, too, it seemed. Though she was getting close to courting age, he wondered if any boy would ever have her. 'Course, then again, if she chewed peppermint gum 'stead of them awful garlic buds, maybe that would help. But that was the least of his worries.

Yet Gabe couldn't dismiss Lavina's remark, and instead of running off to see Bishop Seth Fisher like Preacher King said to, he hurried on home after school, out to Dat's barn, and knelt down next to a hay bale and talked to God as if He might even care to be listening. That prayer and the feeling that followed turned out to be the downright oddest thing he'd ever encountered. When he quit praying, there was an awful ache in his belly, low in the pit of his stomach, like he hadn't eaten in over two days. He was one hungry boy, but when he went in the house and gulped down a handful of oatmeal raisin cookies and the tallest glass of milk you ever did see, none of it seemed to satisfy him.

The hollowed-out feeling persisted, even as he crawled into bed that night. Instead of saying a silent rote prayer the way he was taught to do, he whispered into the darkness a prayer that came straight from his young heart. It was all about how he wanted God to fill him up inside, to make his life count for something more than just working the land, raising dairy cows, and marrying and having a family like his pop and mamma and their dat and mam before them. He wanted a mission to carry out, something far different from the powwow doctoring everyone said he was destined for. He wanted to do something holy and good for Jehovah God.

When he finished his prayer, the emptiness inside was filled with something strong and true. He knew God would answer.

Gabe figured he couldn't tell just anybody what he'd done, 'least not his family. But he did feel homelike enough with one person to tell her about his prayers because he figured Lavina Troyer wouldn't go squealing on him, on account of her childlike way. But it went deeper than that. He felt he could trust Lavina with most any secret. She was the kind of older friend he'd wished he'd had in a *brother*, but God had seen fit to bless him with a houseful of sisters. Maybe that was why he felt at ease around Lavina.

"I'm right proud of you, Gabe," she said when he told her at recess about the praying he'd done.

"You don't hafta be proud, really. I'm just doin' what I believe is God's will."

Her eyes went banjo-wide. "You sound like you've been talkin' to the Mennonites."

He wondered what she meant by that and decided to investigate. Soon he had two fast friends, Paul and Bill—not brothers but cousins—both of them saved and baptized Mennonites. For the next couple of years, he spent as much time with them as he could, sneaking off to Bible studies, even attending Sunday school and church on the People's off Sundays.

He was constantly having to avoid certain farmers who kept after him to come help them locate the best place to dig a well or plant a new tree on their land.

And there was Bishop Seth Fisher. "You're runnin' from God Almighty," the tall, imposing man with graying beard and penetrating dark eyes said after a preaching service at the Esh home one Sunday afternoon. "If I were you, I wouldn't be surprised at nothing, the way you're acting. Out-and-out *glotzkeppich*—blockheaded you are, Gabriel Esh."

Gabe didn't think twice about the bishop's vague, yet somewhat threatening, pronouncement. He wasn't frightened or intimidated by it and wouldn't consider going to meet Seth Fisher privately at the man's home because of it. In fact, Gabe was more determined than ever to follow the new calling on his life. The calling of God.

There came a day of testing, when his own mother was so ill with a high fever and convulsions, Gabe's father declared that her brain might burn up if Gabe didn't at least attempt to exercise some of his supernatural powers over her. But Gabe refused, petitioning God to heal his mamma, quoting the New Testament as he offered a fervent prayer. Angry, John Esh went out and brought Bishop Seth back to the house with his powwow cures and remedies instead.

By the time Gabe was twenty and showing no signs of taking the expected baptismal class necessary to become an Old Order church member, the People wondered if they might be losing one of their own to the world. Bishop Fisher was enraged over the situation—this haughty course the wayward young man had set for himself—and it was mighty clear to everyone that Gabe was avoiding the bishop like a plague. "John Esh's son won't amount to much of anything if he don't join church," the bishop was reported to have said to Preacher King, who in turn told Gabe's father.

So John took his son aside one winter afternoon while the womenfolk were having a quilting frolic. Gabe's father walked him out to the barn, to the milking house. "You know, Gabe, we named you Gabriel for a very gut reason."

"What's that, Dat?"

"Well, honestly, I handpicked the name myself on account of it being your great-grandfather's name before you. You see, son, Gabriel means 'God is my strength'—right fitting for a scrawny lad such as yourself."

He'd heard the story often enough, though never the part his father was about to reveal.

"Your great-grandfather, old Gabriel Esh, was a powerful healer in the community, looked up to and revered by everyone whose life he touched. He died at the ripe old age of ninety-seven, but long before he did, he graciously passed on his gift to Bishop Seth, the bishop we now have."

"Why didn't he transfer the gift to someone in our family?" Gabe asked, knowing that was the way things usually happened.

"Because the woman—your grandmother's sister and *your* great-aunt Hannah—who was most expected to receive it died in childbirth. There was no one else in the Esh family with the same inclinations toward the 'curious arts,' so the gift fell to our present bishop."

Gabe contemplated his father's explanation. "Ain't it true that my great-grandfather could've chosen *anybody*, even someone with no inclination at all?"

"Jah."

"Then why Bishop Fisher?"

256

His father looked down at his work boots. "Seems that after your great-aunt passed away, there was a lot of pressure comin' from Seth Fisher's elderly grandfather for Seth to have the gift. And that's just how it went."

"What sort of pressure do ya mean?" Gabe asked, eager to know. Because he, too, had felt a burden, almost an obligation, to follow through with Preacher King's invitation "to go and see the bishop," even now, after all these years of avoiding the austere man.

"I 'spose it's not for us to say, really."

"But there must be a reason why you think that, Dat."

John Esh shook his head, exhaling into the cold air. "It's just a downright shame that you ain't interested in the bishop's blessing, son. 'Twould give us another healer in the community, and the good Lord knows we sure could use more than one." He paused, wrinkling his face up till Gabe thought he saw the man's eyes glisten. "Such a wonderful-gut honor it would be to the Esh family, havin' our son become the new powwow doctor."

So it was the family Dat was thinking of! Gabe should've known, but he had no idea the "blessing" was so important to his parents.

"God's called me to preach," he said boldly. "To expose the wickedness in high places."

His father's mumblings were not discernible as the farmer walked away, kicking the stones in the barnyard as he headed back to the warmth of the house.

That brought the discussion to a quick end, though Gabe often wondered about the things Dat had said. He searched the Scriptures even more vigorously, together with his Christian friends. It was becoming clear to him that there were certain patterns in families, ways of thinking or behaving that seemed to influence as many as three and four generations from the original sin of a particular family. Some patterns affected the continuation of blessing in a lineage; others gave full sway to chronic sickness and money-related troubles, relationship problems, and barrenness. And there were those who seemed accident-prone or who had emotional or mental breakdowns, all of which seemed to run in families.

On the other hand, there were folk in the community who seemed to enjoy prosperity and health, happy relationships with both their spouses and parents, and had their quiver full of many children. He was so intrigued by the lessons he was learning, he began to teach others, and not long after that, he discovered a column in the *Budget*, written by an Amish bishop in Virginia. The writer spoke out against the patterns of wickedness in the conservative communities, going so far as to say that the black deeds of sympathy healers and powwow doctors were from the bottomless pit itself. The writer's ideas confirmed everything Gabe himself had come to believe.

Week after week, Gabe devoured the columns by Jacob Hershberger and even wished he could go to Virginia and meet the Beachy Amish bishop. But an urgency gripped his spirit, and he began to share the liberating truth of the power of Jesus Christ to break generational bondages to all those who would listen.

There were some in his community who wagged their tongues about the formerly shy and reticent son of John and Lydia Esh. What had happened to transform the frail boy into a self-appointed evangelist, driven and outspoken? Was it truly God's power that had changed him?

Bishop Seth seethed in anger at having been scorned

these many years, more determined than ever to set Gabe straight on the path of his "true calling." Now approaching his mid-fifties, Seth Fisher was more than eager to get the young man alone in a room, just the two of them. The community was ready for a young healer, someone who could carry on the gift into the next generation and beyond. John Esh's only son was the bishop's first choice, though he had his eye on a teenager outside the Amish community, a humble boy nicknamed Blue Johnny.

Lavina Troyer was present, along with her mother and sisters, that warm April day the People had a barn raising at Preacher King's place. The preacher's barn had been destroyed by a lightning bolt six weeks before, and without the aid of telephones or email—though announcements were given in local church districts the Sunday before the scheduled event—word spread, and four hundred men from the county showed up to help build and raise a new barn in a single day.

Gabe, too, was on hand to assist, though no longer living in his father's house due to his unwillingness to join the church. One of his new friends, Paul Weaver, had taken him in, and together the two were working for Paul's father in a carpenter apprenticeship.

The women brought all kinds of food to eat, as was their custom. One church district of women brought meat loaf and white potatoes. Another group brought macaroni and cheese, bread pudding, and sweet potatoes. Other food included roast beef, chicken, ham, stewed prunes, pickled beets and eggs, doughnuts, raisins, applesauce, cake, and lemon pies. Theirs was a set dinner menu for a barn raising, and often the women had to plan ahead for up to seven hundred workers.

So Lavina was there, along with all the women from the Bird-in-Hand Old Order district, including young Leah Stoltzfus and her sister, Susanna Zook, both women with toddlers and babes in arms.

It was Bishop Fisher who took Gabe aside and ordered him to climb the beams and help fit the pieces together at the pinnacle of the wooden skeleton, high above the concrete foundation. Lavina pointed Gabe out to her sisters and cousins. "Watch him work," she said of the lightweight and nimble-footed man who had confided his prayer secret to her years back. She kept her eyes focused on the young fellow dangling perilously in midair.

Right before the nine-thirty snack break, she saw him slip and fall; watched in horror as he skimmed the long beam, breaking his downward course on something that slashed open his side. She cried out when she saw the gash give way to dark red blood. She sped across the yard to the place where he lay, now surrounded by the workers and Bishop Fisher.

"He's hurt awful bad!" she hollered, and one of the women held her back, though she fought them off, thin as she was.

Gabe groaned, still conscious, holding his left side and feeling the sticky substance against his fingers. The bishop knelt beside him and placed his hand on the open wound, whispering something, though neither Gabe nor Lavina could make out what.

"I want no powwowing done . . . on me," Gabe managed to say.

Bishop Fisher straightened, glaring down at him as he

lay there in great agony. "Gabriel Esh, you will repeat after me: 'Blessed wound, blessed holy hour, blessed be the virgin's son, Jesus Christ.' And you will repeat it three times."

Gabe refused. "I choose the healing power of . . . Jesus, my Lord and Savior over . . . your charms . . . and incantations."

This infuriated the bishop, who proceeded to place his thumb inside Gabe's wound. "Christ's wound was never—"

"No! You will not pronounce . . . your witchcraft on me." He paused to gather his strength, to breathe, though it was excruciating, every breath torturous. "In the name . . . of the Lord Jesus Christ, I command you, Bishop Fisher . . . to stop." It was all he could do to raise his voice this way, knowing full well that he was dangerously close to death.

The bishop bent low and whispered, "Choose to receive the blessed gift at this moment . . . or bleed to death."

Gabe could no longer speak, so weak was he from the loss of blood.

"Call an ambulance!" someone shouted in the crowd. "For pity's sake, call for help!"

Gabe recognized Lavina's voice and silently thanked God for his feeble-minded friend as he slipped into unconsciousness.

Lavina was the one who ran and pulled an unsuspecting horse out of Preacher King's barn and rode it bareback to the non-Amish neighbors' to place the emergency call. No matter that she had done so poorly in school and didn't have herself a beau, she could dial the operator. And she did just that, saving Gabe's life.

❖ ❖ ❖

Lily stopped her story, her eyes bright with tears. "I'm sorry, I guess I got a bit emotional just now."

"No . . . no, that's quite all right." Philip was glad she'd paused from her story so he could check on his tape recorder. Sure enough, it was time to flip the tape over. Before pressing the Record button, he asked if she was feeling up to continuing.

"If you hand me that glass of water, I think I'll be able to go on, at least for a while."

Philip was glad to hear it, as he was eager for more, and promptly handed the glass to the woman. She drank slowly, taking several long sips. Then, returning the glass to Philip, she began once again.

❖ ❖ ❖

The Lancaster countryside was ablaze in sugar-maple reds and autumn-radiant oranges, golds, and yellow-greens the year Adele Herr filled in for Mary King, who had been the children's Amish instructor for a little more than two years. Mary, Preacher King's daughter, was getting married, which meant no more schoolteaching, and it was unfortunate because the students had grown attached to her.

It didn't take long, however, for them to switch loyalties and reattach themselves to a bright-eyed brunette woman with a jovial smile and good sense of humor. The children took it upon themselves to make Adele feel right at home, bringing jars of homemade applesauce, beans of all kinds, carrots, corn, beets, sauerkraut, and jellies. In no time, they taught their new teacher to read and speak their language, too.

One day after school, there was a ruckus going on outside the boys' outhouse. Thirteen-year-old Samuel Raber and his stocky younger brother, Thomas, had their fists up, ready to take each other on. Adele rushed outside to put a stop to it, but the boys were all fired up, hungry for a good scrap. "I'll fight ya to the finish!" Samuel shouted, swinging the first blow.

Thomas, who was about the same size, hollered back and swung, too. The two were having it out, right there near the boys' outhouse and the tree swing.

No amount of insistence or pleading on Adele's part could defuse the situation. She was ready to throw up her hands, not knowing what to do, when across the school yard a tall and slender young man came bounding toward the boys. His denim carpenter overalls exhibited a composite of sawdust and what appeared to be smudges of paint and possibly mustard. His yellow hair, cropped around his head, peeked out from under a straw hat. "Sam . . . Tom . . . time to head on home!" the man called to them, breaking up the fight.

Immediately, Samuel and Thomas ran toward the red schoolhouse, glancing over their shoulders as if they thought they'd better run for their lives.

She didn't quite know what to say to the handsome blond man, but she brushed her hands against her skirt and smiled her thanks. "That was truly amazing," she said, finding her voice.

He smiled back, and she noticed the apple green color of his eyes. "Those boys are my sister's youngsters, and she asked me to come down and fetch 'em for her. They're gut boys, really, just full of boundless energy, as you must surely know."

"I've never had any trouble with them until today," she said, glancing at the sky. "Must be a change in weather coming. Sometimes a falling barometer does strange things to children." She smiled back at him.

"Well, weather or no, I'll see to it that they don't cause you any more bother."

"I'm glad you came, because I was about to have someone run and get the bishop."

"No . . . no, you don't wanna do that," he replied, his smile fading.

She didn't tell him that Bishop Fisher was her great-uncle—one of the reasons she was able to land the substitute teaching position. "Why not?" she asked.

"It's a long story." He quickly removed his straw hat and introduced himself slowly and politely. "I'm Gabriel Esh, but my friends call me plain Gabe, and you can, too." His gaze held hers.

"Well, it's very nice to meet you, Gabe. My name is Adele Herr, and I'm filling in for Mary King until next spring."

"Ah yes, she's to be married next month."

"Well, supposedly the wedding hasn't been 'published' yet, but word has it she's tying the knot with the bishop's grandson real soon."

"That she is," he said, still holding his hat in his hands. "Are you from around here?"

"Reading's my home, though I attended Millersville State Teachers' College, so I'm familiar with this area."

Gabe nodded, smiling again. "We don't often get outsiders to teach our children."

"Then I suppose I was in the right place at the right

time, though the parents and the board did scrutinize me, I must say."

"Warned you not to instill worldly wisdom in the minds of their offspring?"

She was surprised. "Why yes. In fact, those were their exact words."

The boys emerged from the schoolhouse, carrying their lunch pails and looking as sheepish as they were besmirched. "We're sorry, Miss Herr," Samuel offered.

"Jah, sorry," said Thomas, his face beet red with embarrassment.

Gabe said, "You boys run along now. Your pop needs your muscle power in the barn."

"Good afternoon, Miss Herr," called Samuel, running.

"Good-bye, Miss Herr," Thomas echoed.

"You won't be havin' any more scuffling out of those two," Gabe promised. He flashed a heartening smile again before excusing himself, then ran to catch up with his nephews.

"Well, one never knows what a day will bring forth," Adele muttered to herself, heading toward the schoolhouse steps.

Adele had her first outing with Gabe two days later. She was twenty-six, and he one year older. Folks had said that Gabe would never settle down and marry till he found a girl who'd be willing to put up with his incessant preaching, his roaming all over the county proclaiming the Gospel. Adele was glad he was still single, because she had been waiting a long time for a man like Gabe Esh to come along and catch her fancy. Only trouble was, he had been raised on an Amish farm, and she was a refined and thoroughly modern Baptist.

Love, they say, is blind, yet she wasn't so sure she wanted to jump into such a peculiar relationship with both eyes closed. So she kept them wide open as they headed off north in Gabe's open buggy, the only transportation he had, what with him still a carpenter's apprentice, with little hope of owning a woodworking shop because of all the traveling he did.

They spent an early evening together, that first date, walking along a wooded area. Ideal for a picnic. And what a picnic it was! Complete with every possible food a young man would enjoy; Adele had seen to that. She even asked Gabe's sister, Nancy—the mother of Samuel and Thomas— to nose around a bit and find out what sandwiches he liked best. Turned out that beef tongue was his favorite, with plenty of Swiss cheese, mayonnaise, and lots of mustard.

After the meal, they hiked farther into the woods, stopping to rest on a stone fence, about three feet high. The sun, sinking fast, shimmered over the rocky surface, providing a warm and cozy spot on that October eve.

"I hope to have a place like this someday," he'd said rather confidently. "It would be ideal for a spiritual retreat, where folks could come and get away from the humdrum of their lives and meet God."

"It's real pretty here." She held her breath though, hoping he wouldn't rush things and say something about the two of them owning a place like this together. Instead, he reached for her hand and they sat in awkward silence. Several orioles flapped their wings and chirped down at them, but she paid them little heed. Her hand fit perfectly in Gabe's, like a glove. Honestly, it was hard to think of anything else.

When Gabriel stood up, she did too, and they walked

hand in hand all the way into the deepest part of the forest, where red sugar maples were so high they had to crane their necks back to see the tip-tops. They laughed together, trying to catch a squirrel, though when Gabe cornered the furry gray creature and put his hand down into a tree hole, she worried that he might get bit. That was the first sign she knew she cared, possibly a little too much.

A few days later, they went for another walk, and the day after that they drove Adele's car to Honey Brook for hamburgers, where no one knew either of them, though folks gawked at the likes of him in his Amish getup and her in a best dress and pumps.

After that, Gabe dropped by the schoolhouse several times a week, usually after school. He said it was to check up on the wood stove or help with anything that might need to be fixed, but, of course, there wasn't anything needing his attention ... except Adele herself. She struggled with her feelings toward him, wondering how such a relationship could possibly work in the long run. Yet her heart longed for his, Plain or no, and they spent joyous hours together, sharing each other's dreams. They talked of everything under the sun, except that one painful thing, too caught up with each other to broach the chasm that kept them truly apart.

Gabe accompanied her with the children on several snowy field trips in late November, and she observed him with the younger students, especially, noting how they seemed drawn to him. "I love the small ones," he said later when she brought it up. "Maybe it's 'cause I never had any little brothers or sisters—since I was the caboose."

It was early in December, a night when Gabe had borrowed his friend's car for a hymn sing in Strasburg. They were listening to the radio, soft music in the background, enjoying the quietude of the moonlit evening, when Gabe said, "I don't know if you know it, Adele, but I believe I must be fallin' in love with you."

Her heart leaped at his words, yet she felt she could not return his ardent affection. Although she cared for him deeply, she could not offer him hope of more than friendship. She knew, as sure as she was a modern woman—"fancy," as he called her—the two of them must remain merely good friends, lest they break each other's hearts.

Gabe was silent for the length of time it took to drive her home. When he pulled into the long, narrow lane of the Troyer farmhouse where Adele was renting a room, Gabe stopped the car and turned to her, reaching for her hand. "I know we've managed to avoid talkin' out our cultural differences, but perhaps with God's help we could work through our future . . . together."

Her eyes clouded with tears. "As much as I care for you, Gabe, as my dear, dear friend, I don't see how we . . ." She paused, struggling with her choice of words. "Oh, Gabe, we're worlds apart, you and I."

"Jah." His eyes held her gaze. "Yet I believe the Lord surely must've brought us together for a purpose."

Adele didn't know what to say to that. Gabe was especially sensitive to God and His ways; she knew it by observing his life and the way he truly relied on the Lord, walking wholly in tune with Him.

"I'm glad for *one* thing," she replied, fighting tears. "We're brother and sister in the Lord, therefore we belong to each other in the family of God. You know what I'm trying to say, don't you?"

"That if we can't be together as husband and wife, at

least our spirits are knit together in the Lord?"

"Yes," she whispered. It *was* a comfort of sorts. Still they struggled with their background differences in the weeks that preceded Christmas, never so much as exchanging an innocent hug or kiss on the cheek, though Adele secretly longed for his embrace.

Adele did not anticipate her father's severe reaction to her friendship with Gabe, during the Christmas holiday. Evidently, word had gotten back to Reverend Herr via Bishop Fisher that Adele was spending lots of time with one of the Amish fellows in the Bird-in-Hand area. This nearly spoiled their family celebration, especially hers and her ailing mother's. "I suspect that you're in love with this . . . this Plain farmer," her father said one evening at supper.

"Gabe and I are true friends" was all she would admit, though with each day of separation came an intense desire to see her Amish friend again.

Upon her return to Bird-in-Hand, Adele told Gabe that she was the grand-niece of the bishop. "Seth Fisher married my father's aunt—that's how we're related. There was a break away from the Amish several generations back," she explained. "Most of my father's people are Baptists. Isn't that interesting?"

"And very unusual, seeing as how they all came from the same Anabaptist roots." Gabe actually took the news of the connection to his People as an encouraging sign. "We're not so far apart, maybe after all."

She smiled at his attempt to dissolve the gap between them. "Three generations ago someone was shunned, excommunicated from the Amish church. I don't see how that's such a good thing."

They joked about it—that they were nearly distant cousins in a vague sense—and Gabe continued to stop by after school or made arrangements to spend time with Adele nearly every day.

For four bliss-filled months they enjoyed somewhat of a dating relationship, though purely platonic, until mid-April, the end of the Amish school year. Three days before she was scheduled to return to Reading, Gabe invited her on a final buggy ride.

"I chose Dat's oldest horse for tonight on purpose," he confessed to her, giving a quiet laugh. "This way we'll have plenty of time to talk."

The night was warm, filled with the sweetness and the promise of springtime. "I wonder what you'd say if I told you I'd like you to think about marryin' me," said Gabe, his eyes intent on her as the horse pulled them forward into the starry night.

Again her heart was drawn to him. "I . . . I *do* care for you, Gabe," she said softly, "but . . ."

Before she could say more, he moved close to her, gathering her into his arms. "Please, my dearest one, you mustn't decide tonight."

"Oh, Gabe, I wish . . ." She yielded to his warm embrace as his lips found hers.

"I know," he said breathlessly. "I know, my darling fancy girl." And he kissed her again.

She snuggled close to her beloved, under the dim covering of a partial moon, and knew in her heart of hearts there could never be another night like this. She would return to her father's house and never see Gabe Esh again. As fond as they were of each other, their love was not meant to be.

They rode in utter silence, except for the occasional snort of the mare and the quaint *clip-clop* against the road. Adele watched the moon come and go under a smattering of clouds, a lump in her throat and a tear in her eye. "Gabe, I don't have to wait to give you my answer. The past months have been the most wonderful of my life. I thought I'd never meet someone like you, someone gentle, who loves children, someone sensitive to the Lord and to me. Oh, Gabe, we both know it can never be."

"Shh, don't say any more. I understand why you feel that way, Adele, but I also believe that if we are both willing, we could make it work." He held his "fancy" girl close to his heart as they watched the moon slide under a cloud, oblivious of what was to come.

❖ ❖ ❖

Lily sighed, still clutching the postcard. "Not long after that night, Gabe witnessed of God's saving power to one Amish farmer too many."

"What do you mean?" asked Philip.

"He went over to Benjamin Zook's place, and right there in front of his uncle and aunt and their four little children, Gabe preached to them of Jesus."

"Benjamin Zook? You don't mean the husband of Susanna Zook?"

"Yes . . . yes, I believe that *was* her name. Do you happen to know them?"

"They are the owners of the Amish guesthouse where I discovered the postcard, and the parents of the young woman of whom I spoke—one of the reasons I made this tape recording. Susanna Zook was related to Gabe Esh."

Her mouth dropped open. "I'd forgotten, but yes, I believe she was Gabe's niece."

Philip was struck by the connection. "What happened at the Zooks' farm when Gabe witnessed?"

"Well, Benjamin was so put out with Gabe's condemnation of powwow doctoring that he went immediately to the bishop and complained. It was Ben Zook who began making the first loud noises toward getting Gabe excommunicated and shunned."

"But if he hadn't ever joined the Amish church, how could such a thing happen?"

She sighed deeply. "As far as Bishop Fisher was concerned, Ben Zook's outrage was the ammunition he needed. One irate farmer and one spurned bishop made for the kindling that was to ignite a roaring fire, to burn Gabe out of the community."

Lily's room had grown dim with the setting of the sun, and Philip was surprised that her tale had lasted well over an hour.

"Do you mind if we stop for now?" Lily said, looking wan. "I'm quite weary."

Philip turned off the tape recorder and thanked the lady for her time. "I hope you will rest now." He stood to go.

She shook her head. "You come again tomorrow, Philip," she said almost in a whisper. "I'll finish the story then."

"Wild horses couldn't keep me away," he confessed.

She extended her hand to him and squeezed it lightly. "You're a good man, Philip Bradley. Why don't you bring along Gabe's grandniece tomorrow. I'd like to meet her."

He thought it interesting that Lily wanted to meet

Rachel, though he had no idea how he might persuade the young woman to accompany him to the nursing home tomorrow. Would Susanna Zook even allow him to speak to her daughter again? That was *one* hurdle he wasn't sure he was willing to attempt.

Twenty-Two

$\mathcal{P}$hilip stopped briefly at the Orchard Guest House on his way back to Stephen Flory's home. Susanna answered the door, looking quite startled when she saw who was standing on her doorstep. "I'm full up, Mr. Bradley," she said before he could even speak.

"I'm not here about a room. I'm here to see Rachel, if I may."

Susanna stood her ground, not budging an inch. "I'm afraid Rachel's not available at the moment."

He toyed with handing over the tape to her, hoping it might find its way into Rachel's hands, but he was no fool. "I'll wait until she *is* available, if you don't mind."

"Well, if you'll excuse me, I have guests to attend to."

Just then Annie spotted him and came running toward the door. "Mr. Philip," she greeted him with a grin. "You came back!"

"Well, yes, I did. But not to stay."

"Do you wanna see where the wasp stinged me? Do ya?"

He leaned over to inspect the tiny mark on her cheek. "All better, looks like to me."

She was grinning, looking up at him with adoring eyes. "Mamma says you saved my life, didja know that?"

He couldn't help smiling now, even at Susanna who appeared to be guarding the doorway with her round person-

275

age. "I was very glad to help."

"You did more than help me," the child insisted.

Chuckling, he stood up only to come face-to-face with Annie's mother. "Oh, hello, Rachel."

"I heard Annie talking so loudly, I had to come and see for myself."

"Mr. Philip's here, Mamma!" Annie tugged at Rachel's sleeve.

Rachel smiled; Susanna scowled.

"Hello again," he said. "I stopped by briefly to loan you something from the woman I visited in Reading today—the one who knew Adele Herr."

With that, Susanna turned on her heel, leaving Rachel, Annie, and Philip standing there together. "I think you will enjoy hearing the story of your mother's uncle . . . and his beloved." He gave the tape to her. "I also believe it will answer your questions, and then some."

"Thank you," she said. "I'm very *gut* at running a tape recorder—it's one of the ways I communicate best."

"Wonderful." He paused, thinking how he should present Lily's invitation. "Before I leave, there's one other thing," he said quickly, keeping an eye out for Susanna Zook, who was bound to return in a huff with Benjamin and order him off. "Lily would like to meet you. She's invited you to come and hear the rest of the story . . . in person."

"Lily?"

"Yes, Adele Herr's close friend. The woman in the Reading nursing home."

"When?"

"Tomorrow afternoon. Would you like to ride along with me?"

"I . . . I don't care much for cars," she said, more cautious now.

"Well, if it's any consolation, I'm a very careful driver."

She thought for a moment. "I might sit in the backseat, if that's all right with you."

"Not a problem."

Rachel's face broke into a spontaneous smile. "Then, jah, I'll go there with you."

Philip could think of nothing else during his restaurant stop for supper. Rachel Yoder had actually consented to accompany him to meet the dear friend of her great-uncle's fiancée. Why should he be excited about something so perplexing?

❖ ❖ ❖

That night, Rachel listened to Lily's recorded story with rapt attention and interest. She was amazed at the parallels between herself and Gabe Esh—his childhood matching hers so completely, though *he* had become a straightforward and courageous teenager and young adult. What had caused him to change, she did not know, just as the People in his day didn't seem to understand either.

She figured she couldn't pick Dat's brain about all that he had heard and seen during the early days of Gabe's "preaching," but she wished she were bold enough to do just that. So much more she wanted to know about the man who had obviously rocked this community forty years ago.

One thing was sure about her parents, though—she noticed they seemed more united recently—'least since Philip Bradley had come to stay at the B&B. Was it because of finding the postcard? She wondered about that till the tape began to make a bumping sound in the recorder, and she turned it off.

The sixty-minute tape seemed to last only a few minutes, and she could hardly wait to hear the rest of the woman's story. To think that her own father had been partially responsible for Gabriel Esh's outrageous shunning. Mighty shocking, it was.

She wondered, too, what Esther and Levi might say about all this if they knew. But she would wait to tell her cousin till after her visit with the Reading woman. Then tomorrow night she would make another taped letter for her Ohio cousin. Such interesting news she would have this time!

After supper, she thought only of the hapless lovers, Gabe and Adele, wondering what was to become of their short-lived relationship, though she knew it could never come to fulfillment due to Gabe's untimely death.

Even though it would mean riding in a car yet another time and traveling with a near stranger, she could hardly wait to meet Adele's friend face-to-face.

❖ ❖ ❖

Susanna would have liked to have had a fit once that Mr. Bradley left. She had restrained herself because of Annie, however, and it wasn't the easiest thing in the world, what with her granddaughter carrying on so about the man who'd saved her life, for goodness' sake!

"It's downright saucy, him showin' up on our front

steps," she ranted to Benjamin in the privacy of their own quarters.

"Why didn'tcha just shut the door on him?" Ben said, looking a bit peeved.

"I'm a kind woman, that's why."

"Then you best not be complainin' to me."

Susanna was put out with her husband. She reached for a bed pillow and pounded at it, pretending to fluff it but gut.

Things seemed to be unraveling around her, and she felt somewhat helpless about it all, beginning with the handsome and tall, smooth-talkin' reporter. Whatever was he thinking, coming back to their inn thataway? Brazen, he was, insisting on talking to Rachel, a widow still in mourning. Couldn't he see how wounded the poor girl was? Couldn't he see that she was suffering, missin' her husband?

"It's beyond me what the man wants with our Rachel," she let slip, not even realizing that she suspected any romantic interest on the part of Mr. Bradley.

Ben shook his head and got out of his chair. "I'd say you're borrowin' trouble, Susie. Ain't no way a good-lookin' fella like that is interested in our daughter; Plain and blind she be."

Susanna dismissed their conversation; she didn't have time for such speculatin'. Other things were brewing in her mind just now.

Susanna waited till Benjamin was clearly asleep, then made her way downstairs to phone a Mennonite van driver a few miles up the road, asking him to come pick her up. It was still plenty early in the evening for what she had in mind. Early enough to pay a visit to a longtime friend. . . .

❖ ❖ ❖

Rachel heard the gentle sound of a car's engine idling in front of the B&B just as she was beginning to nod off. She gave it nary a thought, as quite often a traveler or two would arrive as late as nine-thirty of an evening, coming to book an available room. Usually, though, it was Mam who took care of things after the supper hour, because Dat wasn't much gut to anyone after about eight-thirty or so.

Annie had decided to "be a big girl" tonight and, of her own accord, had gone to sleep in her little bed across the room. Yawning, Rachel lay down and stretched out a bit. She missed Jacob more than usual—having more space in bed upon first retiring and all—and reached for the extra bed pillow and drew it close, hugging it to herself.

A mixture of familiar smells—pungent, yet musty—met Rachel's nostrils, urging her to consciousness, but she felt serene and too relaxed to rouse herself, assuming the pipe tobacco must surely be commingled with her dream.

It was the dreary murmurings, a man's monotone, that startled her out of sleep. "Who's there?" she whispered, fearful of waking Annie.

The chanting continued, and she recognized the voice of Blue Johnny.

"*Was in der Welt*—what in all the world?" Rachel gasped, pulling herself up to a sitting position in bed. She clutched her pillow, wondering how this could be. Blue Johnny, here, in her bedroom?

Then, slowly . . . miraculously, her eyes began to behold a hazy vision of a small girl, curled up on a bed against the wall. Long honey-colored braids fell loosely over the tiny shoulders and back.

What was happening? Was her sight returning?

"Annie?" she managed to say. Then she groped her way out of bed and was met by the blurred figure of a tall, bushy-haired man and Mam, too, holding a large lantern, its golden light spilling over the room. "Why are *you* here?" she whispered.

His features were impossible to identify, yet a radiant glow had settled over him, from the lantern light, no doubt. His dark eyes were silent, hollow pools. "You know I have the power," said Blue Johnny. "And *you* have it, too, Rachel Yoder. You can heal, just as I can."

She felt helpless to oppose the echo of his words. They flowed like warm oil over her sensitive being, enveloping, entrapping her very thoughts. Yet something deep within fought to free her from his sway, and she forced her misty gaze away, searching the room for Annie.

With a whimper, she stumbled to her daughter's bedside and knelt there, stroking the long, silky braids, seeing her little one as through a veil, for the first time in two long years—the skin, fair as a dove; the cheeks, pink as a rose petal. How beautiful her young daughter appeared to her hungry eyes, how very lovely. Or was it just her own imaginin'? It was as she cherished Annie with her cloudy sight that she thought she saw something of Jacob in the little girl. Jah, just the slightest glimmer of his dear, dear face.

"Best not waken her," Mam said.

Even as she continued to touch her daughter's satiny hair, she recalled Lily's tape-recorded story, the amazing account of her own great-uncle Gabe. How the young man with giftings similar to her own had refused the powwow doctors of his day, had rejected the strong inclinations that had come through the bloodline of his family—*her* family—how he'd stood firm against the Old Order bishop.

"No," she heard herself saying, as if in a dream. "I will not accept this sort of healing . . . and the transference neither."

"But, Daughter . . ." Mam was weeping now.

"Don't be foolish, Rachel," Blue Johnny spoke up then. "You don't want to miss out on your little girl's growing-up years, now do you?"

Rachel turned and raised her voice to him. "I'd rather be blind forever than choose the devil's gift."

Annie began to stir, and as quickly as the shadowy vision had come, her sight left her once again. "Please, just go now," she told Blue Johnny.

"Ach, Rachel . . ."

"Make him leave, Mam."

Leaning hard against the bed, she reached for her child's little hand and held it.

"Just remember, Rachel, I have the power to give you full sight," Blue Johnny reminded her. "Someday . . . someday *soon*, you'll come looking for me. Mark my words."

Someday soon . . .

She cringed, forcing the impact of his unholy words from her head, relieved to hear footsteps exiting the room. Then, when the upstairs had become still once again, she rubbed her eyes, thinking that the encounter might've been just a dream. A terrible, awful one at that.

Twenty-Three

❖ ❖ ❖

$\mathcal{P}$hilip felt it awkward for Rachel to sit in the backseat on their trip to Reading, as if he were a chauffeur for an Amishwoman, for pete's sake. Nevertheless, this was the arrangement the blind woman had agreed on, and he found himself stealing glances in his rearview mirror.

At one point, while waiting for a traffic light to change, he caught himself staring at her, wondering what Rachel's hair might look like down, flowing over her shoulders and back, freed from the severity of the bun and head covering she always wore. Free and graceful, and perhaps a bit wavy, as there were hints of some curl whenever a strand of hair fell loose from the twisting on the side, leading back to the bun.

"I think you'll like Lily a lot," he said, making small talk to ease the tension he could feel emanating from her.

Rachel was silent.

"Gabe and Adele seem like real people to me."

"Jah, they do." Her mouth curved up slightly, then resumed its somewhat taut position.

He wondered if she might be feeling more than a little uneasy, perhaps even fearful. "I'm driving well below the speed limit," he offered.

She nodded but still did not speak.

He let it drop, deciding the woman needed space, time

to adjust to the ride. After all, it hadn't been so long ago since she'd lost her husband and young son . . . because of an automobile.

Rachel rode in the backseat of Philip Bradley's car, sensing that he wanted to put her at ease. But she preferred to remain silent, thinking on Lily's riveting story. Honestly, she found it right surprisin' that her own father had been involved in settin' Gabe up for the most unjust shunning ever. No wonder Mam had reacted so severely upon Philip's first inquiring of her. No wonder Rachel's own questions about Gabriel Esh had always been met with guarded remarks.

And what about that dream-vision or whatever it was last night? She'd experienced such a mighty bold feelin'— rare to be sure—risin' up powerful-strong within, and she knew it must've come from hearing the story of Gabe's stand against wickedness in the community.

So, praise be, over the span of years, godly Uncle Gabe had touched her, influenced her to make the decision, once and for all, to turn away from her wavering over Blue Johnny and the other "healers." Cousin Esther would be right proud of her.

Rachel could hardly wait to hear the rest of Lily's story. . . .

❖ ❖ ❖

If Susanna had a hissy fit over Rachel talking to Philip, well, today she liked to have the tremors. After that no-gut New Yorker man came and stole her girl away, Susanna just spun herself in circles every which way, rushin' all over her kitchen, tryin' her best to hunt down stew fixin's, forgetting that most everything she needed for it was downstairs in the cold cellar.

Annie seemed as perplexed at her as Benjamin, and the minute the stew meat, potatoes, onions, carrots, and celery were all chopped up and pushed into a big black kettle, Susanna got off her feet and had to fan herself to beat the band, even though Annie kept on saying, "S'not the least bit hot in here, Mammi Susanna."

❖ ❖ ❖

Lily was perched in the midst of even more pillows than yesterday when Philip and a staff nurse guided Rachel into the older woman's room. But she was smiling as if she had been waiting for their visit with great anticipation.

"I've brought Rachel Yoder with me," Philip said, introducing the two women.

"Very nice to meet you, Rachel," said Lily, extending her thin hand.

Philip watched as Rachel's hand met and clasped Lily's briefly. "I got to hear all about my great-uncle last evening," said Rachel, slipping her hand into her pocket and holding out the tape for Philip. "It was the most interesting story I've ever heard, I think."

"For me, too," Philip added quickly, taking the tape from Rachel.

The nurse located an extra chair so Rachel and Philip could sit while they visited, eager for the continuation of Lily's account of her friend and Gabe Esh.

Lily seemed transfixed by Rachel, and Philip found it intriguing that she would study the blind woman so carefully. "I must tell you something, Rachel," she said at last. "You look very much like your mother's uncle."

"I do?" Rachel said.

"Yes, very much," replied Lily. "In fact, the resemblance is as striking as if you had been his own daughter."

Rachel's eyes appeared to be focused on her lap, but not seeing. "No one has ever told me that."

"I suppose not," Lily replied softly, that faraway look creeping into her gaze once again. "It is truly remarkable. And it is a compliment to you, because Gabriel Esh lived up to his name in that he had the face of an angel. At least Adele thought so."

Philip felt as if he were witnessing the melting away of years as Lily, a peer of Adele Herr's, and the descendant of Adele's loved one sat in the same room together. It was as if they had come *across time* to this very moment.

He noticed that someone had pinned Gabe's postcard to the center of Lily's bulletin board. Obviously, having it in her possession meant a lot to the woman, and Philip was glad he'd had the opportunity to deliver it.

"Let's see," Lily said, "where did I stop yesterday?"

"The shunning," both Philip and Rachel blurted together, which brought smiles all around.

"Yes, the shun imposed on Gabe was the most shameful thing that had ever happened in the church community," Lily remarked. "It tore the Old Order district into pieces."

"What do you mean?" Rachel asked softly.

Lily turned her head toward the younger woman. "Gabe's shunning fragmented the People. I'd never seen or heard of anything so divisive happening among the Amish before. It shook the core of the community."

Rachel sighed audibly. "That may be the reason for so many Amish Mennonites and New Order Amish in our area now. Many of my own relatives are no longer Old Order, as well."

Lily nodded thoughtfully. "I'm not surprised to hear that."

Rachel was silent, sitting with her hands folded in her lap. But Philip could hear her shallow breathing in the chair next to him and wondered what was going through her mind.

"I don't think I told you that it was Lavina Troyer who rented a room to Adele the year she taught at the one-room Amish school," Lily said.

Rachel seemed surprised. "*Lavina* did?"

"But offering the English schoolteacher a place to stay wasn't the only demonstration of Lavina's kindness. She was far wiser than most people gave her credit for, but I'm afraid I've gotten ahead of myself. . . ."

❖ ❖ ❖

Lavina had gone the second and third mile to befriend Adele Herr. She lived alone in her deceased father's farmhouse, bequeathed to her after his passing. At twenty-eight, she was now considered an *alt Maedel*—a maiden lady—among the People, and because she had more than enough room and needed the extra income, she offered to rent out part of the upstairs to the English schoolteacher.

On one of Adele's last days in Bird-in-Hand, at the end of the school year, Lavina was busy cutting off the cream from a gallon jar of old milk when Adele came into the kitchen. A refreshing April breeze was blowing in the window, and the smell of fields and dirt and dairy cows wafted in right with it.

Adele dropped her teacher's notebook on the table and stood staring out across the barnyard. The sun shimmered off the pond south of the barn, casting shadows on a gentle slope that moved upward to scattered willows circled around the sparkling water. "Oh, Lavina, I'm going to miss this beautiful place, and all the children, too," she blurted.

"Well, I hope y'all be missin' me, too," Lavina said, wide-eyed and grinning.

Adele turned and looked at her friend. "Of course I'll miss you. You've been so very good to me. I don't know how to thank you, especially for teaching me all the tricks of the trade—the many canning and cooking hints, and needlework, too."

"We should be thanking *you* for your gut work with our youngsters." The Amishwoman smiled sweetly. "You'll hafta come back and visit sometime. Maybe when you can stay longer, jah?" There was a twinkle in her gray-blue eyes.

"That's very kind of you, Lavina. Thank you." But Adele knew she could never come back to Bird-in-Hand. She headed upstairs to pack up the few things she'd brought with her to Amish country.

There was a private meeting of the deacons, Preacher King and one other preacher, and Bishop Fisher that night. They planned how to oust Gabe Esh from their midst, talking over the way to expedite things the following Sunday when the church membership would gather after the preaching service.

Preacher King went along with Bishop Fisher's idea to

put it to a vote of the People, to forego approaching the rebellious young man in the usual scriptural way, giving Gabe a warning and opportunity to repent. But then, what was there for him to repent of? He'd had a differing view of the Bible from theirs, and he'd refused the powwow gift from the bishop—that's what it amounted to. They'd have to keep a lid on this. If word leaked out beyond the Lancaster community, out into neighboring circles, Plain folk might frown on not only their procedure for shunning, but also the reason for it.

Gabe drove his horse and carriage right into Lavina's yard the day Adele was scheduled to leave. He caught her just as she was loading up her car. "I wanted to come over to say good-bye," he said, helping her lift several medium-sized boxes into the trunk.

She hardly knew what to say. Here was the man her heart had always longed for, and yet she had refused him, rejected his marriage proposal on a most romantic carriage ride.

"Will you pray for me, Adele? For the work God's called me to do?" His eyes searched hers.

She found herself nodding. "Of course I will."

"May I write to you from time to time?" he asked, reaching for her hand.

She thought about that. "Only if you write in Pennsylvania Dutch, okay?"

Gabe didn't question her reasoning, just seemed glad that she would agree. "We'll always be friends, jah?" he said, removing his hat. "Always?"

"In our fondest memories, yes," she replied. "I'll never forget you, Gabe Esh. Never as long as I live."

Gabe moved toward her, his eyes shining. "I love you, Adele," he said once more. "Always remember that."

She longed for one last embrace but felt herself backing away. "I'm sorry, Gabe," she said, reaching for the car door. "I'm so very sorry. . . ."

His eyes were sympathetic and tender, yet the muscles in his jaw twitched repeatedly. "I'm mighty glad the Lord brought us together, even as friends, Adele dear. And I will miss you . . . for always."

She tried to swallow the throbbing lump in her throat, escaping to the privacy of her car before tears spilled down her cheeks uncontrollably. Closing the door, she pushed the key into the ignition, blinking back tears, struggling with the shift. Then slowly, she pulled away, waving a tearful farewell to Lavina who had just come out to sit on the porch.

But it was the vision of a dejected blond man, standing alone in the sun next to a chestnut-colored mare and an open courting buggy, holding his straw hat in both hands, that she was to remember for all her days.

Three long letters arrived from Gabe the first week after Adele returned home. She was thankful he'd remembered to write them in his native language. Her father's indignation over what he perceived to be a continuing relationship had been the main reason for her strange request—that Gabe's letters be written in Pennsylvania Dutch. Yet her response to her friend's correspondence was utter silence.

For two more excruciating weeks, his letters came, but she did not answer them, though they were not filled with declarations of devotion. The young Amishman had honored her heartbreaking decision, filling his missives instead with the things of the Lord, page after page of testimonials of souls finding salvation and divine healing in some cases. Her wonderful Gabe, unfairly shunned, was following God's call on his life, working with a Beachy Amish preacher outside Bird-in-Hand.

Adele began to look forward to hearing from him nearly every other day, though to reply might encourage him, she feared. So she refrained from answering his letters, though it tore at her heart to keep her silence.

In the early part of May, her mother, who had been ill for years, slipped away to heaven in her sleep. Her death was a blow to Adele, and it set her thinking about the brevity of one's life and how each day was unquestionably a divine gift. Her mother's passing also forced her to evaluate her own life in the light of eternity.

So the day after her mother's funeral, Adele crept into her mother's former sitting room and penned her first and only letter to Gabe. As she wrote, she felt as if a dam had broken loose within her, and she realized without a doubt that not only did she love Gabe enough to commit her affection to him, she was now willing to submit to the Plain lifestyle in order to share his life and ministry.

May 14, 1962

Dear Gabe,

Your precious letters, all of them, are gathered around me on my mother's rickety old rolltop desk as I write. My heart can no longer bear not to respond to you.

Although I said before I left that it seemed impossible for us to be together, I know now that I do not want to live my life without you. I am willing to abandon my modern lifestyle for you, dear Gabe, if need be.

Since we've been apart, I have come to understand that in spite of our contrasting backgrounds, we do share life's most important commonalities, you and I. We are similar in our zeal for God, our love for the spiritually lost, and, of course, we both enjoy nature—yes, I miss our many walks together. And we are drawn to children. . . .

If you still feel about us the way you did the night of our last buggy ride, then my answer is yes. I will wait intently for your reply.

With all my heart, I do love you!

Your "fancy" girl,
Adele

Lovingly, Adele assisted her father in sorting through her mother's clothing, furnishings, and personal effects in the week that followed, donating much of it to charity, although the wobbly rolltop desk was put out in the shed, waiting for an antique dealer to haul it away.

Adele waited breathlessly each day for Gabe's response, but none came. Days passed, and still there was no word from the smiling, blond Amishman. She thought that perhaps he hadn't received her letter, though it was not returned stamped "Undeliverable" or any such thing. A thousand times she considered composing another in the event that the first had ended up in a dead-letter file somewhere. But she chose to wait instead, praying that all was well with her dear Gabe, hoping that his silence was not evidence of his waning affection or, worse, that he no longer cared at all.

Late in the afternoon, on Sunday, May thirtieth—two weeks and two days after she had written her letter to Gabe—Adele received a phone call from Lavina Troyer, telling her that Gabriel Esh's life and ministry had been cut short in a car accident. "He was on his way to a preachin' service . . . over near Gordonville," the young woman stammered tearfully. She went on to say that his family would not be offering a funeral service or a burial site "due to the shunnin'."

Stunned and heartbroken, Adele took to her bed with such grief as she'd never known. Lavina arranged to bury Gabe with some of her own money, which originally had been invested by an older brother and set aside for a possible dowry. With the help of a New Order Amish friend's connection at the Lancaster Mennonite Historical Society, she purchased a grave plot and headstone in a Reading cemetery, giving her former school chum a proper burial.

Adele joined the young Amishwoman on the grassy slope, where the two stood just below the headstone, taking turns reading Gabe's favorite Scripture passages at this, their private service. Lavina glanced toward the sky when she said, "Gabe was prob'ly just too gut for this old world, and the Lord God heavenly Father saw fit to take him home." Adele was inconsolable and fell into Lavina's arms, promising to keep in touch "no matter what."

In the years that followed, Adele remained single, throwing herself into her instruction of children, filling up the empty years with her teaching duties and that of caring for her aging father. She never found the kind of love she had experienced with Gabriel Esh and could not forgive herself for having let him go.

Occasional letters were exchanged with Lavina, the unpretentious, simple-minded Amishwoman with a heart bursting with charity and goodness, who, in her own naïve way, had loved Gabe, too. Because of Lavina's compassionate decision to bury Gabe in Reading, Adele was able to visit her beloved's grave, just blocks from her father's house.

Weeks later, Adele heard from Lavina that Adele's letter

had been found among Gabe's personal effects, though it was little consolation.

Every January seventh, Adele ordered abundant flowers, which she placed on Gabe's grave, commemorating the day of his birth. But after a time, a shadow fell over her spirit, and her faith faltered. She spent her remaining years pining for what might have been, disappointed with God, disappointed with herself.

❖ ❖ ❖

A hush fell over Lily's room as she spoke the final words of the heartbreaking story. Rachel brushed tears from her face, and Philip coughed softly, composing himself as well.

"Adele rarely spoke of Gabe after his death," said Lily. "She saved each of his letters, memorizing them over the years. They were her only link to him."

Philip stared up at the postcard tacked neatly to the bulletin board above Lily's head. How ironic that something so small and seemingly insignificant at first had brought the three of them together on this autumn afternoon.

When Lily's nurse came into the room with medication, Philip and Rachel quickly stood and said their quiet thank-yous and good-byes. Philip gathered up his tape recorder, wishing they might've had time to discuss the remarkable tale with Lily. He also wished he'd thought to ask her how she knew Adele Herr but assumed, upon further reflection, that the women had probably met while at the Millersville college or had been close teacher friends. Philip felt, however, that he and Rachel had already presumed to take up a good portion of Lily's afternoon, and it was apparent that the retelling had taken much out of the dear woman. No, it was time to go.

Philip and Rachel settled in for the drive back to Lancaster, with Rachel sitting in the front passenger seat this time. He'd helped her get situated there after their visit with Lily, and Rachel hadn't refused, although he didn't think she was sure at first exactly *where* he'd put her. It seemed a better choice than the backseat. This way, they could talk more readily about Adele and Gabe, if they chose to.

"We should've asked Lily when her friend passed away and where Adele was buried as well," Philip mentioned when they got onto one of the main roads.

"Jah, and it's a pity, really, that Adele died without knowin' Gabe's answer. Receivin' that postcard would've changed her life, ain't so?"

Philip glanced at the young woman sitting next to him. How shy she had seemed when he first met her, yet she was becoming more comfortable with him, he thought. "I have a feeling the postcard would have changed everything, for both Adele *and* Gabe."

She nodded, remaining quiet for a bit. Then—"Why do you 'spose Gabe's message never found its way to Adele?"

He'd pondered that question himself during Lily's recounting of the story. "Well, I really don't know, but it's possible Adele's father, angered by yet another message from the Amishman, impulsively shoved it deep into the old desk that was to be hauled away. But that's only speculation— my spin on it. Who's to know, except that the postcard *had* been jammed into one of the narrow desk drawers."

Her jaw dropped momentarily. "Caught in a drawer, you say?"

"Yes, and remember Adele had sat to write her one and only letter to Gabe on a dilapidated, old rolltop desk? Must be the same one."

"Sounds to me like you missed your calling, *Detective* Bradley."

He chuckled a little. "It's what I do—gather all the facts for a story. So I guess you could say I *am* a detective of sorts. As for Adele's mother's desk—according to Emma at the antique store in Bird-in-Hand, it *did* come from Reading. She was able to trace it back to a Baptist minister's old shed."

"So you did some right-gut checkin' up on the desk, then." Her face broke into a genuine smile, and she let out a little chortle, then caught herself, covering her mouth quickly.

Philip said, "I feel satisfied now, knowing what I know about Adele's and Gabe's love."

"It's ever so surprising that the desk came full circle, so to speak, ending up in my father's house—right under your nose."

Rachel's comment was insightful, and he agreed with her, glad that she'd come along to hear her great-uncle's story on this mild September day.

The sun was creeping ever higher as he made the turn past the white stone wall and into the old cemetery. Towering trees like giant watchmen with wide arms were strewn out randomly across the grassy hillside. "I hope you don't mind, Rachel, but I thought we could make a quick stop . . . to visit Gabe's final resting place."

"I don't mind."

"I was here once before, but I'm afraid I got sidetracked. Now that we've heard the full story, it might be nice to see Gabe's headstone for ourselves." He meant the epitaph, though he had no idea if the Amishwoman would even have thought to inscribe Gabe's marker except for the name, date of birth, and date of death. Yet he wanted to see for himself, and he sensed Rachel was just as curious.

He hurried around the car and helped her out, gently taking Rachel's hand and wrapping it through his arm, while she used her cane with the other. Then, guiding her as carefully as if she were a fragile doll, they walked together over the paved pathway. Getting his bearings, he spied the general location of Gabe's marker, where the groundskeeper had directed him four days earlier. His heart quickened as they made the turn and strolled over a slightly sloping path of grass, under a shining sun.

Gabe's marker was unadorned, devoid of crosses and angels, as were others near it. Only slightly weathered, it was rounded at the top, a plain tombstone befitting an Amishman. "What's it say?" Rachel asked, her arm still linked through his.

Slowly, his eyes scanned the inscription as he read the words, silently at first:

GABRIEL ESH
Born January 7, 1935
Died May 30, 1962
Shunned by men, Blessed by God.
Loved by Adele Lillian Herr.

Philip was deeply moved as he read the words on the headstone aloud to Rachel. She was especially still, her eyes open in the dazzling light of the sun. A breeze skipped across the grass, rippling her skirt and apron, and for a moment it seemed as if she could actually see.

"Will you say Adele's *full* name again," Rachel said softly.

Philip looked down at the marker once again. "Adele Lillian Herr."

She breathed in quickly, gripping his arm.

"Are you all right?" He placed his hand over hers, consoling her.

"Jah, I'm fine, really. But I think maybe you missed somethin' important—it's there for all to see."

"What do you mean?"

"Lily . . . short for Lillian, ain't so?"

He was stunned by this beautiful blind woman's insight. Of course—Lily was Adele Herr!

Twenty-Four

$\mathcal{I}$t seemed as if they stood there for hours, motionless, lost in thought, absorbing their discovery of Lily's true identity.

When they finally turned from the gravesite to walk away, both were contemplative, seized by the poignancy of the moment. Philip wondered why Lily had wanted to keep her identity hidden. Why hadn't she wanted them to know?

Continuing to make their way down the gentle slope, he took great care to point out the uneven places beneath their feet, for Rachel's sake, then fell silent again, considering the events of the day as they approached the car.

It was Rachel who spoke first, breaking the near-reverent stillness—and when she did, it was as if she were reading his thoughts. "Lily didn't want to be known as Adele, 'least not to us." She sighed audibly. "She must've suffered terribly—losin' Gabe thataway—must've felt she had to mark time, keep standin' still, not movin' forward at all in life, choosin' her middle name instead. It was a way to hide—go into herself—protect herself from the awful pain."

Philip was struck by Rachel's profound evaluation. *She seems to speak from experience,* he thought.

She stopped, turning to face him, though her eyes were downcast. "I know all too well what Lily . . . Adele, has gone through her whole life long. She simply couldn't move forward with livin'. That's the reason for her secrecy."

As Philip helped her into the car, he wondered what secrets Rachel may have pushed down into her own soul, hidden from the light.

The sun slipped behind a cloud just as he started the car and headed back in the direction of Lancaster, making it easy to concentrate on the road and on the lovely, perceptive young woman by his side.

"Adele *did* get Gabe's message of love before she died," he heard Rachel saying. "She got it just in the nick of time."

Soon they fell into a rhythmic and pleasant ebb and flow of conversation such as he had not recalled ever engaging in so fully with a woman. They talked and laughed about each other's childhood and religious training, their parents and siblings, their hopes and dreams. . . .

And Rachel shared with him her dedication to Jesus Christ and how she loved to listen to Bible tapes and occasionally the taped sermons sent her by Esther, her Ohio cousin. "Walkin' with Jesus makes all the difference in the world."

Philip found himself lost in conversation with the intuitive and bright woman, and by trip's end, he had nearly forgotten that she was both blind and Plain.

❖ ❖ ❖

Stephen Flory and his wife seemed pleased to be treated to supper that evening. Philip touched on the high points of his and Rachel Yoder's visit with Lily, "who quite amazingly turned out to be Adele herself."

"No wonder I couldn't find her obituary," Stephen joked.

Philip nodded. "No wonder . . ." He told them he would be heading back to New York tomorrow. "I'll catch the first train out," he said.

"So your work here is done?" Stephen wore a boyish grin.

"I believe I have the makings of a terrific human interest piece." He was thoughtful. "I don't know exactly what I'll do with Gabe's and Adele's story, but I'm sure it'll come to me . . . in time."

"Maybe after it simmers awhile," Deborah spoke up.

"Maybe . . ."

❖ ❖ ❖

Rachel was ladling out the chicken corn soup for supper when her thoughts drifted back to Philip Bradley. She supposed she oughta be caught up in the astonishing story she'd heard over the past two days—one on tape, the other in person. But she didn't feel it was so wrong to focus mental energy on someone as kind and appealing to her as was the writer from New York. Mighty interesting, he was, especially for an Englischer.

She found herself wondering about his human interest story on Gabe and Adele, but she had little hope of ever bein' able to read it. Not unless Susanna would agree to read to her, and if not, maybe when Annie got a little older. Still, she felt awful sorry for him havin' to return to such a busy place as New York. She'd allowed herself to enjoy the strength in his arm as he led her through the cemetery where

Gabe lay buried and the smell of his subtle cologne, something she'd never smelled on Jacob—never. Which wasn't to say she didn't like it a lot.

Something about Philip Bradley made her feel alive again, like she didn't want so much to mark time anymore. Like she could begin to think about movin' ahead a bit. One tiny step at a time. Jah, and she felt ever so confident with him by her side.

Yes, now that she thought of it, Rachel was mighty glad he'd picked their Orchard Guest House B&B in the first place. . . .

Twenty-Five

While waiting at Lancaster's Amtrak station for his train to arrive, Philip toyed with the idea of calling Rachel. He hadn't stopped thinking of her once since he'd dropped her off last evening. And he didn't think it was so much a romantic thing he felt; he just wanted to hear her voice one more time. So he took the risk of getting Susanna Zook on the other end and called anyway.

"Orchard Guest House" came the soft, sweet voice.

"Rachel?"

"Yes?"

"It's Philip Bradley, the man who—"

"I know who you are," she interrupted, surprising him.

"Just wanted to say good-bye before my train leaves. And it was very nice to meet you—to get to know you."

"That's gut of you to say, Philip. I pray you'll have a safe trip home. May the Lord bless you always."

He smiled at her quaint expression. "And you, too," he said without even thinking. "Oh, and please tell Annie good-bye, too. I hope her wasp sting is healing nicely."

"Jah, it is."

He heard some commotion in the background—voices, as if someone wanted to use the phone. "Is something wrong?"

She fell silent.

"Rachel?"

"No, it's *not* Rachel, and you're not to bother our daughter again, you hear?"

He felt his eyebrows jump up. "I'm sorry, but I was having a conversation with—"

"Not anymore you ain't" came the terse reply. "And for your information, Rachel's not blind . . . not really. She suffers from a mental disorder, some sort of hysteria. So it ain't in your best interest, I wouldn't think, to search out a . . . a woman such as Rachel."

Philip was dumbfounded. "I understood she was blinded in the accident."

"Well, you're quite *wrong!*" the woman said emphatically. "She's mentally impaired . . . doctor says so."

Mentally impaired?

Rachel was far from it, and Philip knew it without a doubt. Susanna was obviously disgusted with him and rightly so. He'd taken her helpless, widowed daughter out of the city, exposed her to the heartwarming story of their wayward ancestor, brought her safely home, and was only interested in saying an innocent farewell. "I'm terribly sorry to have bothered you, Mrs. Zook."

"Jah, and so am I." And with that, she hung up the phone.

Once his bags were safely secured in the baggage compartment above his head, Philip browsed through a magazine he'd purchased, though not seeing either the ads or the articles presented.

He could not shake the words Susanna Zook had fired into his ear. Rachel not really blind? How could that be?

What kind of woman would make up such things about

her own daughter? He dismissed the strange statements, assuming they were the product of a desperate woman's defense—to keep her widowed daughter safely secluded from the outside world. Surely that was all Susanna was attempting to do.

Instead, he chose to concentrate on Rachel's spiritual declaration, some of her final words to him on the phone.

May the Lord bless you always. . . .

Rachel's voice echoed in his thoughts as the train pulled away from the station, past warehouses and industrial buildings. Within minutes, the landscape became gloriously different. Visions of nature's beauty and simplicity framed the picturesque farmland and gentle, rolling hills, all of it representative of his Lancaster County experience.

Leaning back, he realized anew the wonder of God in his life—the grace and goodness he'd let fall by the wayside of his hectic existence, smothered and choked out by his own personal goals and ambitions. He thought of a young boy, kneeling at the altar of repentance, his heart innocent and true.

Lord, forgive me, Philip prayed silently. *Thank you for waiting for me to come to my senses.*

Lulled by the swaying of the train, he closed his eyes and thought of the delicate woman with an occasional curl in her honey brown hair. What a delightfully old-fashioned young lady. Her innocent approach to life was refreshing, and Rachel's adorable little daughter—well, they were quite a pair.

Please, Lord, watch over Rachel and Annie. . . .

Philip caught a cab to Times Square, checking in with his editor before heading to his cubicle. "Wild and wacky stuff," Bob said, chewing on a pencil. "Do people really live like that?"

"You'd have to see it to believe it, but yes, they do, and quite cheerfully, I might add."

He purposely did not mention the human interest piece. He liked Deborah Flory's suggestion about letting it simmer for a while. Trudging back to his small enclosure, he felt as though he could use some simmering, too. Not this week and not the next, but when the leaves started to change in Vermont.

He picked up the phone and dialed Janice. "I'm back," he said. "Is Kari around?"

"She's standing right here, dying to talk to you."

"Well, put her on."

"Uncle Phil, hi! It seems like forever since we talked."

"Forever—yeah, I know." He stared at a wide bank of windows just beyond the next row of cubicles, spying the sides and tops of buildings, one column of them after another, as far as the eye could see. "Do you and your mom want to watch the leaves change with me?"

"In London?"

"In Vermont . . . at Grandpap's cabin in the woods."

"But you promised London," she insisted.

"London can wait."

"Okay, if Mom can get away."

"She'll say yes, trust me," he said. "It's been a long time since I sat still and watched green turn to red. Maybe too long . . ."

❖ ❖ ❖

Philip was packing for the trip to Vermont when the doorman rang his apartment. "You have a registered letter downstairs, Mr. Bradley. Would you like the mail carrier to bring it up?"

"I'll come down. Thanks."

When he had signed for the letter, he noticed that the return address was Fairview Nursing Home in Reading, Pennsylvania.

"Lily?" he said aloud, waiting for the elevator.

Quickly, he opened the long business-style envelope and discovered a typewritten letter addressed to him.

Dear Philip,

I was quite relieved that Shari, our receptionist, had saved your business card. I never could have found you, otherwise, to properly thank you for Gabe's postcard . . . and for your visits.

Perhaps by now you know that I am Adele Herr. I didn't intend to deceive you, but years of great sorrow and denial on my part had taken their toll, and I grew to trust few people. I must confess that I have lived an embittered, hopeless life, and by your coming, I know how wrong I was.

The postcard is a reminder of God's faithfulness to me, that He had His hand on me from the beginning, though I allowed great disappointment to rob me of my faith. I have given myself to my Lord and Savior once again.

So thank you, Philip. The message from Gabe, though quite belated, has altered my life and given me a reason to live.

I wish you well, my friend.

Sincerely,
Adele Herr

Philip refolded the letter, his heart filled with gladness,

and he thought again of the Scripture reference Gabe had so aptly placed next to his signature, some forty years ago.

He who began a good work in you will carry it on to completion until the day of Christ Jesus. . . .

Epilogue

❖ ❖ ❖

*T*hings seem a bit unsettled 'round here since our New York guest left for home. Mam's on edge more than ever, 'cept she still does insist on having frequent prayer times as a family, where Dat reads one pointed Scripture passage or another, directed toward me.

There's plenty of apple-cider makin' and apple-butter churnin' in the area, and I have to say that I hope we'll be making some candied apples, too. 'Least for Annie's sake.

We're hosting ever so many more guests, now that it's peak foliage, and I'm right grateful to be keeping busy. Still, it's mighty hard to tidy up the southeast guest bedroom or take a walk with Annie over the footbridge without thinking of the young man from New York. Seems the longer time goes, the harder it is to believe everything that happened while Philip Bradley was here.

Most surprising is the story behind it all—how a humble young fella, born sensitive and timid as anybody, mustered the courage to stand up to Bishop Seth Fisher and all the preachers, too! In the end, the obvious heir to the powwow "gift" chose to follow the call of the Cross, becoming a joint heir with Jesus.

It's a pity that Gabe died so awful young, missin' out on his sweetheart for a lifetime. I 'spect sometime here real soon, they'll be meeting again over yonder for all eternity.

Gabe was surely right, after all, 'bout what he wrote: *Soon we'll be together, my love.*

Thinking 'bout the Glory streets and that wonderful-gut heavenly reunion to take place over yonder, I'm surprised that Jacob doesn't come to mind just now. Still, it's Philip Bradley who takes up much of my thoughts here lately, though not a soul must ever know—not even Cousin Esther—how brave I felt when I was with him. And even though he's a fancy Englischer and long gone, just thinking back to the way he said my name—like it was right special somehow—how we laughed together on the ride home from Reading, the way he saved Annie's life . . . well, every speckle of that memory leaves a right pleasant feeling.

Every so often, I catch myself thinking: Wouldn't it be something if Philip came back around—workin' on some project or another? 'Course, the way Mam talked to him on the phone—grabbing the receiver out of my hand like she did and tellin' him I wasn't really blind, that I was mental—who knows what he thinks 'bout me now? Well, next time—if there ever *is* a next time—maybe I won't be so timid-shy around him. Maybe not . . .

I still don't know if that dusky vision of little Annie was real or not, don't know if Blue Johnny ever truly came to my room that night. Mam refuses to talk about it, so I 'spect it *did* happen. I do know *one* thing, though: Powwow doctoring is not of God. For sure and for certain.

Thanks to Lavina, we've been attending my former church again. Clear out of the blue, the dear woman offered to pick up Annie and me in her little carriage for Sunday preaching at the Beachy church. I'm learning as much as I can about God's healing plan for His children, trusting, too, for His perfect timing for me. Esther sends me wonderful-gut Scripture verses on our taped letters, back and forth. I've still got plenty of growin' to do in the Lord before I discover all He has planned for me. But I do have a strong feeling that the postcard was sent by an unseen, yet divine hand, arriving at just the right time—across the years—winging a message of truth to each of us.

News travels fast amongst the People, so it's not surprisin' how many folk have heard Gabe's story. In a way, he's still preachin' the sermon God gave him back when, maybe more powerfully than ever before. Sometimes I think my great-uncle must be looking down from on High and smiling at the way the Lord has overcome evil with good. Here in Lancaster County, we call that Providence.

Acknowledgments

❖ ❖ ❖

Space doesn't allow me to describe the way in which this story took root in my heart, but I can say with assurance that God planted the seeds in me, regarding my study of various types of "sympathy healings," to include powwow doctoring and other kinds of alternative healings. Out of my inquiry came a better understanding of the "curious arts" and the tools that Satan uses to seduce and ensnare.

I don't often talk about my writing "pilgrimage"—the process by which I craft a novel—but I can say that the Holy Spirit is always on time, preparing the way for research and inspiration as well. And without certain key people of God, this book would be languishing in a file.

So it is with great appreciation and thanksgiving that I recognize my wonderful husband and first editor, Dave, who literally made it possible for me to meet book deadlines. Always my friends and discerning editors, Barb Lilland, Anne Severance, and Carol Johnson offered gracious support and prayerful encouragement; so did BHP editorial, marketing, and publicity teams. My parents, Reverend Herb and Jane Jones, helped with numerous book resources and prayer, along with other prayer partners: Barbara Birch, Alice Green, Carole Billingsley, Jean Campbell, Judy Verhage, Bob and Aleta Hirschberg, and John and Ada Reba Bachman.

Special thanks to nurses Kathy Torley and Rita Stahl, who answered medical questions. I am also indebted to Marianna Poutasse, curatorial assistant at Winterthur Museum, who shared her knowledge of antiques.

In addition, I extend heartfelt gratitude to the countless readers who have written to me this year, offering prayers of encouragement, sharing Scripture, and requesting more stories. May the Lord bless and keep each of you always.

WELCOME TO LANCASTER COUNTY

Torn From Her Family and Home, Katie Must Search Her Past to Find Answers to Her Future

In the quiet Amish community of Hickory Hollow, time has stood still while cherished traditions and heartfelt beliefs have flourished. But the moment Katie Lapp finds a satin baby gown hidden in a trunk, she uncovers a secret that could shatter the tranquil lives of everyone involved.

Following Katie Lapp from the eve of her wedding, through her banishment from the close-knit community, and into her search for a mother she never knew, THE HERITAGE OF LANCASTER COUNTY provides a dramatic and powerful look into a life of faith, a search for truth, and a promise of peace.

Through vivid characters and heart-warming prose, author Beverly Lewis recreates the simple life of the Amish in this trilogy of hope and reconciliation that shows us that even when we think we are far away, God's love is always present.

THE HERITAGE OF LANCASTER COUNTY
The Shunning
The Confession
The Reckoning

FROM BESTSELLING AUTHOR
BEVERLY LEWIS

A Young Girl's Hope Binds a Family Together

Based on diary entries from Beverly Lewis' childhood, *The Sunroom* is the tender story of Becky Owens, a talented young woman of twelve who must face the possibility of losing the one she holds most dear. The daughter of a Lancaster County preacher, Becky knows the power of sacrifice and so offers, in a desperate bargain with God, to give up her most valuable possession for her mother's life. As her journey of faith continues, she comes to a new realization of a love beyond limits in an inspiring tale few will forget.

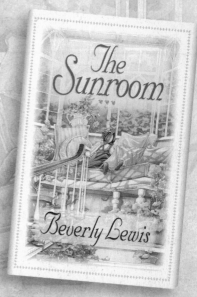

Can Love Dissolve the Differences Between Them?
THE SEQUEL TO *THE POSTCARD*—RELEASE DATE OCTOBER '99

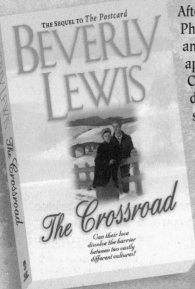

After returning to New York, journalist Philip Bradley cannot forget Rachel Yoder and her little daughter, Annie. Her appealing way of life and cheerful Christian witness beckon him amid hectic deadlines and his fast-paced lifestyle. On sabbatical, Philip returns to Lancaster and immerses himself in the ways of the Plain People as well as in the affections of Rachel. Will he choose to remain with her or will the differences in their lives be too great to overcome?